# MEN at RISK

# MEN at RISK

## *Stories*

## Samuel Atlee

CREATIVE ARTS BOOK COMPANY
Berkeley • California

*Men at Risk* is published by Donald S. Ellis
and distributed by Creative Arts Book Company.

For information contact:
Creative Arts Book Company
833 Bancroft Way
Berkeley, California 94710
1-800-848-7789

ISBN 0-88739-406-X

Library of Congress Catalog Number 2001097458

Printed in the United States of America

ACKNOWLEDGEMENTS

Some of the stories in this collection first appeared in the following magazines: "Artist on a Roof" in *Sou'wester*, "Bingo Swine & Flypaper Sisters" in *Writers' Forum*, "An Erawan Monkey" in *Vignette*, "The Field Desk" in *Farmer's Market*, "The Girl from Blue Hawaii" in *Chiron Review*, "The Goodman Keilworth 1938" in *Potpourri*, "The Inn of the Three Gorges" in *Mobius*, "Overture from a Faithful Booster" in *Flyway*, and "Righteous, Bold as Lions" in *Flying Horse*. "Krishna's Kid Ivory" appeared in different form in *The Missouri Review*.

The author gratefully acknowledges the generous support of the National Endowment for the Arts.

This book is for my children.

# Contents

# MEN at RISK

# Artist on a Roof

I suspect I was the first one outside Mrs. Farley's family to hear about the impending invasion. I was at her farm, about ten feet above her on the roof of the garage, looking down at her. Imagine a small, thin woman in her fifties, with gray hair. Her features are fine and her mouth is small and delicate. She often used a rake at the farm, and I marveled at the sight of this long awkward thing with dangerous teeth, transformed in her hands into a deft jeweler's tool, as light as a pencil, something one handled with respect. She scratched the ground carefully with the teeth, as though inscribing her initials onto gold. She looked up. "When the Chinese come," she said, "we'll be ready. And believe me, it's possible. Don't be fooled by all this stuff you hear. Capitalism, democracy. Pooh! In a matter of months we might all have to wear khaki suits and work on road gangs. Just like that. Some people might work in the orchards, but everyone will work. And when they come, we'll be ready. They'll make you and me foremen because we know how to work with our hands. At least we'll get something to eat."

Mrs. Farley had hired me to put a new roof on the farm's garage, and I'd almost finished stripping the worn shingles and rotting tarpaper off the old roof. Mrs. Farley walked over to a pile of the shingles and bent down and began to gather them up. She carried them over to a plastic trash barrel and dumped them in. Then she straightened, and drew a small, gloved hand across her brow.

"How are we going to get rid of this junk?" she asked.

I looked down at the shingles in rough piles all about the garage. I suppose I was making a mess. Some of the shingles had broken apart and crumbled into powdery pieces in my hands, or else the October wind had caught them and thrown them slapping against the side of the farmhouse with a loud *thump*.

"You know it doesn't bother me," she said. "But Mr. Farley would really be horrified. He just can't stand messiness. I'm afraid if he saw this, he'd probably ask you to leave."

Even though I'd only met her husband a few times, his was suddenly a threatening presence, and Mrs. Farley's mention of him was like being reminded, as a child, that soon your father would be home. Mr. Farley was out of town at the time, on a fishing trip to Florida with his brother, but nonetheless I thought I better climb down and start to clean up before he suddenly appeared.

"He's so neat, you know," she said. "He's neat about everything. If I don't fold his socks just right he gets angry with me, and all his shirts have to be neatly stacked just so in his bureau drawer. He won't have his shirts on hangers. He says they look sloppy. If you don't think he's neat, just look at that swimming pool of his."

She was right, for Mr. Farley was indeed conscientious about his pool. There were never any leaves or spiders in the water, and he trimmed the grass around the pool so closely that the lawn took on the well-groomed appearance of a putting green. No blade was out of line.

It was at the pool that I'd first worked for Mrs. Farley. She'd wanted a painting of the pool as a birthday gift for Mr. Farley, and since it was supposed to be a secret, I hadn't been able to paint at their house. So one day when her husband was out, she called me and I went over to take some photographs, which I painted from. Acrylic on hardboard, and the view is cool and simple. One looks out across the pool as across a pane of glass, almost level with the water. It's as if you are floating in the deep end; the trees and hedges are dark and loom above. The pool is sheltered, clean and inviting.

Later, Mrs. Farley told me that her husband was pleased with the painting. I enjoyed doing it for them, but when jobs like that are slow I don't mind doing house painting or roofing, either. Mrs. Farley's an old neighborhood friend of my mother's—the house where I grew up is just down the street—and since my mother moved away after my parents split, she tries to look after me. Odd jobs, that kind of thing. And recommendations.

I climbed down from the roof and began to help Mrs. Farley put the shingles into a pile. Even though the farm doesn't belong to Mr. Farley, but to her as a sort of hobby, it was important for his sake that we kept things neat.

"We have a daughter about your age, you know," she told me, bending down to pick up a scrap of paper. "Actually, she's a little older. She's thirty." She straightened and held the piece of tarpaper before her face, scrutinizing it. "She married a man who played the saxophone," she said. "Can you imagine, the saxophone? I think he was in a band that played rock music, in Texas. He was nineteen years old. She was twenty-six when she married him, and then three months later they had a baby boy." She threw the paper onto our pile and looked up at the peak of the roof.

"I've never seen my own grandchild," Mrs. Farley said. "My daughter's husband lives in New Hampshire now. They aren't divorced, but they should be. My daughter can't do anything on her own. Last week she called me up and asked me to send her money. When I asked her where to send it, she gave me the name of some motel on the Nebraska Turnpike. I mean, she had the baby with her, and it gets cold there. She wants to move to Arizona and build a house from tires. Old truck tires, tractor tires, I don't know. She had two dogs with her, three cats, and the baby. When I asked her why she was moving, she said it's because Aaron—that's her husband—wanted to become the first mushroom grower in New Hampshire, and he dug out the basement of the house, and it fell in. Not all the way, but some. I imagine they're on drugs. If Mr. Farley knew I'd sent her money, he'd kill me. I think the only reason she called was because she knew he wasn't home. Mr. Farley won't talk to her."

I kept moving and tried to clean up the trash, exposing the matted brown grass around the garage as I worked. For a moment Mrs. Farley stood quite still, staring into the garage. Inside there was a dusty, littered assortment of junk, old crates, and other trash left there by the farm's previous tenants.

"If my daughter ever comes to visit me she'll have to stay here," said Mrs. Farley. "My husband won't have her in our house. That's why I wanted you to fix the roof. For her car." She dropped the shingles she had gathered and looked at me. "How long do you think it will take you to finish?"

"A week, maybe. I'll work as fast as I can."

"Oh, but you don't have to hurry." Then she gathered up a few more shingles, dropped them on the pile, and walked over to her station wagon and took off her leather gloves. She climbed into her car and started it up. Then she put the car in gear and drove away.

— ❋ —

Roofing requires patience. Before putting on the new roof of galvanized steel, first I had to repair the rotted planking. Once exposed, many of the old planks turned a crusty warm black in the sun, and proved sturdy enough to remain on the roof. The badly rotted planks I removed. They were brittle and dusty in my hands. I replaced them with smooth fresh planks of pine, still tarry-smelling and white, that oozed moisture when I hammered them into place. This took three days, and I worked alone. The pile of old shingles was still in front of the garage. When the work on the planks was completed, from a distance the roof presented a patchwork pattern of sullen blacks and bold new whites, like a crossword puzzle.

When I arrived at the farm the following day, my station wagon was loaded with the new galvanized sheets. Both Mr. and Mrs. Farley were there, gathering up the shingles and loading them into the back of a rented pickup truck. Mrs. Farley had on her leather gloves, a pale blue blouse, and a heavy tweed skirt. Her husband wore khakis and a flannel shirt, and he was suntanned from his fishing trip. Mr. Farley tossed the shingles angrily into the back of the truck. Mrs. Farley had told me that, before he left, her husband had suggested she hire a contractor for the job of replacing the roof. Instead she hired me.

It was obvious he wasn't happy with her decision. Mr. Farley'd come home from Florida and found his wife's farm a mess; the piled shingles and scattered tar paper were evidence that some dangerous stranger had been clambering about on the now hideously outraged roof. Mr. Farley clomped back and forth from pile to truck, from truck to pile, carrying over-large armfuls of the shingles, perhaps to emphasize his distrust, his perturbation. I watched him for a moment and then got out of my station wagon and walked up to the garage.

Mrs. Farley was standing by the back of the truck. She looked up and gave me a merry smile. "Go ahead and do your work," she said. "We'll do this. And don't look so agonized. We're having fun."

I went back to my station wagon and started to unload the galvanized sheets. I pulled them two at a time through the back window, then carried them over to the side of the garage, and stacked them neatly on cross ties of wood. I was hoping Mr. Farley might appreciate my care. He paused by the pickup truck and watched me. And indeed, his dark eyes, even his full head of bristly crew-cut hair, seemed to relax as he watched me carrying the sheets. They were of uniform size, their shiny corrugated surfaces were spotless, they blazed with sharp reflections of the bright morning sun. The sheets fit snugly one on top of the other beside the garage, and I was relieved that, by bringing the new roof with me, I seemed to be able to interpose it between Mr. Farley's anger and myself.

Later I climbed up the ladder to the roof. A single wormy plank at the peak had caught my eye. I had let it go before, assuring myself that it would hold; wary now, I decided to remove the rotted plank and replace it with a crisp, firm new one. As I nailed the fresh plank to the beams, the hammer rang out loudly in the still October air.

"Don't you think it's a little too late for that kind of thing?" said Mr. Farley. He was standing at the front of the garage, looking up at me. "It's perfectly clear what you're doing. You take a couple of the old planks out and you stick a couple of the new ones in. I suppose that might fool a lot of people. But don't you think you ought to do the whole roof? If it were your own garage you'd do it that way, I bet. You'd put all new planking down and then you'd put on fresh tar paper and then the galvanized sheets. But you're not going to do that here, are you? I guess you think you can fool my wife. She doesn't know any better so you figure you can get away with a half-assed job."

"I don't think that's a very nice way to talk," said Mrs. Farley.

"I don't care if it's nice or not," he said. "I just can't stand seeing this young fellow make a fool of you."

"Stop being so silly," Mrs. Farley said. "He knows what he's doing. He's putting on a new roof and it'll be just fine. He's going to build me a new roof for my pretty little garage."

Again Mr. Farley looked up at me. It was obvious he was angered by his wife's last remark. His expression was blank and unfriendly. He thrust his hands deep into his pockets and walked over to the cab of the truck.

"Come on," he said to Mrs. Farley. "I can't stand to sit here and watch while somebody ruins a perfectly good piece of construction." Then he opened the cab door and stood for a moment staring up at me. "You're just like all these dopes," he said. "No sense. It's a crime they let you people wander around. Why should I have to clean up everybody else's mess? Come on," he said, motioning to his wife. "I don't want to see you cry when that roof comes tumbling down. I don't even want you to be here."

Mr. Farley climbed into the truck and slammed the door. His wife put her gloves into her pocket and got in. I could see them sitting together as the truck drove out the lane.

— ❋ —

I figured the thing to do was to finish up quickly and split. But the problem was, it was going to take me another two or three days, and I didn't want to spend each day perched up there on the roof, listening to an angry husband. As a kid, I'd heard enough of that.

Splitting altogether, the job undone, just wasn't an option. I remembered the first time I'd met Mrs. Farley at her farm to discuss the roof. "I just want a regular roof," she'd said, "nothing fancy, nothing garish. What I want is something functional." I wondered, a little, how I might make a roof look anything less like a roof. And Mrs. Farley seemed, in her way, to be asking for my approval. Not for the idea of the roof, but for the farm itself. "Do you like it?" she asked. "Don't you think it's nice here?"

I'm not certain I was enthusiastic enough. There's the garage, some fifty feet from the smallish run-down farmhouse, which itself sits halfway down a hill at the bottom of which lies a stagnant pond. It's not a bad piece of real estate, I suppose, if all it's for is to house a wayward daughter. Mrs. Farley was a decent, generous woman, and why shouldn't she have a place where she could get away from her husband's railing? Even when the roof was done, I knew he wouldn't like it.

When I was thirteen my mother fell in love with a man named P. G. McNair. P. G. had made a fortune selling or trading some kind of commodities, and at the age of fifty-five he set his sights on my mother. It was his only ambition, and P. G. wasn't a man to be denied. My mother is a vivacious woman. I didn't know then, though I could have guessed, that together my parents were unhappy. My father was a traveler for a home products manufactory—ceiling tile, flooring, that kind of thing—so he was often not at home. When he was at home he drank, and he drank more after my mother left us. He had a terrible car accident out in Indiana, and my mother came up with P. G. from Florida for his funeral. Afterwards, I stayed on; I had some money then, and I had friends, and it didn't seem like such a lot to get my own apartment so I could finish out the last year and a half of school, and then go on to college after that. Living with P. G. and my mother down in Florida in their condominium would have been a temporary thing, anyway. I mean, they encouraged me to come, but it just didn't seem right. Mrs. Farley and my mother were great friends, before this happened, as I've said. I think they're still in touch.

The day my mother left, that night, my father called me into the living room for a talk. That morning he'd left the house early, and before I left for school P. G. showed up. My mother had all of her bags packed back in the bedroom and I helped P. G. carry them out to his car. I don't think she took anything other than her clothes, not even a photograph. It was a relief, at the time, for her to go, for things between my parents to end.

"You change your mind, just call me," my mother said. "P. G. and I can be back up here in a day. If he gets too bad call a neighbor. Or go some-place else. In time, he'll be better."

"I'll be fine," I said.

"Matthew," said my mother. She looked at me and I knew she was feel-ing all those things—worry, guilt, whatever. Still, I had to hurry for school, so I kissed her good-bye and shook hands with Mr. McNair. I knew P. G. was going to make my mother happy, and she deserved it.

"Now our real life can start," my father said, that evening when he called me in. Whatever this real life was, it seemed to consist mainly of microwave dinners, football, and Jim Beam. Work for my father and school for me. It couldn't have been easy for my father, trying to express this enthusiasm I know he didn't feel.

"I'm going to think of some things," he said. "Some things we'll do together. Watch me. Just watch." Then he clapped his hands together once, as if—poof!—for him at least, the entire matter had been settled.

—— ❀ ——

As it happened, I had two days at the farm to work alone. The galva-nized sheets fit together with a splendid snugness when I laid them, one beside the other, over the renovated planks; overlapped slightly, they laid their fluted edges one on top of the other with a precision that was complete. I was thrilled, for such exact cohesion is so rarely achieved in one's work . . . in life even. I nailed the galvanized sheets onto the planks with squat, wide-headed nails. After two days I'd completed one side of the garage. Now from the road, the wide inverted V of the roof looked like an open book, laid face down on its pages: its back was a dull black—the planks—while the front cover was the brilliant polished silver of the sheets.

The next day when I arrived for work, I found two cars at the farm. Mr. Farley's new midnight-blue Mercedes was parked in the center of the gravel drive. Its chrome gleamed, its bumpers blistered with morning light. Even the tires appeared to have been scrubbed. Mrs. Farley's old Chevrolet wagon, with its white paint chipping and its fenders crowded with dark scabs of rust, was almost hiding in the tall grass of the field where she had parked it. That Mr. Farley endured his wife's rather eccentric taste in automobiles was the only thing about the two that suggested any compromise. Mrs. Farley was planting roses in the garden beside the house. She'd brought along a bag of sand, and as she stood in her woolen skirt, up to her ankles in the dirt, she spooned the sand out with gentle care and then mixed it into the soil with a trowel. She might have been preparing the mix for a cake. When I climbed out of my car and slammed the door, she looked up and waved.

Mr. Farley was waiting for me at the garage. He was pacing, stopping every now and then to peek over the eaves at the side of the roof I'd finished. I wasn't much inclined to face him, and I dallied gathering up my tools. Finally I started walking toward the garage.

At a range of twenty feet he sighted in on me. "Do you really know what you're doing?" he barked. "I'm just asking you," he said, more mildly. "Tell me the truth, no funny stuff about it. I won't hold a grudge. Do you, or do you not, know what it is you're doing?"

I looked away from Mr. Farley to the roof, and there was only one answer I could give him. "Yes," I said, "I do know what I'm doing."

The poor man was stunned. He looked at the garage roof slowly, then nodded. For a moment a smile struggled with the sternness on his face. Then he walked over to his Mercedes and got in, and drove off.

"I'm sorry he has to be like that," said Mrs. Farley. She stood below me in front of the garage, holding her gloves. "I apologize," she said. "He just can't help it. Last night he picked up the phone at home, and it was my daughter. She called collect. He wouldn't talk to her, so five minutes later when the phone rang again I picked it up. She was calling from a motel in Pasadena. She said she'd lost one of the cats and she'd given my number to people along the way so they could call me in case they found the cat. She said they should call me collect. Mr. Farley's sort of upset."

"It's not your fault," I said.

"When can you finish the roof?" she asked.

"Tomorrow, for sure."

"Then you can give Mr. Farley your bill in the morning."

She took her car keys out of the pocket of her skirt and walked over to her car. She opened the door, and with an irritation I was surprised to see from such a restrained woman, she slapped her leather gloves down onto the front seat. "Some people," she said, "never change. Not in a thousand years. Try your best not to be one of them."

— ✳ —

My last day at the farm I spent several hours finishing up. The front section of the roof, above the open stalls, went more quickly than I'd anticipated, and in a few hours I'd practically finished both rows of sheets.

Late in the morning, Mrs. Farley's station wagon came bumping down the lane. I'd been alone all morning and was glad to have the company. Only two of the galvanized sheets remained before the roof was finished.

Mrs. Farley backed her station wagon up to the garage. After she shut off the engine, I was surprised to see that Mr. Farley also climbed out of the car. I had thought he might not ride in his wife's old wagon, but here he was, a brown hunting hat on his head and thick work gloves on his hands.

"Good afternoon," said Mrs. Farley. "The roof looks beautiful. Don't worry about us. We just came down to clean out some of this old junk."

Mr. Farley removed two plastic trash barrels from the back of his wife's station wagon and carried them into the garage. He ignored me, yet that in itself seemed a good sign. He began to gather things up inside the garage, while I watched him through a chink in the roof. Today, this cleaning up didn't appear to bother him.

After he'd filled one of the barrels, Mr. Farley appeared again in front of the garage. He loaded the barrel into the back of the wagon. Just then his wife came out of the garage, carrying a section of rusty pipe, and one of the broken roof planks I'd discarded. She slid these things carefully into the back of the wagon. "Save these," she said to Mr. Farley. "And this one, too." She removed a big, old-fashioned light bulb from the pocket of her skirt, and set it on the roof of her wagon. "Some day these things might be valuable," she said. It struck me as peculiar that she should want to save the bulb, let alone the plank or pipe. Why should she be preparing herself for a time when such things would be available no more?

Mr. Farley seemed to share my confusion. Just as I was about to start nailing down one of the last two sheets, he looked up at me suddenly and winked. It was an amused wink, a single rapid shudder of his eye. It shocked me, yet at the same time it told me, with absolute clarity, that he considered his wife a fool. She would save anything; she knew nothing about farms or real estate or junk; and when it came to really cleaning up, he had to do the work. His single wink seemed to promise us a happy complicity of men. But just as suddenly Mr. Farley's expression changed.

"Do you have your bill?" he asked.

I'd made the bill out earlier that morning, so I put my hammer down and walked over to the edge of the roof and handed it down. Mr. Farley unfolded it and scanned the bill. Then he pocketed it in his shirt.

"I didn't think you had it in you," he said, his voice straining with the effort to be friendly. He eyed the roof. "It looks good, though. Is it all right if I send you a check?"

"Sure," I said. Then I watched the Farleys walk beneath me into the garage. What, I wondered, had happened to him?

One last sheet remained. I clambered back to the top of the roof, and as I bent down over the sheet, through the gap between the last uncovered planks I could see just a bit of Mr. Farley's leg below me, then a hint of Mrs. Farley's moving hand. I lifted the last sheet into place, closing off the view. I hammered in one of the nails, holding it stiffly for the first few tentative taps, then dropping the hammer down hard from a height, each stroke rewarding me with a firm, loud *bing* from the head of the nail. As I hammered, I could hear Mrs. Farley talking below me inside the garage.

"When the Chinese come," she said, "we'll be ready. They'll appreciate us because we know how to work with our hands. They'll make you and me foremen because they'll see right off that we know what we're doing."

I stopped hammering and waited for Mr. Farley's reply. Yet he too was listening, and he'd noticed that the thud of the hammer had stopped above him. I took a nail from my shirt pocket and held it against the smooth sur-face of the galvanized sheet, then gave it a few cautious taps to assure him that I was working.

My little signal worked. Confident that I could no longer hear him, Mr. Farley said to his wife, "Yes, we will. And when the Chinese come we'll be at the top of their lists. They'll think we're special because we were prepared."

He was perfectly serious, and I was thrilled. For the first time, Mr. Farley had agreed with her. I struck another nail hard with a series of rapid blows, driving it down until it was flush with the surface of the sheet. I imagined myself perched above them, providing the Farleys with this sense of shel-ter; it was as if I held up the sky above them. Seen from a distance, we might have looked like the stiff figures carved into a stylized Roman frieze, perhaps commemorating Labor, or even the building of Rome: above them on the roof, myself, the solemn workman, my hand, hammer-laden, frozen in mid-stroke; below, the members of the household, their arms outstretched beneath the stony folds of robes, their faces fixed with smiles—they were laughing at some private joke. Just above them, my last nail went in like a shot.

# *Krishna's Kid Ivory*

It was three o'clock in the morning when Durning arrived for the first time in Delhi, just off the Lufthansa flight from Hong Kong on its overnight trip through to Frankfurt. Deplaning alone, he found the Delhi airport so underlit and empty that he felt like he was descending through a tomb, a feeling that persisted once he'd cleared customs and was on his way to the Ranjani Oberoi in a taxi, being ferried at low speed by an invisible driver through a landscape that was dark, flat, and vacant, so deserted-looking that he wondered if this was a city of the dead. Where was the teeming India of legend? Asleep, Durning gathered; there wasn't a single cone of welcoming light in the whole inky landscape. Delhi was, it seemed, a city of operatic odors. The smell of an open sewer was suffocating, but as they drove on it gave way to other tart scents: curried cooking fumes, wood smoke, rotting vegetables. Dazed with fatigue and disoriented, Durning saw on the horizon the black skeleton of a gallows—which turned out to be a jungle-gym outside an elementary school once they drew abreast. The broad black avenue his taxi drifted down wasn't unlike some jungle river. When at last they pulled up to the Oberoi, the big hotel was ablaze with light.

They were not expecting him. The marble-floored lobby was empty, and the front desk clerk seemed taken aback by Durning's arrival. He was a small, immaculate Indian with a neatly clipped military mustache. Durning felt the man was picking an odd time to get snooty. Where was the fax confirming his reservation? When had that reservation been made? "I'm afraid, sir," the clerk said, "we seem to have no record of you. And no room to offer you, either."

"Then what do I do?" Durning asked. "I've never been to India before and I don't know where I am. Did my brother leave a message for me? We're supposed to meet in Vrindavan tomorrow evening."

"I'm afraid no one left a message." The clerk studied something behind the counter. "If you wouldn't mind double occupancy," he said, not looking up.

"Excuse me?"

"It's the middle of the night, sir. The room's a two-bed suite. Take it or not, it's all I can offer."

Durning was too exhausted to look elsewhere. He checked in, and afterwards took the elevator upstairs. Inside the room, he discovered that he was definitely not alone. The suite was vast, almost vulgar with its gaudy chandelier and gold-painted moldings, and its thick expanse of turquoise-colored carpet. His roommate was a huge African in a canary-yellow shirt, who sat with his legs crossed, lounging on one of the queen-sized beds. Evidently he too had recently checked in, because his luggage was by the door. A red and white pack of Marlboros lay on the night table, and the African lit one with a chunky Zippo. "Hel-lo," he said, offering Durning an enormous salmon-palmed hand. "Magumba-bumba-ticka," he said. Then he leaned back, smiled widely, and took a long satisfying drag on his cigarette.

Durning sat down on the bed opposite and rubbed his shoulder, which was sore from the two vaccinations his doctor had given him before he'd left Kansas City. Courtesy of the doctor, too, there was a satchel full of Nivaquine pills and Paludrine, for malaria, stuffed inside his duffel. He tried to relax and leaned back a little on the bed, feeling dazed. He noticed a fat gold Rolex on the African's wrist. He wondered, was this fellow a businessman, just up from the Congo? There was a thick leather-bound book on the blue coverlet beside him, and after a moment the African pawed it over and popped it open to a page, which he scanned. Then he stubbed out his cigarette and, with a nod to Durning, began to read out loud in a strange African tongue. He had brilliant white teeth and his voice was rich and liquid. Could he be a clergyman, perhaps? The African raised a big black hand and began to intone specific sentences, lifting one finger after another, slowly, as if he were ticking off important points about which Durning might be tested later.

That seemed appropriate because the whole trip was something of a trial. And not just the flights, to Los Angeles first and then forever on to Hong Kong, followed by the Lufthansa flight, which hadn't taken off until midnight. Two days ago Durning's brother, Henry, had called him collect from an ashram in Vrindavan. He had been expelled, he was in some sort of trouble, he had no money, and he wanted to come home, though he said he couldn't travel alone. Since their parents were dead, home in this case meant Durning's house in Overland Park with Tracy, his wife, and their two children. Not that Henry wasn't welcome—or was he? Henry was Durning's only brother, a pure fuck-up who'd always had a nose for trouble. Perhaps that assessment itself lacked a certain charity, thinking of Henry's misadventures in that way, but that's what they were, and as Durning saw it, that pretty much summed up the differences between them.

How could two brothers be so opposed? Durning, the college jock, the real estate salesman, with two kids and a wife, a seven handicap and a black BMW parked beside his razored lawn. Three years younger, Henry had never held down a job. Ever since adolescence he'd always seemed slightly dazed, befuddled. He'd gotten two misdemeanors for vagrancy and shoplifting when he was twenty, then did a six-month stint in jail from which he'd emerged a born-again Christian. By then their father was dead and the family just grew apart. Henry was a construction worker, a dishwasher. He'd pumped gas; he'd been in communes in Texas and California. Nothing worked out for him for very long. After their mother died, Henry headed to India with his inheritance, living first like an old hippie on the beach in Goa, then on to Vrindavan and the ashram. He kept in touch with Durning through letters or postcards maybe once a year.

Now Durning found himself in a strange country, having traveled halfway around the world to fetch his brother. Tracy was clearly ambivalent about the prospect of Henry's visit, struggling openly with what she thought they should do. What they both wanted, privately, was for Henry to disappear. "How come you have to go after him?" she had asked. After all, who would know if they simply ignored him, if they didn't accept Henry's collect calls?

"He's my brother," Durning said. "I have to do something."

"Who says?" Tracy replied.

But of course she gave in. "Go get him," she said. "If he's really in trouble, I guess the only place he should be is here with us."

The last time they were together was just before Henry's departure for Goa, two years ago, when his brother had visited for the weekend. What Durning remembered of his stay was all unfortunate. Durning had fetched Henry from the Kansas City airport in his brand new BMW. On the way home they'd stopped at a mini-mart because Henry was thirsty, and then Henry had spilled his cream soda all over the new BMW's leather seats. Henry tried to ·clean up the sticky mess with his shirt, which he removed—and which was surely his only clean one.

Durning's children thought Henry was weird. Most of the weekend he'd sat on the sofa in the living room staring off into space. Was it drugs? Then late one evening, after Tracy and the kids had gone to bed, Henry started talking to Durning about the beatings. How when they were kids, Durning had gotten up in the middle of the night, regularly, and gone over to Henry's bed and thrashed him. "I did no such thing," Durning had replied, flabbergasted. "Yes, you did. It went on for years and years." Henry was practically crying when he finished. "I don't remember anything like that," Durning had said, which was the truth. A thing like that, how could he forget it? And why bring it up now? Was it Durning's fault that Henry had turned out this way? It was typical, Durning felt, the way Henry tried to make everyone else feel guilty and responsible.

When Durning awoke it was daylight and the room was filled with Africans. The suite seemed to have been transformed into a sort of welcome center for the United Nations: there were six or seven Africans dressed in native clothing, all loud vertical stripes and bold colors. One goateed man in a purple robe wore a jaunty cap. There was a lot of loud, upbeat conversation—none of it intelligible to Durning—but the sense of excitement inside the room was genuine. A few of the Africans stood gazing down at the silent American in his bed. Then they drew aside and a good-looking Indian woman in an orange sari strode forward. Her jet-black hair was mostly hidden but her sooty eyes and cheekbones were striking.

"You're joining us for the tour?" she asked, in perfect English.

"What tour?"

"To Mathura, and to Agra to see the Taj."

"I have to go to Vrindavan," Durning said.

"What luck, since it's right on our way." The woman held out her hand. "I'm Mrs. Merchandani, the guide."

"And who are all these people?"

Mrs. Merchandani smiled down at him. "Poor you," she said. "This must be altogether confusing. These gentlemen are divinity students from the famous seminary in Bangui. In the African Republic. They're on a special grant here to study the religions of India. They haven't been keeping you up?"

"Not really," Durning answered.

"I gather they're holding some kind of competition. The one who gives the most heartfelt reading from the Bible gets all the others to pay for his meals. I understand Mr. Magumba is leading the competition at present. Mr. Magumba's your suite-mate."

"What language do they use?"

"Sango. It's their native tongue, but they also speak French. You mustn't worry yourself, though. I can give you the tour in English. Won't you join us? We'll also be visiting Mathura, the birthplace of Krishna. The Govinda festival there is afoot. Vrindavan is only a few kilometers."

"What time will we be there?" he asked.

"Just this evening," said Mrs. Merchandani brightly.

Something in her enthusiasm was so profoundly pleasant that Durning found himself desperate not to disappoint her. And why refuse a trip to the Taj, as well?

"Chop-chop," Mrs. Merchandani said. "The sun's well up now and the traffic en route will be terrible."

— ❋ —

All of India seemed to live by the roadside. Leaving the turmoil of Delhi behind them, Durning thought the landscape might open up, but life lapped up here in the sun-bleached countryside on even the remotest stretches of highway. There were food stalls and other small shops crammed up along the shoulder of the road. Delhi itself, by day, had been astonishing. Looking out the window of the minibus at the flocks of bicycles and the old-fashioned, round-nosed automobiles and the vast seas of pedestrians, Durning was overwhelmed—someone must have gone mad here to let all this happen.

Mrs. Merchandani was right, because the roads were jammed up everywhere. Even the main road to Agra was only a narrow two-lane passage through trees, congested with traffic. Plus, there were terrible accidents every twenty miles, most involving livestock. Several times the minibus had to drive slowly around some poor splayed-out beast and the truck or the bus that had felled it. At each accident scene a furious debate between drivers was in progress, surrounded by an enthusiastic crowd of onlookers. There was dust everywhere.

Inside the bus the Africans were in high spirits. Mrs. Merchandani had used the small microphone at the front and made several announcements to them in Sango, and then Mr. Magumba had followed with a morning prayer. There were evidently lots of comic sights outside the windows, because shortly the Africans were full of jokes and jolly laughter. Durning was sitting in the center of the back row of the bus. Mrs. Merchandani worked her way rearward and joined him. He wondered how she managed to keep her orange sari so immaculate in such a dirty country.

"It's a three-hour trip," she said. "If you'd like to catch up on your sleep a little."

"I was wondering," Durning asked, "how it is that you speak their language?"

"My husband and I were stationed in Africa. I studied there."

"Did you like it?"

"We loved it," she said.

"Were you there long?"

"Five years."

"Your husband," he said. "What did he do? Was he a diplomat?"

"My husband was in the military. And you, what takes you to Vrindavan?"

"Family," Durning replied. "My brother."

"Oh?" Durning could feel the pretty woman studying him. "If you don't mind, I'd have to conclude that you're not so enthusiastic."

"It's a long story," Durning said.

"And this is a short ride," said Mrs. Merchandani. "You'll have to pardon me, but I do this trip so often that I sometimes get bored. The people are the thing I like. And I do rather enjoy your company."

"Thank you," he said.

Durning noticed out the window that there were billboards all along the highway. One, in English, advertised Ford tractors. Another, in Hindi, featured a suave, mustached Indian gentleman, with romantic good looks;

it was an advertisement for men's hair tonic painted in bright pastels on the side of a restaurant. Through the haze of diesel exhaust, Durning spotted in the distance a tin-roofed shantytown. The makeshift village was built around a kidney-shaped drainage ditch, and people were squatting there, shamelessly relieving themselves. At the other end of the ditch women were on their knees, washing laundry.

"They are rather like children, aren't they?" Mrs. Merchandani said.

"Who?" Durning asked.

"I find these Africans so enchanting."

As if to demonstrate her point, the man sitting to their right turned and spoke to Mrs. Merchandani with great delicacy. He had a broad, high brow and that morning had nicked himself several times on the chin while shaving. When he was finished, the man turned to Durning and offered an impish grin.

"Mr. Tutu wants to know if you understand why so few Africans emigrate to the United States."

"No," Durning said. "Ask him to tell me."

Mr. Tutu blurted out his answer and the entire bus suddenly exploded into laughter.

"A joke," said Mrs. Merchandani. "Mr. Tutu claims it's because they're afraid they'll all be turned into hockey pucks. Ice hockey he means, I gather."

"That's weird," Durning said, offended.

After the laughter died down, someone in the front of the bus called back to Mrs. Merchandani and spoke to her at length. There were whoops and catcalls. Mrs. Merchandani blushed, and turned her face away and looked out the window.

"What is it?" Durning asked. "What did he say?"

"Mr. Jabala was inquiring. He wanted to know if you're aware that there are still cannibals in Africa. On the upper reaches of the Congo. He says white meat is very tasty to the people there. That in the jungle, there are men still as wild as the wildest of beasts."

"How reassuring," Durning said. "Is Mr. Jabala hungry?"

"I think he's only trying to frighten you."

"Tell him he's doing a good job."

Luckily, at that instant, Durning looked up and saw the accident about to happen. He was trying to get a handhold on the back of a seat, when a second later their bus smashed into the back of a big truck. The collision threw him down the center aisle of the bus, like a stone shot from a cata-pult. Afterward the bus lurched over to the side of the road with a groan.

Durning sat for a moment in the aisle. The Africans, too, seemed some-what disoriented by the collision, but after a moment they began to get out of their seats, and a few of them helped the dazed American to his feet. Durning was surrounded by these big black men, when suddenly a great laugh exploded again among them—evidently they were amused by the absurdity of the entire scene. Embarrassed by his fall, Durning felt victim-ized by their amusement, tinged as it seemed to be with ridicule and hos-tility. Brushing himself off, he turned and straight-armed the exit.

He strode a few paces down the roadway into a crowd of filthy people and stopped. The air outside was humid and foul-smelling. Where, exactly, could he go? He felt sick with shock from the crowd, the heat, and the excitement of the accident. But having come to the decision that he want-ed absolutely nothing more to do with any of the people in his party, he looked back and watched as Mrs. Merchandani carefully shepherded the Africans across the buzzing two-lane traffic and into a decrepit restaurant called the Blue Haven Café. By now the driver of their bus had climbed down too and was quarreling with the driver of the truck he had rear-ended. For the time being, it didn't look like their tour was going any-where. The sky in the distance was a sullen gray, but at the horizon it dis-solved into a mist of luminous blue.

Durning recrossed the road and followed the little group into the restau-rant. Inside the air felt thick with cooking fumes, and a ceiling fan beat nois-ily through the haze. A waiter in a dingy white jacket was serving tea and a plate of sticky cookies to the Africans, who were seated with Mrs. Merchandani around a table. Several of the Africans looked up, their mouths open as they chewed. They waved to him and cheered, one of them doing a comic imitation of a man pitching forward like a diver. Why were they all so jolly? he wondered. And why couldn't he be more like that?

"I hope you're all right," Mrs. Merchandani said. "You seem to be cut a little. Sit down here and let me have a look."

Durning obeyed her, then felt her fingers as she gently tested above his eyebrow. He smelled alcohol as she tore open a Wash'n Dri towelette from her purse, then felt its sting against his forehead. When she was finished Mrs. Merchandani neatly applied the towelette to her manicured fingers and left it in a little ball on the edge of the table.

"Perhaps now you'd like something to eat?"

"Thank you," Durning said. "What about our bus?"

"Mr. Dawali, our driver, is investigating that at the moment. If our vehicle cannot be fixed then he will telephone and order another. Mr. Dawali is very competent."

Presently the waiter returned with two tin trays in his hands and several others balanced on his forearms. He began to set these out before the Africans, who had grown rather sullen and quiet. There were chickpeas and samosas, along with rice in a chunky yogurt dressing. The food smelled delicious.

"These are *thalis*," said Mrs. Merchandani. "A *thali* is a ready-prepared meal. Like your TV dinners in the United States. Would you like one?"

"Sure," Durning said. He had just realized that he hadn't eaten anything since yesterday, and he was famished.

Mrs. Merchandani was drinking a glass of muddy tea. "In this business," she said, smiling, "one learns to grow unflustered."

"Have you been at it long?"

"Six years," she said. "For some time it wasn't necessary that I work. Then it was."

"What happened?"

"My husband died. We have two children, one boy, one girl. My husband had a military pension but it proved insufficient. And touring is something I like. I like people, and I'm good at it."

"I can tell," Durning said, moving aside as the waiter placed a steaming tray before him.

"My husband was the chief of security for Rhajiv Gandhi," said Mrs. Merchandani proudly.

"That's a big job, isn't it?"

"Too big. Too big for one person with a staff of only eighty. They've changed their methods dramatically since Mr. Gandhi's assassination, though. India is too disparate and too passionate a nation when it comes to issues of national security."

Presently Mr. Dawali approached Mrs. Merchandani and spoke to her in Hindi. Then he snapped to attention and departed from the restaurant.

"It seems we aren't going anywhere just now," Mrs. Merchandani said. "Our bus cannot continue the journey. Mr. Dawali has already telephoned back to Delhi for another." She turned to the table and repeated this news, in Sango, to the Africans, most of whom had finished eating. A small dish of toothpicks was being passed around among them.

"Gandhi," Durning said. "Wasn't he blown up?"

"Exactly," said Mrs. Merchandani. "How keen of you to remember."

"How awful," he said.

"Yes," said Mrs. Merchandani. "There was nothing left of either one of them."

"I'm sorry," Durning said.

"I know you are. On the whole, people are." Then Mrs. Merchandani looked into Durning's face, in a way quite unlike anything he'd ever experienced. That is to say, it was the deeply resigned expression of a woman whose husband had been turned into confetti.

"They executed them," Mrs. Merchandani said.

Durning suddenly had to stand up. He had eaten too quickly and his stomach was doing wild hot flips. He stumbled over to the grubby counter where the waiter was resting.

"Do you have a bathroom?" he asked.

The waiter gave Durning a wink and a merry chuckle. "But don't you see?" he said. "All of India is a bathroom, sir."

— ❋ —

It was an hour before the replacement bus arrived. Given the delay, Mrs. Merchandani suggested that a choice be made between Agra and Mathura, as there wouldn't be time to do justice to them both. The Africans elected to see Mathura, which to Durning seemed very odd—how could they? But to them, evidently Agra was simply the site of a splendid tomb, whereas Krishna's birthplace was alive with temples and celebrations. Durning had composed himself by now and along with the Africans he and Mrs. Merchandani filed out of the Blue Haven Café and boarded the bus. The new driver was a richly bearded, turbaned Sikh. Mr. Dawali was left behind by the roadside with the damaged vehicle.

Traffic seemed to improve on this leg of the journey. Durning dozed, and when he awoke with a jolt heard the loud snoring of the Africans all around him. Mrs. Merchandani was sitting in the front of the bus in the seat immediately behind the driver. Durning's suite-mate, Mr. Magumba, was sitting on the aisle in the seat directly beside him. Magumba was a big

man, and how uncomfortable this narrow space must be for him! Presently
he looked up and cast an amused glance Durning's way. He was still wearing his dark slacks and his canary-colored shirt from last evening.

Mathura was on the right bank of the muddy Yamuna River. Through
the window Durning could see a sun-baked village of low houses with a
crowded bazaar and innumerable temples. Colored streamers hung from
the buildings' eaves. Their bus snaked down a hill and through the crowded alleys, dislodging pedestrians as it inched ahead. Mrs. Merchandani used
the microphone at the front to make a lengthy announcement to the
Africans. Then the bus stopped, and the Africans began to file off. Mrs.
Merchandani repeated some of her announcement in English for
Durning's benefit.

"As you know, Krishna is the most human of all the Hindu gods. In
his mature years, we know him as the wise philosopher whose teachings
are embodied in the *Bhagavad Gita*. But here, in his early days, we see him
as a child stealing curds and butter and being punished for it by his mother. Govinda is the festival of his birth, and devotion is expressed in reen-
actments of Krishna's childhood attempts to get at the pot of curds and
butter, which was placed beyond his reach. The earthen pots containing
his favorite foods are known as *matkas*. You'll see them suspended between
buildings high above the streets. The young men form human pyramids,
some of them rising several tiers. Finally one of them will reach the *matka*
and break it open. There is an additional incentive because the *matkas*
contain cash."

Here Mrs. Merchandani stopped, clicking off her microphone and
handing it back to the Sikh. She and Durning were alone now on the bus.

"Perhaps you'd just like to wander," she said. "It's a fascinating village."

Durning climbed out of his seat and joined her at the front of the
vehicle.

"Your brother?" she inquired, with the air of someone who has just
remembered something vaguely. "In Vrindavan. I suppose he's what you
would call a hippie?"

Durning was so startled he didn't know how to reply. "Hippie?" he
repeated. In his own ears the word sounded weak, American, and foolish.
He was embarrassed by it and suddenly felt that he should have made his
journey to fetch Henry alone, without the intrusion of these Africans or
this meddlesome widow. "I say that because Vrindavan is only famous for

one thing. The ISKON temple. The International Society for Krishna Consciousness. Is that where your brother is?"

Durning nodded.

"There are students there from the world over," Mrs. Merchandani said. She put her fingers very lightly on Durning's wrist. "It's really quite difficult to gain admission. Is your brother a student there?"

"Yes," Durning lied.

"How wonderful," she said. "Then you must be very proud of him."

— ❋ —

Durning had begun to feel like an ugly American, conspicuously unreceptive to almost everything he saw. Was his presence here, even, among these faithful a sort of lie? He walked through the village with no particular destination in mind. In a wide unswept alley he happened upon a crowd of sweating, nearly naked boys, their bodies glistening as they whooped and piled gleefully onto one another's shoulders. They were trying to reach an earthen pot that was suspended from a cord strung above them in the street. How much fun they were having, their laughter and camaraderie and their shrill cries! When at last one boy reached the *matka* and broke it open with his fist, small colored packages and coins scattered about the alley. The youths shrieked with pleasure as they scrambled after them.

Had there ever been boyhood moments like this for him and Henry? Frankly, Durning could not recall. Their father had been a bully, a drinker, and was rarely pleased with his sons; for him, severity had been everything. Durning could clearly remember giving up on Henry, just as their father had done, when early on Henry had removed himself from the competitive race for honors that was at the heart of their relationship as brothers. Durning had goaded him, had tried to cajole him to compete. Had he hit him, in the hope that Henry might strike back? Distantly, it seemed to Durning that this was possible, though not in the manner Henry had described.

It was late in the afternoon by now, and the heat was blistering. At a dark opening off an alleyway, a fetid stench burned Durning's nostrils. Further on, the alley opened into a marketplace crowded with people and the rich aromas of sweets and spices. The spices were arranged in wide paper cones on cloths covering the ground, the mounds of saffrons and curries and cinnamon arrayed like so many rich daubs of pigment. Crowds of people scrimmaged all about Durning in the street. He wiped away the sweat leaking into his eyes, and suddenly felt that he had gone as far now as it was possible for him to go. When he imagined strolling back through the village to find the minibus, a feeling of weakness overtook him.

He backtracked through the village. Mrs. Merchandani and the driver were standing in the shadow cast by the bus, sipping coffee from Styrofoam cups. When the Africans all returned, they looked as if they'd been dancing. Had they been moved by what they'd seen at the temples? Mr. Magumba and the goateed man in the cap were covered with sweat. They passed Durning, giggling. How good-natured they were, how uncomplaining! Durning tried to imagine what sort of city Bangui might be, where these men had come from. Were there dusty mimosas around a deserted square, in the distance the roaring of a lion? Now the Africans struck Durning as both brave and virtuous, so far from home, yet still ready with their easy affability, while he, Durning, remained aloof and alone.

He was out of his element, and it humbled him to be among people who felt so casually at home in this world. What, after all, did he know? It suddenly seemed to him that his knowledge of the world was small, and all interior, made up of safe, prescribed compartments—the closet that contained his suits and ties, say, or the glove box and the trunk of his cherished car. Nothing in his life had prepared him to be out and abroad in an alien country. And though she was, perhaps, overly inquisitive, even Mrs. Merchandani struck him as quite gallant in the way she handled her misfortune.

Hilarity reigned once more inside the vehicle. Evidently Mr. Tutu and Mr. Jabala had had a comic encounter of some kind in the village, and they were both trying to recount this amidst squeals of childish laughter. Mr. Tutu ended up on the floor, waggling his head and gasping for breath, while all around him the other Africans jeered and guffawed. Finally, the driver closed the door and turned the bus back into traffic.

Durning grew excited when they approached the environs of Vrindavan, which wasn't far. Dusk had settled quickly over the countryside, and by twilight the town's tumult seemed strangely beautiful. Crowded, yes, and filthy, but after the day's misadventures their arrival nonetheless had for him the atmosphere of a homecoming, of at last meeting Henry, which would make everything clear. Durning was startled when the bus jerked to a halt before the creamy face of the ISKON temple. The modern building was lavishly floodlit.

Mrs. Merchandani made an announcement to the Africans. She must have said something serious and rather flattering about Durning, because afterwards the Africans eyed him with a newfound curiosity. Durning rose, and the other passengers followed him single file past the driver.

"We shall wait right here for you," Mrs. Merchandani said. "Good luck."

Durning crossed the street and approached the temple. He wondered if he would find Henry waiting inside for him, or out here in the hubbub of the street. He passed through the crowds of people scrambling on the sidewalk, then walked back and forth, looking for his brother. There was a queue of taxis at the curbside. People passed him carrying enormous bundles, trailed by strings of goats. Finally he spotted Henry standing in a corner by the gate in the shining God-filled air. It was hard to miss another American, and Henry had the attitude of someone who had been waiting there all day.

At home, Durning might have crossed the street to avoid meeting such a man. Could this disheveled person with the vacant look really be his brother? Henry wore frayed blue jeans, some sort of leather sandals, and a T-shirt that was stained and faded. His hair was dirty and long, though his face was clean-shaven. He had about him the look of someone utterly and completely lost. He looked like a beggar. For a moment Durning wanted to turn away, but he knew he was being monitored, and such an indifferent act struck him as truly loathsome. He looked back and saw the minibus, where the Africans stood chatting in a huddled group. He wondered, was Mrs. Merchandani watching him through her window?

"Henry!" Durning shouted, when he was practically upon him.

Relief took hold of his brother's face. Yet Henry didn't appear to be looking at him. In fact, his eyes had a rheumy look.

"What happened to you?" Durning asked.

"I can't see," Henry said. "I've got some infection."

"Oh, my God," Durning said.

"Maybe it was the malaria water in the cistern. We went swimming there, this girl and me. I haven't been able to see much of anything for two weeks."

"Jesus, you should have told me on the telephone."

Henry moved his sandaled feet, which were filthy, but didn't answer. "Maybe back home they can help me." Then he held out his hand for his brother to guide him.

"Your suitcase—or don't you have one?"

Durning led Henry back through the crowd to the bus. The Africans observed them with quiet interest, then drew apart so the brothers could board. Durning climbed up first and guided Henry up the narrow stairway. He climbed into the first seat, opposite Mrs. Merchandani's seat behind the driver. Then he pulled Henry in behind him, helping him down onto the cushioned bench. Durning could feel Mrs. Merchandani's black eyes upon them.

"I thought you might bring a limo," Henry said, laughing. "Who are all our friends here?"

"It's a tour bus," Durning said. "It was the easiest way for me to get down here. Anyway, how much can you see?"

"Shadows, mostly. But I can hear things. One of the doctor-types thinks it will clear up okay, if I can get the antibiotics at home."

The Africans filed back onto the bus, looking down at Henry as they returned to their seats. Perhaps they mistook him for some holy wanderer. As he passed them, Mr. Magumba gave Durning a high-five sign and grinned. It was an event in that black face. His enormous hand fell for a moment on Durning's shoulder.

"This is weird," Henry said. "You and me together here, in India."

"Tell me," Durning said.

"Who are these people? Where'd you meet them?"

There was a polite cough from across the aisle, and Durning realized then that Mrs. Merchandani had been waiting for him to introduce her. "This is Henry, my brother," he announced. "Mrs. Merchandani is our guide." Henry reached his bony hand into the aisle and Mrs. Merchandani shook it. Then the driver pulled the door closed with a slapping hiss and began to edge the bus back onto the road.

"Your brother here has been telling us all about your adventures," said Mrs. Merchandani. "Perhaps, if you feel up to it, later you can share them with our other guests."

"What's she talking about?" Henry whispered.

"I guess she's just curious. Actually, so am I. I mean, what went on here? You told me on the phone that you were in some kind of trouble."

"No money, for starters," Henry said. "These people might be all full of hugs and kisses, but they still have strict rules."

"You said something about an expulsion?"

Henry took a breath and let out a long sigh. "I guess this is the part where you let me know how I'm a stupid fuck-up, right? How I don't fit into your neat little scheme of things."

Durning was stung. "I just want to know what happened to you," he explained.

"I told you, we went swimming. We had a slight difference of opinion, all right? The big cistern is off limits. So are some other things that you don't know about, and never will. Even the enlightened ones have family rules we all have to follow."

Henry's inference made Durning bridle. "So," he said. "Is that why you got thrown out? For skinny-dipping with some babe?"

Before Henry could answer, Mrs. Merchandani suddenly broke in. "I think you should be ashamed of yourself, Mr. Durning. Have you nothing more you can give to your brother?" Then she sat back with a serene sense of her own moral certitude.

Durning was angry. *Nothing more he could give to his brother? My God,* hadn't he come halfway around the world to fetch him? And who was taking Henry back to look after him? Still, in his heart he knew that Mrs. Merchandani was right. Henry was Durning's only brother, and he should be cherished, not reviled. Henry might be weak, and undependable, but he had retreated and survived where Durning surely would have crumbled. These thoughts came to Durning in a rush and, eyes slightly blurring with tears, he turned back to Henry.

"Just ignore me," Durning said. "We're going home now." Then he grabbed Henry's hand and watched as the bus plunged on through the darkness.

# Righteous, Bold as Lions

Myers shambled along the side of the road, slump-shouldered, his head stuffed with equal parts of whiskey and frustration. He was drunk enough that he couldn't remember precisely where he was or why he was here—though that was okay since it was generally how he preferred things these days. The one thing he did know was that if he didn't soon get some relief, he was just going to have to jump in front of one of the passing semis and put an end to the whole mess.

Something had been keeping his pain in check, something pleasantly numbing that had settled over his brain like a welcome mist, but now the whiskey was wearing off. Whimpering like an infant, Myers suddenly remembered that he was on his way to buy some wire snips, to cut open his teeth, which had been wired shut since he'd shattered his jaw. As he waited at the intersection, girding himself to cross the street, a yellow Land Rover suddenly pulled up, spraying gravel. There was a handsome logo on the passenger-side door, of three palm trees in silhouette, and TRANS-PORTERS INTERNATIONAL painted in red letters above. Myers watched as the electric window came down, and he could see someone inside smoking, the tip of the cigarette glowing like an incense stick. "Lift?" a man's voice asked. "You'll turn into a duck if you keep standing there."

Myers realized that it was raining. Also, he hadn't noticed that he was standing in a ditch, but he looked down now and sure enough, there he was, in a culvert flush with rain. Who in their right mind would stop to pick him up, anyway?

"You don't look too good," said the man kindly. "Miserable, would be my guess. Though I'm not a betting man myself."

Myers wanted to tell the guy to buzz off, but he couldn't speak. He made a try at opening his mouth, but that set the muscles in his jaw to screaming, so he quit. Anyway, the best he could manage through clenched teeth were mumbled words that sounded like someone talking in their sleep, so he'd pretty much given up talking altogether.

"Stand away from that culvert and step inside the vehicle," said the man with military authority. "You appear to be a person dependent on the kindness of strangers," he said.

"You bet," Myers thought as he climbed in. He needed a lot of help, no doubt about it. He was in bad shape all the way around, having lost at least twenty pounds since his accident. How could he fortify himself, when food meant sucking down milkshakes through a straw? He climbed inside the front seat of the Land Rover and was able to get a view of the driver for the first time. The man bore a shocking resemblance to President Jimmy Carter: the chipmunk grin and boyish hair sticking out from underneath a Marlins baseball cap. Cool blue eyes appraised him.

The man pulled the Land Rover back onto the road. It was an automatic, Myers noted, as his back sunk into the comfy seat. Empty beer cans rolled around on the floor. Myers noticed a high-powered rifle and a gray laptop computer between the seats.

"Where to?" asked the man. "Liquor store or hospital? Hospitals are generally an okay place to get reoriented, if you're sick." He coughed, his phlegmy hacking thick with cigarettes. "By the way, my name's Garnett," he said, though he made no effort to shake Myers's hand.

Myers shook his head vigorously in disagreement, because he didn't want to go to the hospital—not ever again. If he knew anything at all, it was that hospitals were expensive, and the one thing he didn't have right now was money. Hadn't he just been thrown out of his apartment, because he was broke?

Myers leaned back and put his head against the seat, watching the wet pine trees zipping by. The steady hum of the Land Rover was soothing. He knew Garnett was talking to him but he couldn't make out his words. He felt himself sliding down into a very deep hole, and before he could mention how grateful he was for the ride, he passed out.

— ❈ —

He awakened with a jolt, startled by the loud growling of a cat. It was a big cat, and it was close. In fact, it seemed to be immediately behind him inside the Land Rover. Half-turning in his seat, Myers looked back and saw that there were no other seats in the vehicle. In fact, a heavy steel cage lashed over tightly with a tarpaulin took up the entire back of the truck. The cage was as tall as the ceiling of the truck, and Myers could hear something big back there, moving around inside its cage.

"Not much smell now, is there?" Garnett asked him with a grin. "That's the way I like it, personally. I can't stand it, having an animal crapping away back there while I'm driving across the country. Agnes, she's just waking up; she's been sleeping for two days. I'll introduce you when we stop. Agnes is a fourteen-month-old mountain lion that I'm delivering to the wild game park outside San Diego. That's what I do. I mean, that's our business, the people I work for. Bears, birds, you name it. Big animals, mostly, though. You want one moved somewhere, you call us. We're professionals. To tell you the truth, I ain't been feeding Agnes much, but she'll get along just fine. About the worst I ever had is monkeys, let me tell you. I had to steam clean this entire vehicle after I unloaded them."

Myers looked around, wide-eyed, but said nothing. Maybe at the next stoplight he could just climb out.

"Now, now," Garnett said in a soothing tone. "Stop worrying, young fellow, you're safe. Agnes is on one side, we're here on the other. Anyway," he said, "if she gets too feisty, I'll just put her out again." He took one hand off the steering wheel and pointed down at the rifle beside him on the floor. "Animal rights people wouldn't be too happy with me, I guess, but what they don't know can't hurt them, right? And I never lost a client, not once. Never mistreated one and never lost one, neither. Our vehicles are ventilated, top and bottom. There's water back there, too; it's automatic, because we got a tank right on top. I'll have to show you our brochure."

Myers tried to dismiss the man and turned back to the windshield. Waking, he'd discovered a whole new universe of pain: the haze inside his head had cleared, but now his jaw ached again, and everything was as excruciating as it could be. Suddenly the big cat snarled again, making Myers jump. For a moment he wondered if he'd pissed his pants.

A few miles farther on, Garnett turned off the highway into a motel, where a row of cabins sat far back among the trees. The rain had stopped. Garnett climbed down from the Land Rover and came around and helped

Myers out. Garnett stood Myers up, then led him around to the back of the truck.

"You busted your jaw, didn't you?" Garnett asked.

Myers nodded. Garnett held up the keys to the Land Rover, which were attached to a remote, and flicked a button, locking down the doors on the truck with a little squawk. Garnett had the laptop and a black toilet kit beneath his arm. "Stand back a sec," he said, holding up the remote as he thumbed another button. Myers watched as the electric window on the back of the Land Rover came down a few inches and then stopped.

"Handy, huh?" Garnett asked. "I can open and close this thing without even being near the vehicle. Makes my deliveries a snap. It's extra-heavy glass back there, unbreakable. That's Agnes in there, inside. Take a look. But not too close, okay? Believe me, she's something, in the wild. That's nine thousand dollars' worth of animal back there, friend. I got the paperwork right here to prove it."

It was dark inside the cage. Myers couldn't see well, but he could hear something pacing around in there. He leaned a little closer, sensing something on the other side. Then a large, wet, black nose passed by the opening in the glass and vanished. The big cat's head looked larger than a basketball, and Myers drew back, stunned.

Garnett thumbed up the window again with his remote. "I guess you can't see her too good, so you'll just have to trust me. Come on inside, we'll fix you up."

Garnett grabbed Myers by the arm and led him across the parking lot to the door of his room. He rattled the handle on the door a few times and then produced a key. Then he pulled Myers in behind him and hit the light. Inside there were various broken objects scattered about on the floor: a splintered chair, a table with broken legs, a cassette player with tape spewing out of it in glossy loops like intestines. After helping Myers to the couch—aside from the bed, it seemed to be the only unbroken piece of furniture in the room—Garnett brushed aside some fast food debris on the sofa and sat down beside him. There was a telephone beside the couch on the floor, and Garnett opened up his laptop and fiddled with some wires until he'd established a connection.

"I got to check my e-mail," Garnett said. "Could be my next assignment from the office, who knows?" He tapped cheerfully at the keys. "By the way," he said, as he took something out of his pocket and handed it to

Myers. "You dropped this inside my truck."

As soon as he saw it, the page from the yellow pages that he'd torn out, Myers remembered where he'd been, and what he'd been up to only a short time ago. He'd been on his way to the hardware store to buy a pair of wire cutters, to clip away the cursed steel that locked his mouth. Earlier that morning he'd been thrown out of his apartment, but at the time he'd been unable to defend himself, to complain or explain or do anything except stomp away. That was the last straw, as he saw things. With his jaw clamped shut, his own silence rendered him powerless. For three weeks now he'd been unable to speak. He even remembered, distantly, waking up inside the hospital, some big nurse looming over him in the harsh light. She droned on, giving him some complicated speech on how he should feed himself, what he could eat and when, and so forth. Myers hardly remembered any of it; it was like he heard everything quite clearly, but after a second the words just fell away. What was the use? Then he was getting into the Land Rover and now suddenly here he was, in a ruined motel room with Garnett, who hadn't bothered to explain the carnage inside the room, but who was pretty clearly a man in some sort of deep trouble too.

By now Garnett had finished with his e-mail and was stomping around, looking for something. Finally he went into the bathroom and came back carrying a hand mirror.

"You got any idea how you look?" he asked Myers.

Myers didn't have to look. Beneath his eyes, he knew, his face was still swollen and discolored from his surgery. He had made a point of not looking at himself since he'd come out of the hospital because he'd never seen himself looking so ridiculous. Not only that, but it was simple stupidity that had gotten him into this to begin with. He hadn't been in a fight, even, but had simply passed out outside a tavern, shattering his jaw on a curbstone when he fell.

"Uhhgg!" was the best response Myers could muster. Finally, using grunts and hand gestures, he asked Garnett for something he could use to write. After a moment Garnett offered him the laptop.

"Go ahead," he said, lighting up a cigarette. "Write me a memo, if you like."

With only the slightest hesitation, Myers took the laptop onto his knees and typed: *broken jaw can't talk can't sleep can't eat do you have dope or booze or a pair of pliers if not then a gun with bullets please?*

Garnett studied the screen and laughed out loud. Then he opened up his toilet kit and began to survey its contents, picking up brown bottles, squinting to read their labels. A dusty shaft of sunlight came through one of the windows and fell on his brown hair, and Myers noticed that it was streaked with gray. "Shit, I don't even know what half this stuff is," Garnett said. "All this gear in here's for Agnes, or the other animals. Gets them to sleep, you know, when we're on the road. Mostly I just put it in their food. I doubt you want a tranquilizer that strong, though on second thought maybe you do. Hold on a sec." Garnett got up from the couch and went over to the shabby dinette, and came back with a bottle of bourbon. "See if you can get some of this into you," he said, handing Myers the fifth.

Myers quickly unscrewed the cap, tilted back his head and did the best he could to pour some of the bourbon through his teeth. Misery and pain had propelled him into a state of such complete neglect that he didn't care how much he spilled down his clothes. Just thinking about the whole wasted junk pile of his life made him want to puke, yet he was unable to scream out his frustration. Once he'd broken his jaw—the coup de grâce—there was no longer any doubt that his life was a total failure, so he'd decided to stay drunk for a long time, then probably kill himself.

Myers' parents had supported him after he got out of high school, but two years ago they'd pulled the plug, telling him it was time he make it on his own. Now he was twenty-three years old, a maintenance man at the local community college, earning minimum wage cleaning up after his contemporaries at the school. He'd been living in a basement apartment owned by a Pakistani dry cleaner, who that day had thrown him out for not paying his rent. He'd been drunk much of the time the past three weeks, and he was always alone. Nights, when he wasn't hanging out in the bars, he sat at the table in his kitchen, scribbling long furious letters to Petra, his ex-girlfriend. Just three months ago, Petra had left him, though she'd left a likeness of herself behind. Petra fancied herself something of an artist, and out of papier mâché she had constructed a life-sized version of herself, complete with eyes and mouth and painted nails, a wig and pieces of her own discarded clothing, which she'd left for Myers in their kitchen with a Dear John note safety-pinned to the collar of its blouse. Now it seemed entirely appropriate to Myers that such a ridiculous loser like himself should pass out on the street and end up with his jaws wired shut, sipping what sustenance he could through a plastic straw.

He was feeling a little better now, in fact. He kept tipping up the bourbon, letting it run through his teeth and down his throat. He offered the bourbon to Garnett who took a long pull on the bottle himself.

"You might wonder," Garnett said, as he wiped his mouth on the back of his wrist. "Been a good few months since I had another guy to shoot the shit with, you know? I'm on the road, mostly, and none of these animals can talk." He took another long draught from the bottle. "New York to Chicago. Chicago to Des Moines. Then back again. I keep in touch with the head office by e-mail and telephone. It's not a bad life, I suppose, though it's not exactly what I had in mind. Though who can remember, really, what they had in mind?" He handed the bottle back to Myers and rubbed his chin. "You're all right," he said, "even though you can't talk. Why don't you write down what you want to say here on the computer?"

After a moment, Myers tapped out on the screen: *Thanks for the fuel.*

Garnett took a long drag on his cigarette and blew a plume of smoke towards the ceiling.

"I guess I'm away from home too much, that's one thing," Garnett said. Myers didn't know what to say to this, so he just sat there, watching Garnett's face working, breathing through his nose.

"Well, shit," Garnett said, standing up now and walking around in a tight circle. The sun was dipping behind the trees and shadows were beginning to lengthen in the room.

Finally Myers wrote: *I guess you know some people here in town?*

"Right," Garnett said. "Ain't that the truth." At first his face was blank but then it opened into a cheerful smile. Then he got up and stared at a spot on the ceiling, the smile sticking to his face like something he'd put on. Myers was immediately sorry that he'd asked the man this simple question.

"I guess I'm still trying to get a hold on this," Garnett said after a while. He kicked the corner of the sofa and tried to laugh, but now he looked like he wanted to tear something apart with his bare hands. "I came home from another run two days ago and found this guy is shacked up with my wife. Nancy, that's her, is at this very moment sleeping with a man named Max Zugg, a big worthless lunk with the mind of a muskrat. The year Nancy and me moved out here from West Virginia, before I started all this varmint transport work, we'd go to the movies Friday nights, and we were always running into him, Max Zugg, and sometimes I'd catch him watching her. You know, I didn't think. I was gone a lot, and me and Nancy, we had our problems—people do—but Nancy is a good person, and I never thought Nancy would let a creep like that come into our home. Not my house, she wouldn't."

Garnett went over to the bed and picked up a pair of shoes, holding them aloft by the laces. His blue eyes were popping in his head. "These shoes came off my front porch," he said. "I came home and this man's shoes are parked outside my door. He's living in my house, for God's sake! He's sleeping in my bed! Right now, I'm staying here in this motel, getting drunk and trying to find the guts to put a stop to this. Kill them or kill myself, that's the question." He tried to light a cigarette but his fingers were shaking. "Damn," he said. "I'm sorry. I didn't bring you out here to tell you all my troubles. Why don't you say something?" he asked.

Myers stared at him until Garnett asked, "So, do you have a family?"

*Kicked me out,* Myers typed.

Garnett nodded. "Girlfriend?" he asked.

*Split on me,* Myers wrote.

"What else?"

The fact was, Myers didn't know what to say, because he had only questions of his own to ask. Were things really this bad, for everyone? Everybody Myers met these days seemed to be stricken by heartache and betrayal—although admittedly, mostly these were the experiences of people he met in taverns. Still, couldn't Myers tell Garnett something about his life, about Petra and the likeness that she'd left him? He began to write something on the laptop, trying to make some sense out of things, but what came out instead were simply words—*shit fuck damn*—that only expressed the blackness inside him, his own failings and the deep cavern of his own bitterness. Mostly it was just a dark impulsive pounding, then he stopped.

Myers noticed now that the shadows on the floor had fused together and night had filled the room. The screen on the laptop glowed with an eerie light. Beside him on the sofa, Garnett seemed to be reading every word.

"I hear you," Garnett said, laying his hand on Myers' arm. "That's the sad parade of souls, and I think it's time that you and me got even."

— ❈ —

Myers sat slumped on the sofa, feeling nothing. Garnett had produced another bottle of bourbon, and had been drinking steadily for most of the last hour. Myers could hear the man outside, crunching around the parking lot of the motel. By now it had turned into a cool evening. Then Garnett came back into the room holding the bottle, and even in the awkward light Myers could tell that an artificial calm had come over him, though he knew the man was drunk. "I'm going to get my house back," Garnett announced. "One way or another, I'm going to take care of things. You don't mind coming along?"

Myers nodded in agreement. Garnett had gone out of his way to lend him a hand, and even though he'd only known the man a short time, somehow Myers felt closer to him than he had to anyone in quite a while.

Myers followed Garnett outside, where the air was sweet and cool. "I got a way to get them out of my house," he said, conspiratorily. "I'm just going to need you to watch, okay?"

Even if Myers had wanted to ask him for details, he couldn't. He climbed into the Land Rover and watched Garnett go into the motel room one last time. When he came out, Garnett lingered in the doorway, staring back into the gloom of the littered room. "Fuck it," he said. "Fuck everything." Then he slammed the door and climbed into the truck. Myers could hear the big cat behind them in the cage, its malevolent presence as it snapped and hissed and paced.

"I ain't been feeding her too regular," Garnett said, seeming guilty. "She'll get her fill, though, I expect, tonight."

Myers wondered what the man meant by that. He sat back and watched as they drove north on the highway, eight or nine miles, up through Waynesboro. As drunk as Garnett must be, he still drove carefully, slowing down and stopping at every light. On the other side of Waynesboro, Garnett pulled off the road into a pleasant suburban neighborhood, with young trees dotting the lawns amidst a sprawl of two-storied houses. Garnett turned left, then turned left again, and coasted the Land Rover to a stop. He fingered his electric window down and gazed across the street.

"There she is," Garnett said. "It's no mansion, but it's mine."

Myers nodded vigorously in agreement. It was a nice house, a clean white-stuccoed ranch, and because Garnett was so proud of it Myers wished that he could talk so he could tell him so. A cool breeze was coming down off the hills, rustling the leaves on the new trees.

Suddenly Garnett punched the Land Rover into reverse and backed the truck into the driveway. There was a front door, and a second, patio door facing the street by the garage, and Garnett backed the truck right up to it. He moved the Land Rover so close to the house that for a moment Myers thought he was going to drive right through the building, but he stopped.

The two men climbed out. "Just stand clear," Garnett said loudly. "Agnes is probably a little wired tonight." With that he began to dig around beneath his seat, and came up a moment later holding Max Zugg's shoes. They were black oxfords, very worn. "I've been following those no-good cheats around," Garnett said, his face suddenly twisting with rage. "He comes home here every night to see my wife," he said. "This is my house, damn it, and I don't like what I've been seeing. It's tearing me up inside and I can't stand it anymore. I'd like to be dead, is what I'd like." He sobbed once, but caught himself. "At night, when I stand outside the window, I can hear them in there screwing."

Myers looked at the man, who was trembling. "But why stand out there and listen?" he wanted to ask.

"In just a minute, I'm going to let Agnes out and give her the run of the place," Garnett said. "Either I'll chase them out or I'll get done in myself. I don't give a shit, to tell the truth. Really, I'm a desperate fuck and I don't care. Watch me!"

For a moment the two men waited there, at the back of the truck, staring at one another, and it felt to Myers like his whole body, even his lungs, was vibrating with the deranged, drunken danger of what was happening. To let this animal out seemed, well, little short of crazy.

Presently Garnett walked around to the back of the Land Rover and thumbed down the remote, lowering the window several inches. Then he dangled Max Zugg's shoes just outside the opening. The cat went ballistic, snorting and snapping and circling inside, until Garnett shoved the shoes in through the glass. Myers could hear the animal tearing the shoes apart inside. The cat was moving around in there so violently that the Land Rover began to rock on its frame.

"Maybe I'll just look in on them first," Garnett said. "See who's home, maybe give Nancy a running start." Myers saw the crazed expression on Garnett's face. He wanted to stop the man, but before he could grab him, Garnett ran up the steps of the house by the garage and let himself in. He was so distracted that he was still clutching the remote to the truck in his hand, but with the other hand he threw aside the screen door so viciously that the door popped off its hinge.

Myers watched, and for a while nothing happened. He saw that the blinds over the windows in the front of the house were drawn, and he could see a lamp on inside, in what must be the living room. Then there were muffled voices, a cry. Quick, jerky shadows began to move around inside the house behind the shades. There were more voices, loud, and the sound of breaking glass. Suddenly a woman screamed.

After a moment the front door burst open, and a frightened-looking woman in a white slip scrambled out, quickly followed by a man, who was bald and barefoot and wearing shorts. Before Myers could get a look at them the couple clambered off the porch and disappeared around the corner of the house into the trees.

Myers heard glasses and plates crashing to the floor inside the house. After a while the crashing stopped, and then everything was quiet.

"I can't take it!" Myers heard Garnett screaming from inside. "I can't!" he sobbed.

Suddenly Myers heard the electric window on the back of the Land Rover going down. Inside, Garnett must be using his remote, though Myers had no idea what the man was up to.

"Agnes?" Garnett called, in a plaintive voice. "Come here, baby. Come inside to Papa. Let's put an end to all this pain."

Myers scrambled clear of the vehicle, and once the window was down the whole way the cat sprang free. It moved so quickly that Myers didn't really see it bound out of the Land Rover and up the stairs—it was just a blur that burned his optic nerve as it passed. Panicked, Myers let out a strangled cry, which was all that he could manage. He wanted to tell Garnett to run. He felt a strange, terrible, hot thrill run through him as he waited for Agnes to make her move.

# The Inn of the Three Gorges

Call me Edward. My Chinese name is Kao Tsui Mae, but like all Hong Kong school children I was told to take an English name as well. I chose Edward, strong and simple, not an elaborate name like Hilton or Regency that some boys took, making you think maybe their fathers were taxi drivers who'd named their sons after Hong Kong's big hotels. In Mandarin, my family name sounds to an English-speaking person like the name of the farm animal that produces milk. "Mr. Cow, your table is ready." Would you like to be addressed like that? In America, I became Edward Koh.

I am happy to be in America, now that Hong Kong belongs to China. You think these mainlanders can be trusted, that what happened in Tianenman Square was just an accident? Really, to them such things are only like a bee flying up the nose of an elephant—when the government gets tired of this annoyance, it draws in a patient breath, then raises its massive foot. That is why my father left his village of Triple Gorge in 1950, after Mao and the Communists came in. My father moved us very quietly to Hong Kong, where we could live safely and be free.

Look at this photograph, will you? It's a picture of me and my brother and our two sisters, which was taken by my father in Hong Kong in 1960. Four little Chinks in a row. Isn't it nice the way my father arranged us, from smallest and youngest—that's me in the black sweater—up to the oldest and tallest, my brother, Alex, on the right? Alex also went to the University of Oregon; today he runs the family business in Hong Kong, importing textile machines. Our sisters, Grace and Lena, are in the middle between us. Lena is married to a Frenchman and lives in Paris; Grace married an American engineer and lives in Tampa, as I do.

Like my father, I'm ambitious. I have been a consultant engineer, manager of a cement plant; now I own a restaurant. I possess my father's nose and the heavily lidded eyes of a Chinese, though I wear my hair combed back and lightly oiled, in the manner of Humphrey Bogart.

Even as a youngster, I wanted to live in the United States. Growing up in Hong Kong, *Bonanza* and *Gunsmoke* were my favorite TV shows. Though when my mother found hidden in the bottom drawer of my dresser my cowboy hat and holster with matching Colts, she was badly shaken.

My mother brought my hat and holster into our dining room, placing them before her on the table where our family gathered for meals. Even then there were many fish tanks in our flat, for my father believed good Feng Shui would bring us luck—goodwill flowing everywhere, with five thirty-gallon tanks.

In Hong Kong as in Britain, real guns were not allowed, so my mother's hands were cautious as she held up my shiny Colts. "Such weapons," she said, feigning fright. "You want to grow up to be a criminal, robbing jewelry stores and banks?"

"No, I want to grow up to be a cowboy. I want to ride a horse like on TV."

"You want to be an American, Chinese boy?"

"Yes," I said. "I do."

"Ah," my mother whispered, though I could see she was struggling with some other fear.

"Where did you buy these things?" she asked. "Where did you go, and when?"

"I bought them at the toy shop on Nathan Road."

"Did you go near the train station, you little fool?"

My mother was always worried about the train station in Kowloon, and the bus terminal, or any place where people from Hong Kong might come into contact with Chinese from the mainland. It was a common worry in those days among mothers in Hong Kong that their children might be kidnapped and taken back to Canton, where the gangs would put them into slavery. It was well known that in every train station in China there were beggar children who were blind, or who'd lost a hand or foot—gangs controlled them all. The newspapers were full of stories about children who'd been abducted and disappeared.

"I don't go near the station," I said. "I never go anywhere like that."

"Then you're a good boy," said my mother, and gave me back my guns.

— ❋ —

In the fall of 1968, when I was twelve, my father learned by letter that his aunt had passed away in Triple Gorge, the village on the Pearl River where he'd been born. My father's parents had died during a famine when he was still an infant, so he'd been raised by his aunt. Her family was the only family my father had in China. This happened at a very difficult time, when it was dangerous for offshore Chinese to travel through the country. The Cultural Revolution was in full swing, and Red Guards were rampaging across the land.

My mother didn't want my father to make the trip, but he insisted. It was his familial duty, he said, to pay his respects as his aunt's adoptive son, regardless of the danger. Undoubtedly his aunt would have been cremated before he arrived, but still, he must go and show his face to his cousins.

My parents argued about his trip all night, but my father was very stubborn. Finally, seeing that he was going regardless, my mother hatched a plan. My father was to wear old clothes and travel on the train just like a peasant; even his wristwatch she made him leave behind. He was to carry no cash other than what it took to buy his ticket. He would be allowed one suitcase, an inexpensive vinyl bag, but with nothing for himself inside. Instead, my mother filled it with gifts for the cadres in Triple Gorge, should my father need them. She bought an American camera, a cashmere sweater, boxes of candied fruit. Her one concession to my father was a small photo album of our family, which he was to take along so he could show his cousins how we looked.

The following day, my father took the train without incident and arrived in Triple Gorge. The village must have seemed smaller to him than he remembered, though it was basically the same aside from the revolutionary slogans decorating every house. No one recognized him because it had been nearly twenty years since he'd last been in the village.

After strolling through the town, my father found his aunt's house, where several people from the neighborhood were waiting inside with his cousins. His aunt had been cremated already, her ashes scattered by the Pearl River two days before. There was an old photograph of her on the hearth; rows of wreaths with consolatory words on them formed a fan-shaped space. Candies, fruits, and tea were laid out among the flowers.

One of my father's cousins, Ming Li, came and secured a black crêpe band around my father's arm with safety pins. "Your auntie didn't suffer," she said. "In the morning we found her still in bed. She didn't answer. She died peacefully in her sleep." Tears trickled down Ming Li's cheeks and she wiped them off.

"It's a happy death," said Wang, a locksmith who lived next door.

"This old woman was blessed," said a middle-aged woman, a colleague of Ming's who worked at the tractor plant with her. "Such a clean and peaceful parting."

Ming Li came and put a hand on my father's shoulder. "Don't be too sad," she said. "It was time for her to go. She had a good life, and she loved you very much. We're so happy you came to honor her."

My father nodded, feeling that she shouldn't be treating him as though he were still a child. Then Ming Li pulled him aside and said in a low voice, "We're having a small memorial banquet here this evening. I've invited one of the cadres, the secretary, so you must be careful what you say. Anymore things here are never what they seem."

The funeral banquet was held inside the cousins' house that night. Along with a few neighbors, the secretary of the local cadre came to eat and drink rice wine. The secretary was a small, lumpy man about my father's age, and wore a homemade army uniform with a Mao button on his collar.

In the beginning, the table was very quiet. "Your auntie was an honor to our village," said the secretary finally, raising his cup of wine. "The whole commune is going to miss her."

"Eat this," Ming Li said, offering him a dish. She had prepared diced chicken, fish, and noodles, and roasted cashews for the children—fresh vegetables were in short supply. To my father, Ming Li seemed high-strung and jittery: hostess nerves, no doubt. He wondered if the secretary was a family friend, or maybe Ming Li's suitor, since she'd never married. But then, under the new regime, perhaps everything in the village was communal, even funeral rites.

Little cousins played in the bedroom while the adults ate their meal.

Occasionally one of the children burst into the room and grabbed a handful of cashews, then disappeared.

"Perhaps you don't remember me," the secretary said to my father, seeming amused. He tilted his cup back and drank more of the wine.

"No," said my father. "I'm sorry, but I don't. Are you new here to the village?"

The secretary chuckled, though it was possible my father had offended him and hurt his feelings. "No, Kao Tang Woo," the secretary said. "We went to school together here, though you obviously don't remember. I was a poor farmer's boy then and lived outside of town. Wang Fou's my name. I was in the class group just beneath you."

"Oh, my goodness, I'm sorry," said my father. "You know, it's been so long since I lived here."

"Yes," said the secretary. "Isn't it in Hong Kong that you live? What do you do?"

"Oh, I'm just a common laborer," my father lied.

"Do you miss our village here, with its beautiful improvements?"

By no means had my father seen everything in the village, but to him the place looked the same, or worse. Regardless, he said, "Certainly, I miss it."

At that moment one of the children burst from the bedroom, dragging my father's suitcase, which Ming Li had put away in there for safekeeping. The zipper on the vinyl bag was already opened, my father saw; no doubt the children had been searching inside of it for sweets. Sure enough, a moment later one of the older boys came into the kitchen, holding the American camera my mother had bought for my father's trip.

"Ah," the secretary said. "Let me have a look." He tossed back another cup of wine and grabbed the camera.

The secretary took the camera and examined it, then began to snap the button and rewind it, over and over like a child. He looked through the viewfinder, giggling, as Ming Li refilled his cup of wine.

"Whose camera is this?" he asked, burping loudly.

"It's mine," my father said. "Rather, it's what I brought with me, as a gift to the village."

"Yours?" the secretary said, and he gave my father a peculiar look, curling his lip. "If the camera's here, it's public property. Give it to me, Kao Tang Woo."

Suddenly there was a shriek from the other room. One of the children had fallen inside as they were playing, and he was screaming. "Ah," cried Secretary Wang, and suddenly he stood up. But before he could move another step he threw up—a yellowish shaft of liquid food, which splashed on the edge of the table and the dirt floor. Immediately Ming Li ran to the pantry to get a cup of tea to help sober the man up, while one of the other cousins took a broom and dustpan and began to sweep up his vomit, which was filling the small room with a sour scent.

Secretary Wang sat down, sick and embarrassed. My father had the odd sensation that he was somehow to blame. Then the table grew quiet as my father's cousins scurried about, clearing away dishes and trying to clean up. Soon the secretary excused himself again and staggered outside. They could hear him vomiting again in the street.

Holding the broom, Ming Li cast a worried look my father's way.

After a moment the curtain to the street opened again and the secretary stuck his face inside. His cheeks were livid, strings of spittle dripping from his chin. "That camera and the bag it came in and all its contents," he said, staring at Ming Li. "Have one of the children bring it to me at the Commune Administration Building, immediately!" Then the secretary vanished.

— ✳ —

Early the next morning my father was dragged out from his auntie's house. He had spent a restless night, tossing and turning on the wooden bed, filled with vague apprehension. There was already a large crowd gathered at the front gate. Two Red Guards took my father by the arms, and other Red Guards, about ten of them, followed behind. These Red Guards were generally strangers to the village where they were stationed, so they didn't mind roughing people up, even killing them if they felt like it.

The Red Guards led my father through the village to the school, the only two-story building in the town. According to Ming Li, my father looked calm; he neither protested nor said a word. About fifty people had already gathered in the schoolyard.

"Please let him go," Ming Li begged. "It's all our fault, for writing him about his auntie. He never should have come. He only wanted to show us his respect."

"Out of the way!" commanded a tall young man, evidently the leader of the Red Guards.

"Please let him go, brother," Ming Li cried. "Have mercy on him, I'm begging you!"

"Shut up," the tall leader said, and he suddenly slapped Ming Li across her face. "He's a Hong Kong snake and you know it! If you and your family don't stop interfering with us, we'll make you parade with him. Do you want to do that?"

There was silence as Ming Li wept, covering her face. She and the other cousins were swallowed up as the crowd pressed in.

The Red Guards took my father to the front entrance of the school, where two tables had been placed. On one of the tables stood a tall paper dunce cap with black characters on its side. "Down with the Capitalist Roader!" it read. My father stared at the crowd silently, clenching his teeth.

A young man in glasses raised his hand and started to address the crowd. "Friends, we are gathered here this morning to denounce Kao Tang Woo, who is an evil Hong Kong devil come back to revile us."

"Down with Bourgeois Pigs!" a woman Red Guard shouted. People in the crowd raised their fists and repeated the slogan.

One of the Red Guards went on. "First, Kao Tang Woo must confess his crimes. He must reveal his attitude. Then we'll make the punishment fit his attitude, all right?"

"Right," some voices replied.

"Kao Tang Woo," the Red Guard cautioned. "You must confess everything, you hear? It is up to you to save yourself."

My father was forced to stand on the bench. Then the questioning began. "Why do you practice business, stealing from men with your bourgeois poison?" the leader asked.

"I've done nothing," my father responded calmly.

"Shameless bastard! He just came here to laugh at us!"

"Friends!" cried the Red Guard's leader. He motioned to the group behind him, and suddenly Secretary Wang came forward, carrying my father's vinyl suitcase. "Look at this!" Wang cried, holding the bag aloft. Then he began to pull things from the suitcase, first the camera, then the cashmere sweater, scattering them across the platform where my father stood. "Look at what this Capitalist Roader brought into our village! Bribes, he's selling bribes! He even tried to poison me last night, then sat and did nothing while I puked!" Wang handed the items down into the crowd and they were passed along from person to person, even the small boxes of candied fruits. "Look at this!" a Red Guard cried, holding my father's photo album above his head. "Take a look at these photos!" he said. "The stupid fool incriminates himself! Here is hard evidence of his corrupted life!" With that the Red Guard began to tear photos from the album and throw them out into the crowd, where people scrambled to pick them up.

"Evil capitalist!" someone yelled.

"Cut him with a cleaver!"

"Take his head!"

At last my father spoke. "Friends," he said. "I apologize if I have offended you. Perhaps, from your point of view, it was incorrect of me to visit here, to come back to this village where I grew up. But I came out of family duty, to show my respect for the old woman who raised me. Is there something wrong with that?" My father paused, looking down into the faces before him in the front row. "Are such things prohibited now in the new China? Believe me, I meant no offense."

"Take this, Capitalist Roader!" A heavyset Red Guard struck my father on the side of his head with her fist, silencing him at once.

"You were wrong to come here!" a man said from the crowd, his forefinger pointing at my father.

"But I meant only respect," my father said, struggling as he straightened.

"Shut up!" the tall Red Guard yelled at him. "You don't get it, do you? Does it mean nothing to you that you've been brought here to be judged?"

"You cannot judge me," my father muttered. "I don't live here anymore." It must have seemed incomprehensible to him that his heartfelt journey had suddenly gone so terribly awry.

Before he could say more, a large bottle of black ink was poured over my father's head, and one of the young Red Guards slapped him hard across the face. "Silence, dog!"

My father was swearing and blubbering. "Fuck your mother!" he cried, trying to wipe the ink from his face. "What kind of place is this, you animals!"

"Bourgeois dog!" someone yelled.

"Serves you right!"

Subjected to this torment, after a while my father became another person. He was still standing on the platform, his face and shoulders covered with black stains. He turned his eyes, searching for the faces of his cousins, but they were nowhere to be found.

"Down with the rich traitor!" a farmer shouted in the crowd.

Again the tall leader stepped in. "In order to help Kao Tang Woo get rid of his counterrevolutionary airs, we'll shave his head." With a wave of his hand, the leader summoned other Red Guards behind him. Two of them came forward and held my father's arms, while a third, brandishing a razor, chopped roughly at the hair on my father's head.

"Don't, please!" he cried.

"Cut him!" someone yelled.

After four or five rough strokes my father's head looked like the body of a poorly shaven lamb. There were chop marks against his skull and in several places he was bleeding.

"Look at all these photos!" someone shouted. "The house, the yard, the car, the clothes! Who could call himself Chinese and live in such outrageous splendor!"

"I've told you the truth," my father muttered. "I only came here to honor my dead aunt. I meant you no dishonor, please!"

"Liar!"

"Comrades!" cried the tall Red Guard, turning to the crowd. "How shall we handle this parasite, who sucks the lifeblood from his country?"

"Burn him!"

"Cut his neck!"

"Make him drink doggie piss!" a small boy shouted, drawing a titter from the crowd.

Then one of the Red Guards tried to put a placard around my father's neck. He climbed onto the table with the placard, but my father elbowed him aside, knocking the young man to the ground. The tall Red Guard rushed over to my father and slapped him, viciously, several times across the cheeks.

"So," he said. "You're a stubborn man, aren't you?"

"Go to hell," my father said, raising his eyes. "May your ancestors eat only donkey shit!"

After this the Red Guard slapped him, again and again, as my father's arms were held behind him. Finally my father fell to his knees on the platform, but was pulled back to his feet.

"Friends!" the tall Red Guard resumed. "Let us continue the denunciation!"

"Give him another one across the face!"

A few angry farmers began to move forward toward the platform, waving their fists in the air.

"How he scorns us!" they screamed.

"Hold back," the Red Guard called down to the crowd. "We can easily subdue this man with words, but it's his spirit that is evil! What shall we do with him?"

"Feed him to the dogs!"

"Let's cut off his cock!"

Evidently, some people had begun to talk to each other in the crowd. Some said they thought my father was a strong man for enduring so much torment. Others said they should just let him go. But still, there was no stopping the Red Guards. Sometimes their denunciations went too far, and later the cadres themselves were punished if things got out of hand—yet who could stop them?

"Comrades!" the tall leader spoke. "We know the crimes this Bourgeois Pig has committed. Shall we let him go home, or should we teach him a lesson?"

"Kill him!" one of the farmers shouted.

"Why should he be rich while we are poor?"

Finally two Red Guards pulled my father off the platform by his arms. Another one picked up the tall hat.

"Please," my father muttered.

One of the Red Guards slapped him again across the face.

"Won't someone help me?" my father begged. "Please!"

It was no use resisting. Within a few seconds the dunce cap was firmly planted on his head, the big placard around his neck. The words on the placard read: "I am a Capitalist Roader! My crime deserves death!"

"Now we shall lead him through the village!" the tall Red Guard said.

The crowd laughed and boys threw stones at my father as he passed. One stone struck the back of his head and blood began to drip down his neck. Farther down the lane, old people who couldn't follow the throng stood on chairs, watching, smoking their pipes. They were going to parade my father through every street. It would take hours to finish, since the procession would stop for a short while at every intersection so the peasants could denounce him. Some spat in his face.

"Kill him!" someone screamed.

"Look! The Capitalist Roader has shit himself! He stinks!"

And so it went, that afternoon, until the Red Guards took my father's body back to the school. Some people whispered that he'd had a heart attack, but really, did it matter? At nightfall, a crowd was still gathered in the schoolyard, examining the ground. Beside the platform, my father's body lay against a hedge. One of his feet had been chewed on by a dog, and a whitish bone in his arm stuck out several inches. Beyond him, some ten feet away, the dunce cap lay on the ground, and flies were gathering.

That was the way things worked. Since my father's cousins had all fled in fear, there was no one to retrieve his body so it could be buried. Often as not, the village dogs had their way—tearing pieces off and then chasing after each other until evening came or they grew bored.

— ❋ —

As I said, now I live in Tampa. It's also where my sister Grace lives with her husband, Roy, the engineer. Next door to them my mother built a three-bedroom house she decorated in the Chinese fashion, which I share. Fish tanks, mirrors, fish tanks. There is even a Feng Shui master here in town! As for me, when we moved to Tampa I opened up a restaurant.

It is true that as a boy back in Hong Kong, I once dreamed of owning a saloon in the style of *Gunsmoke* or *Bonanza*. But of course Tampa is not the Wild West, and we are practical people, we Chinese. Instead, I opened a Chinese-style restaurant in the American vein, which I call The Inn of the Three Gorges. No MSG, every night a different special, plus speedy takeout from my handy drive-thru window. I buy my fortune cookies from a baker in Atlanta.

That is my father's story, and my story too. Inside my restaurant, though, in my office just behind the kitchen, I've set up a small shrine to Kao Tang Woo—an old photograph of him with candies, fruits, and tea, forming a traditional fan-shaped space among the wreaths. It is a good thing, is it not, to honor your forebear?

# Bingo Swine & Flypaper Sisters

Pulitzer's celly in the county jail was a ponytailed half-Samoan from El Cajon named Ahrens, currently on his third go-round, serving fourteen months for a phony truck registration and for bopping his wife on the head with a socket wrench (thrown). Ahrens weighed about two-sixty and was vain and antisocial. Since he didn't like watching television in the dayroom he mostly slept, snoring away night or noon like some great beached mammal, his snorts and growls echoing off the hard block walls of their cell. In his three weeks in blues at the George Bailey Correctional Center, Pulitzer had rarely slept—despite hopping down from his bunk nightly in a fury of frustration to try to awaken Ahrens by flushing and reflushing the stainless steel toilet twenty or so times. That never worked. Nor did clapping his hands or shouting. Of course this was on nights when Ahrens had forgone a talking jag—he told Pulitzer all about the profitable chop-shop he'd run outside—or when he skipped altogether one of his frequent and rather terrifying attacks of claustrophobia. Claustrophobic, in jail? On those nights Ahrens kept Pulitzer awake with his rapid up-and-down pacing and his frantic dialogues over the cell intercom with the ill-tempered guards. ("Don't call us again unless you are actually bleeding . . .") Agitated, with his chest still aching from his car wreck, Pulitzer thus contemplated for long hours the dim light from the cell's single slit-like milky window. Outside was the parched landscape of San Ysidro, about a half-mile from the border and Tijuana. It was the first time in recent memory that Pulitzer was sober, so when at last he did sleep it surprised him that he didn't dream of booze; he awoke instead several times with a start, feeling his lungs fill pleasantly with the dream-smoke from his much-missed cigarettes.

To Pulitzer, the place resembled a madhouse more than a jail. Breakfast at four-thirty, lunch at ten, dinner at three-thirty in the afternoon. Lockdowns and clean up. Twice every day a voice came over the intercom and then behind a protective grill a window slid open in the wall of the dayroom; about half the block lined up there to receive medication from the nurse. Lithium, Thorazine, and Antabuse. Inmates stood around afterward bargaining pills for sodas or extra chocolate puddings. Shortly most of them were either wired or in bottomless gloomy funks. One wild-haired felon from Boston spoke to no one and was known among the inmates as "The Indian," since after meds he trotted briskly round the crowd gathered in the dayroom, round and round like a Plains warrior about to descend on the encircled wagons. A woman's shrill cackle came regularly from somewhere down the cellblock, which was unnerving because they were all men.

After a few days Pulitzer finally wised up. He was in the psycho block. Since he was older (forty) and a first-timer without priors, they'd decided to stash him somewhere relatively quiet where he'd be safe. His fellow inmates were nonhostile, subdued; there were blacks, whites, and Mexicans in roughly equal numbers. Pulitzer had been a fifty-one/fifty when the police first brought him in, which meant he had to spend his first forty-eight hours inside a rubber room, where the guards could check him every twenty minutes. He did vaguely recall some drunken mention of suicide just after his arrest. But what was he going to do now, hang himself with his tongue?

So what brought Eastern-bred, degree-rich Pulitzer to a jail in San Diego? Alcohol and his wife or, more specifically, two motor vehicle counts for drunk driving and one domestic charge for violating a restraining order. It was his second jail stint in fifteen days. The first one had been a simple overnighter in the downtown lock-up before Rose, his wife, had bailed him out. Strange, because she'd had him arrested to begin with, just for banging on her door. The second arrest, he'd been out on Plaza Boulevard, sitting quietly curbside a few feet from the desnouted accordion of his BMW, so drunk he'd blown a .32 on the arresting officer's breathalyzer. At .35 you immediately became a cast member on *Star Trek*. One thing he'd learned: when they inflated, airbags hurt. Wham! All in all,

Pulitzer supposed it was a good time for him to be in jail.

He'd been in San Diego just a month. Rose, his wife, was from the Philippines, and since their separation she'd been working as a cocktail waitress in a Navy bar. She was eight years younger than Pulitzer and he had come to San Diego to try to get back together with her, but things hadn't worked out. Prior to leaving New York on his cross-country trek, Pulitzer had listened carefully as his psychiatrist recommended to him a sort of triple-play: (1) stop drinking, (2) resolve his marriage, (3) get a job. Pulitzer was now 0-for-3. While his wife was at work flirting for tips and waiting tables, Pulitzer ate dry tacos and rice in George Bailey and wondered when the court might spring him. He was a drunk, true, but he still felt like he'd been suckered.

— ❄ —

Delacorte, the arresting officer, probably felt like killing him, he'd spent so much time driving Pulitzer up and down the county before finally getting rid of him around three in the morning at the George Bailey Jail. First they went south from the scene of the accident to the station in National City, where Pulitzer was booked. Pulitzer was drunk and restless and couldn't sit down comfortably because of the handcuffs, so he kept getting up and wandering around the room. "Sit down," said Delacorte. "You commence to annoy me." Then Pulitzer muttered something about his chest hurting from the airbag and suicide, maybe, which necessitated a second drive north to the County Medical Center, where after a half-hour wait blabbering Pulitzer was examined by a dazed-looking Pakistani physician. "Yes," Pulitzer answered, "I guess I'm pretty miserable." Had he wanted to kill himself? "Maybe," he said. "I mean it's possible. Doesn't everyone, now and then?" Back to the squad car, which had a hard plastic shell bench in the back seat and was murderously uncomfortable. The hairs on Delacorte's neck looked like they were standing on end. "You shit your pants, Pulitzer," he said. "Do you know that? You stink." Pulitzer said nothing. "If you'd just kept your mouth shut I could have taken you down to city and you'd probably be out on bail by now." Pulitzer didn't mention that there wasn't anyone—not Rose, certainly, and thus no one local—to come and bail him out. Instead he asked, "You suppose some real crime's afoot right now, like murder? I mean while we're riding around. Do you have a family?"

"Fuck off," said Delacorte.

At the downtown jail, Pulitzer was extricated once more from the cruiser and taken inside. Everything around him looked like red neon and chrome and steel. After a few minutes they were told that, because Pulitzer had already been classified a fifty-one/fifty (potential danger to self and others), they'd have to go elsewhere because all the rubber rooms downtown were full. Delacorte examined the ceiling tiles while Pulitzer slumped numbly against the wall. He wasn't exactly sober yet but he did feel lousy, which was probably a good sign. Back to the cruiser then, for the thirty-minute ride south down I-5 to Bailey. "You getting paid by the mile by any chance?" Pulitzer asked. Because of some ordinance that forbade police officers from entering local detention facilities with their weapons, Delacorte had already disarmed and rearmed himself several times, on each occasion opening the trunk to either withdraw or deposit his Glock automatic. "We going to Mexico?" Pulitzer asked. A moment later Delacorte pulled the cruiser into a parking space and stopped. He leaned over in the front seat, sorting through something in the glove compartment. Pulitzer couldn't see properly through the Plexiglas shield. Then the door opened.

Delacorte stood there on the gravel, a pair of latex gloves on his hands. "Out," he said. "Come here." Pulitzer climbed out of the car and suddenly smelled alcohol and felt the policeman dabbing at his forehead. "There," said Delacorte. "That's better." "What is it?" said Pulitzer. "Your head, dummy. You must have banged it." Then they went inside and the administrative guards at Bailey took Pulitzer's photo and booked him in.

"I'm going now," said Delacorte. He was poised to leave.

"Thanks," said Pulitzer. He stretched out his hands, which were still cuffed, and Delacorte shook one.

"Good luck," said Delacorte. "Take care of yourself."

The rest of the evening was a blur. Pulitzer was forced to shower two, maybe three times, and the next thing he knew he was standing naked in a square, tan-colored room with a blue quilted sort of shawl over his shoulders. It looked like the sort of thing movers used to protect furniture and came to mid-thigh. It was cold. There was a high ceiling with a bright fluorescent light, and a round hole in the middle of the floor. That was it. Every now and then one of the guards came by and looked in at him through the small thickly-glassed window in the door. There must have been something posted there outside—what, his biography?—because the guards paused there and peeked in at him and Pulitzer could hear pages being turned. Pulitzer stood there for a long time in his bare feet feeling chilly. Then he noticed the stuff on the walls.

It was really pretty indistinct and he couldn't focus on it. Sometimes it was there and sometimes it wasn't. When he saw it, there were pages and covers and mastheads from lots of old magazines and newspapers—someone must have pasted these to the wall and then painted over them with this filmy tan paint. They were there but Pulitzer couldn't read them. Each time he tried to focus a little more it all disappeared and then there was just the blank tan wall, nothing. But they were there. He was sure of it because he kept seeing them, and it wasn't for another week when he was brought by the empty rubber room again, this time manacled and on his way to court downtown, that he realized that the walls were blank, uniformly tan and opaque and anonymous, and that what he had seen in there that night on the walls was alcohol poisoning, hallucinations. By then he knew that George Bailey was clean and modern and only two years old, and at any rate it was against prison regulations to paste anything to the walls.

— ✵ —

After ten days in Bailey Pulitzer yearned for human contact, which was a paradox seeing that he was in enforced proximity to fifty-four other human beings. Ahrens, his cell mate, mostly slept during the day, and his grotesque snoring made their cell uninhabitable. Trying to adjust himself to the noise seemed to Pulitzer a wifely enterprise and unnecessary. When Pulitzer had asked Ahrens how his wife stood his snoring, he responded: "She loves it. Can't sleep herself without me in the room." Well, she was without him now, because he and Ahrens were both in jail. Anyway, it was pretty clear that they came from different backgrounds and that Ahrens didn't like him.

Thus abroad, either in the dayroom or on the long balcony that extended the length of the second tier of cells, Pulitzer met an odd lot of other inmates. Many spent their time watching cartoons or MTV on the televisions bracketed to the dayroom's ceiling, out of reach. Their conversation was reluctant and amazingly neutral. Traveler, who was two cells down from Pulitzer, a tall good-looking kid in his twenties, planned trips; after scouring the classified pages of the San Diego newspaper for hours, he would join Pulitzer on the parapet and discuss with great enthusiasm the merits or demerits of different destinations—Paris, Moscow, London. "Dat boy ain't goin' nowhere," one black inmate told Pulitzer. "C'ept across the ravine." "Ravine?" asked Pulitzer. "Donovan," said the man. Donovan was the state penitentiary about a half-mile down the road from Bailey, and sure enough one night after lock-up the guards came and took Traveler away. That was one virtue of Pulitzer's sleeplessness: he got to hear it when other guys checked out.

Pulitzer had two children in New York from his first marriage, but his phone call to them proved a disaster. The last time he'd seen them, five weeks ago, he'd been drinking so heavily he couldn't take them for the weekend as he was supposed to, and they had to settle instead for a quick lunch. The telephones on the dayroom wall made only collect calls, and after being asked his name by a recorded voice, and then listening to the familiar ringing of the phone, Pulitzer heard his thirteen-year-old daughter, Marcie, pick up the receiver and get this: "Will you accept a collect call (pause) from Pulitzer (pause) from a correctional facility?" That last line made it difficult not to tell the truth, but Pulitzer—leery of his ex-wife because he was in arrears on child support and owed her a lot of money—lied anyway. "I'm in Denver, dear," he told Marcie. "I had a car wreck and I'm in jail." "What are you doing in Colorado?" said Marcie. Clark, Pulitzer's fifteen-year-old son, seemed more impressed. "Jail, huh?" he mused. Pulitzer imagined Clark trying to fit him—Pulitzer—into some scenario that included cells and inmates. Then the line went dead and Marcie wouldn't accept any more of Pulitzer's calls.

Aside from his brother, who was an attorney and was working, rather reluctantly, Pulitzer thought, to help spring him, there didn't seem to be much of anyone interested in hearing from him. Not Rose, for sure, and his parents were dead. Was there anyone whom his drinking and general foolishness hadn't offended? Delacorte, who'd arrested him for God's sake, had exhibited the only kindness Pulitzer could recall: his deft patting with an alcohol swab at Pulitzer's bloody head.

It was what he deserved, Pulitzer reasoned. How to make a bad situation better? By making it much worse. Thus the car wreck. Before the crash, when he wasn't harassing Rose he seemed determined that the final act of his life be played out in a grungy motel room with two dozen empty fifths of Jack Daniel's. A fifth a day or more. And it wasn't cheap.

Three days later Pulitzer called his children again. He timed the call so he reached them when they'd just come home from school, and this time things went much better. They spoke for half-an-hour, mostly about Pulitzer's accident. "You're in San Diego, right?" asked Marcie. "Correct," Pulitzer said. "What about Rose?" said Marcie. "Did you see her? I hate her guts." "I did see her but I'm not going to see her anymore." As he said this Pulitzer realized it was probably true. They chatted on and Pulitzer felt his heart throb, rise up like a bobbing apple. He loved these kids, and he was so embarrassed for them, for himself. In his mind they were his very furniture, a floor, and a roof above him.

Just then there was some commotion behind Pulitzer on the second tier in the cell block. Laughter, hoots, applause. In one of the cells two inmates had pulled down the pants of another inmate and had him bent down over his bunk. Nothing was happening except a pantomime of ass-fucking. Someone let out a long demented wail of passion.

"What's jail like, Dad?" Marcie asked.

Pulitzer paused. "Maybe I can tell you more about it later."

"Mom's not here," said Marcie.

"Out?"

"Her singles group," Marcie said. She laughed. "Fat chance."

"Who knows, maybe she'll get lucky," said Pulitzer. "Give her a shot. By the way, what are they saying? You know, about me?"

Marcie's voice grew sullen. "You mean Grandma and Grandpa?"

"Yes."

"Grandma started to say something demeaning about you but I cut her off. Clark and I just won't stand for it. We love you, Dad, and you're going to get a lot better now."

There were tears in Pulitzer's eyes when he left the telephone. "Demeaning," Marcie had said. Not a bad word for a thirteen-year-old, let alone the very welcome show of support. It improved Pulitzer's mood a hundredfold.

— ❄ —

Taxis are yellow. Trees are green and so is grass. The sky: blue. In the morning the chatter of birds outside the window was almost deafening. It was so alive, so new. When he was released from George Bailey, everything Pulitzer saw in the real world looked bright and neat and freshly minted. Colors and sounds assaulted him. He asked the cabby to stop at the 7-Eleven a few miles from the jail so he could buy supplies. There was fresh-brewed coffee—not that undrinkable jail house chicory—and cigarettes. Pulitzer noticed that there were pints and fifths and gallons of booze, gin and scotch and rum, the bottles gleaming, a veritable crystal altar of the stuff. Where was it now, his brand? There. Black Jack. The dark thick-shouldered bottle, brown and rich in its solitary splendor. Pulitzer let it pass and paid the cashier. Outside, the first drag from his cigarette nearly put him on his back.

For the past twenty-four hours people had been talking at him, instructing him. "Your release from the county jail is conditional," the judge had said. That had been yesterday. "Conditional in the sense that you are obliged to observe the orders of this court. You're to spend ninety days in an alcohol treatment center. You are to complete the state's three-month drunk-driver course. You are to attend domestic violence classes and stay away from your wife. Do you understand?"

"Yes, sir," Pulitzer said.

"You have the opportunity to turn things around for yourself," said the judge. "If the past month is any indication, you've probably made a mess of your life. You are to abstain from liquor, from any liquor, for six months. I don't know how much damage you've done already, Mr. Pulitzer, to yourself and others. Am I clear? Do you intend to follow the instructions of this court?"

"Yes," said Pulitzer. "I do."

"Then you're dismissed."

He was led out of the courtroom, but had to wait. By then it was late in the afternoon and he was taken back downstairs, still in manacles and cuffs, to sit with other prisoners in a holding tank. Then a bus back to Bailey. Then another holding tank. That's what jail was mostly: waiting. No one was in any hurry. When he got back to their cell it was after lockdown and Ahrens was already in fine fiddle, snoring up a storm. Pulitzer didn't care, he wanted to celebrate. But with whom? Time passed; Pulitzer waited. When he was released, finally—his paperwork was in order, he could leave the block now and get his clothes   Ahrens was still asleep. Pulitzer would have liked to get some memento of the experience for his kids—

he often bought them T-shirts when he traveled—but unfortunately the jail didn't have a gift shop.

Now it was morning and the taxi dropped Pulitzer at the front door of Coronado Volunteers. It was a big building like a two-story suburban ranch and there was a long empty parking lot to one side. There was a flagpole, and roses and geraniums and impatiens bloomed everywhere in planters by the door. Pulitzer went inside. There was an office to the left. A large big-armed man in a mint-green sport shirt sat behind a desk. There was a sign on the desk, like a no-smoking sign, with the word "whining" crossed out with a thick red line. I guess they don't want to hear my story, thought Pulitzer.

"Yes?" said the man.

"I came to apply," said Pulitzer. "I'd like to get in here."

The man looked at him. His brown hair was close-cropped in a no-nonsense military style. Nothing about the place—this man, this room—seemed even remotely friendly. Pulitzer had chosen Coronado Volunteers simply because it was in the suburbs, and not downtown. Perhaps he had made a mistake.

"Where you coming from? Federal, state, or county?"

Was it that obvious? "County," Pulitzer replied.

"Application's on the desk." Then the phone rang and the man turned to answer it.

Pulitzer filled out the form and waited in the large hall outside the office. It was an Alcoholics Anonymous meeting room, he guessed: lots of chairs, a podium, different stuff written on the walls. Slogans for the undrunk. Two men went past Pulitzer and out the door. On the wall by the office there were lots of things in frames, letters, commendations, photos. A roll of honor. One letter was dated 1962 and was signed by then-Governor Pat Brown. Coronado Volunteers seemed to have proven its worth. Pulitzer shook his leg. He had to piss; his bladder was out of practice, still back in jail where the can was only a few feet away.

"Come on in," he heard.

Pulitzer handed the man his form and sat down in the chair opposite. The man looked at Pulitzer. Everything about him was noncommittal. Then he looked at Pulitzer's application. Pulitzer noticed a short hairline scar at one corner of the man's mouth. There were lots of frames in here too. Pulitzer crossed his legs. Christ, did he have to piss!

The man looked up from Pulitzer's paper. "I don't know," he said. "We're sort of full up. Give me a good reason why I should let you in."

"I just got sentenced yesterday," said Pulitzer. Suddenly he felt relaxed. "I'm supposed to stay someplace for ninety days. Like here. I mean, a place like this."

"Uh-huh." The man looked at Pulitzer, but Pulitzer could detect nothing in the gaze. "Try again, huh?"

Pulitzer felt himself withdraw, felt things closing in on him. He was in the right place, wasn't he? The man seemed in no particular hurry. He was neither hostile nor helpful. "I sort of made a mess of things," Pulitzer said. Maybe this was it. Still, he wasn't supposed to whine, was he? "I had an accident a while back and wrecked my car and . . ."

"Later. Is there anything else I should know?"

Pulitzer thought. He wanted to get this right, damn it, now. His bladder had suddenly quieted; he could feel it concentrating, too. He felt dumb, stupid, humiliated. He felt like he ought to have an answer. It was a simple question, wasn't it? Then he had it, and he knew his answer was correct.

"I'm an alcoholic," he said. He said it candidly and without inflection.

"Is that so?" said the man. Pulitzer thought he saw a slight smile disappear from his lip. "If that's the case I'll check. We might have one more bed for you up in our imperial suite. Can you pay?"

"No, I'm afraid not."

"Dandy," said the man.

— ❄ —

Pulitzer spent the rest of the day arranging himself. He had no suitcase—it had been stolen from his car after the accident—so unpacking only took a moment. There was a fiberboard bureau beside his bunk, a closet, and three identical beds in the smallish room, each made neatly and covered with a thin blue spread. No one appeared to have many possessions. There were no pictures on the walls and the linoleum floor was bare. Down the hall were dormitory-style showers and the toilets. Pulitzer was on the second floor and out a rear door from his room was a patio strewn with barbells and weights. Coronado Volunteers sat halfway up a hill so the view from the porch was good, overlooking a trailer park and, farther on, a K-Mart with an empty lot. There was the expressway, and Rose's apartment was only a mile away—Pulitzer could go there if he wanted. But what was the point? Dennis, a barrel-chested Indian with tattooed arms, gave Pulitzer a pillow and sheets. Pulitzer would meet all of his roommates soon enough: Mark, a sunny California kid, a surfer, a millionaire's son, a dope dealer and two-time felon; Dennis, the Indian, who'd been shot and then killed a man in self-defense (and who was about to be made casino-rich from his share of the reservation); and then there was the Doctor, who was probably nuts.

People were watching Pulitzer, he knew. He was the new kid on the block. He wasn't frightened exactly, just wary. He spent the rest of the afternoon talking with the Doctor on the backyard patio downstairs. It was a gorgeous day and the yard was full of flowers: roses, daisies, mums, nasturtiums. Pulitzer knew these things because he'd worked summers for a landscaper during college. When was that? A long time ago, it seemed. The sun was high and bright and it felt wonderful just to sit beside the Doctor in a chair and feel the warmth on his hands and face.

The Doctor told his story. That's what people did at Volunteers, they talked, often with little or no prompting. Confessed to all sorts of things, anything, dissecting themselves in public like laboratory frogs laid out cruciform for the class to see. The worse the tale, the better. The Doctor? He was on his third marriage, he and his present wife had two infant kids, he'd lost his medical license for cocaine abuse and booze. His most recent residence had been Rancho LaBrea, a posh rehab like the Betty Ford Clinic, but the Doctor had run out of money. Both of his former wives were crazy, he said; he'd been bankrupt twice. "So I was in my Mercedes this one night with a fifth of Absolut," the Doctor said. "I tore off the cap and threw it out the window. I threw it out the window. That meant . . ."

Pulitzer knew what it meant. So you drank the whole thing, so what? The Doctor was lanky, athletic-looking, and prematurely gray. His features were blunt yet he had a rather feminine mouth. Not exactly good-looking, but not bad. Other men came and went and introduced themselves to Pulitzer. The Doctor was still talking. That phrase about the Absolut cap going out the window was provocative, all right. But after a few weeks Pulitzer had heard it so often—the Doctor was keen on sharing during meetings—that every time Pulitzer heard the story again it commenced to make him sick. Aside from that, later on the Doctor confided to him that he wanted to secretly drug his wife; the man had little range and didn't seem to listen. Finally the Doctor got almost as bad as the carpet-swatch confessors—these were people who were called on too often during meetings who had no recent life trauma to report save the urgent one of telling the decorator if their decision was for that chocolate shade, or beige. Shit.

There was a kitchen and dining room off the meeting hall, with chairs and Formica tables, and presently dinner was served. Meatloaf, mashed potatoes with gravy, peas. Excellent, Pulitzer thought, a major improvement over the chow in jail. More men stopped by and introduced themselves. There were twenty-two of them in total.

"You got a college education, huh?" one said.

"I do," Pulitzer answered.

"Make a lot of money once?" another asked.

"Sure, sort of," said Pulitzer.

"My, my," said another. "Graduate degree?"

"Yes."

"Thought so. What's your name?"

Pulitzer told him his real name.

"I don't think that will do," someone said. "Here we're supposed to be anonymous."

"Right. What do we call this nice college boy? You listen to him? He e-nun-ci-ates, even. You got fifty bucks you can spot me?"

"No," Pulitzer said.

"That name's got to go," said Dennis, the Indian who had given Pulitzer his sheets. His plate was already empty and he pushed it away a few inches on the table. "You running for office or anything?" he asked.

"No," Pulitzer said.

"You in business?"

"I was," said Pulitzer. He didn't want to admit to these men that he'd been an executive once.

"Prize fellow, huh?"

"What's that?"

"It's what we're going to call you. Pulitzer."

"Add some prestige to this fuck-head group. You a doper?"

"No," Pulitzer said. "Just booze."

"Well, now. Isn't that the cat's pajamas?"

There was a framed sculpture of a pair of praying hands hanging on the front wall of the main meeting hall at Coronado Volunteers, and at the mandatory men's-only meeting that Tuesday night, new residents like Pulitzer were required to stand beneath the hands and relate their biographies for the two years previous. Big Mike was the resident manager and ran the meeting. Big Mike was the man who'd interviewed Pulitzer that morning, if it could be called an interview. Maybe the interview was now, Pulitzer thought. "The bloodier the better," said Mike. "No bullshit. I want the crap in your underwear and the cops and the tragic pussy in your life. Got it? Tell the truth or you're history, gentlemen."

The Doctor went first. When he finished everyone clapped. Then there was a ratty-looking tool and die maker, a vet, who had just gotten out of the hospital and was so weak he could barely stand. Then a former running back from Nebraska. Pulitzer listened in startled awe as they spun their tales of woe. Then it was his turn at the front of the room.

"My name is Pulitzer and I'm an alcoholic," he said. He was so nervous he felt his voice crack as he scanned the blank waiting faces of the men seated before him. "Two years ago I was working for an insurance company in New York. I've always been in business. I started drinking in earnest five or six years ago when my first wife and I separated. I got married again three years ago to a woman who comes from the Philippines but that didn't work out. I was drinking a fifth a day or more and was a danger to myself and others." As he proceeded with his narrative, Pulitzer felt a slow confidence begin to build, his words coming out more firmly and smoothly. A sort of rhythm developed. Nothing was too much for these men. The rudest detail produced only laughter. They seemed to hold nothing against him, and it was good, he guessed, to have all this stuff aired and accepted publicly. "I've lost two jobs from drinking and offended just about everyone I know," Pulitzer said finally. "I've been thinking about it and I'd like to stay here and learn how to live sober. That's it. Thanks for listening."

Pulitzer walked back to his seat and felt his cheeks flush, and then he heard the room fill with loud applause around him. As he sat down he felt his eyes smart with gratitude.

— ✳ —

It was sheer luck, but Pulitzer had picked well. Coronado Volunteers had a boot camp aura but it seemed to work. Reveille at seven, lunch at noon, dinner at six, followed by a meeting and lights out at eleven. No long hair or beards, no hats, no shorts, no shades. If you couldn't live with the rules you were put on restrictions, and if you still couldn't live with the rules you were thrown out. The men were encouraged to find jobs. "This place ain't on the tour," Big Mike told them. Mike ran two meetings a week for the house residents and prided himself on an unsentimental approach; he was a much-decorated Marine who had done two stints in Vietnam, and he spoke of his ten-year addiction to alcohol and cocaine only with reluctance. Not that it compromised his authority; it *gave* him authority. He was successful now, he had made it through. "This place ain't on the tour," he repeated. Big Mike said everything twice either to avoid questions or because he doubted the mental acuity of his charges, which was likely a good bet. "You come in here with nothing," he said. "Most of you, anyway. In a year only three out of ten will still be sober. That's a fact. Here's the pattern. You got nothing so you come here. And you're lucky to be here; most drunks we don't take. You get sober and then you get a job, and you get some money. Then you have to get a car because you need some pussy. Then you get the car, and pretty soon you have the woman. Then something fucks up with the woman so you get drunk. So you get drunk. Back where you started, see? I've seen it a thousand times."

There was a certain arrogance to Volunteers, at least among San Diego rehabs. Aside from its bucolic suburban setting, it remained aloof and refused to take state or federal funds. That had been mandated by the founders, all ex-drunks, in the Fifties; these same men and women had buried twenty-five-year tokens and empty fifths in the foundation blocks of the building, in the hope that the gesture might inspire other men to stay sober.

Of course all this meant that Pulitzer had to work, which was a sharp reminder of his rather reduced circumstances. Still, he was able to pick up occasional painting jobs or other chores through the people who came to meetings, and he paid his rent and maybe had enough to go to a movie, too, a few blocks over the hill in Chula Vista. Chula Vista had a nice village feel to it with a wide palm-studded main street and a post office and a pharmacy, but most of the businesses catered to the Mexicans who came over the border to shop; there were bridal shops and jewelry stores, and a lot of photographers' studios. Most of the men in Volunteers had already had their pictures taken elsewhere.

There were house chores to do. Pulitzer swept, cleaned toilets, and mopped floors. In the morning he put up the flag and at sunset he took it down, folding it neatly with the help of another resident. It occurred to him that he hadn't handled a flag with such reverence since after President Kennedy's death, when he was in grade school, and he and his classmates had imitated the crisp flag-folding technique of the honor guard everyone had seen on television—left, right, left, right. Now it wasn't patriotic: it was a task assigned on the Coronado Volunteers' weekly chore sheet, and if Pulitzer forgot about it, it was irresponsible, and another sign that he'd fucked up.

One afternoon when he was taking a break from his house duties and smoking a cigarette in the dining room, Big Mike came through and asked him to go upstairs and alphabetize the books in the television room's small library.

Pulitzer was annoyed. "Why?" he said. "Can't you see I'm busy?"

"Doing what?"

Pulitzer didn't say.

"Just do it, all right? We've never had but a handful of executives like you in here. You might get some thoughts as to your future, if you know what I mean."

Pulitzer was surly but did as he was told. What was he anyway, a child? But strangely enough, after a few minutes he warmed to his task. After all, there was a time when books had been his life; it was what had led him to his career in business. Had Big Mike known something Pulitzer should know? Or was Pulitzer such a thoroughly predictable dog: fetch and have his ears scratched? But rather than contemplate his future—it was unimaginable, just now—Pulitzer marveled at the titles: there were the obligatory inspirational tomes and AA recovery tracts, but the bulk of the books were well-thumbed thrillers and science fiction. It seemed most house residents preferred a different galaxy altogether. Well, why not?

To his surprise, Pulitzer didn't think too much about drinking, though that was all anyone ever talked about. He didn't, really, want a drink. His accident had scared him so—after it he realized how lucky he was just to be alive—that he seemed to be, sort of, a new person, someone who'd survived. Of course jail had helped that too. But who this new person was, exactly, Pulitzer wasn't sure.

Saturday nights were a big event at Volunteers. Come Saturday, one or maybe two hundred people packed into the main meeting hall for dinner and the featured speaker. Afterwards there was bingo. Most of the speakers were from out of town—Los Angeles, Las Vegas, even San Francisco—but they were all ex-drunks who told their life stories, some with such poise and expert timing that they might have been stand-up comics. In his third week at Volunteers, Pulitzer was assigned as a collector during bingo; he gathered wagers into a small wooden bowl, fetched coffee or soda for the players, and read off the winning numbers to the bingo master if one of the players at his tables won. It was a prestige assignment at Volunteers. The other three collectors, two of whom were convicted felons, were all good-looking, well educated, and polite. Pulitzer was flattered to be among them. What's more, in an evening he made eight or nine dollars in tips. Most of the players were old, but occasionally there was a good-looking younger woman he and the other collectors could ogle. One of Pulitzer's regular players was a sweet-natured blue-haired widow in her seventies who wore beautiful jewelry, tipped generously, and called forty-year-old Pulitzer "baby." Pulitzer imagined her taking him back to her home to spoil him, even tucking him in at night. But then Pulitzer remembered he hadn't been with a woman in three months—not since the last time with Rose—and the fantasy took a sudden left turn into uncharted waters and Pulitzer had to shake his head to clear his mind. The last thing he needed at this stage was something complicated.

When they weren't gathering bets or hustling coffee, Pulitzer and the other collectors convened at a separate table in the front of the room to smoke and gossip. Pulitzer hadn't lived in a dormitory with other men since college, and the camaraderie and fooling around was sometimes fun.

"I hate this shit," said Mark. "Look at these drones, will you?"

"What, you wouldn't be playing bingo on a Saturday night in the real world?"

"This is the real world," Mark said. Mark was twenty-six and one of Pulitzer's roommates; he'd done two tours of the California penal system that had made him careful about everything, even combing his hair.

"I know I have to eat shit, it's just a question of the elbow room at the table."

"We're pigs," said Tasker. "We're swine." Tasker was a former salesman, a brawny guy from Indiana. The final grace note in his marriage had been throwing a twenty-seven-inch television set through the windshield of the brand new Buick he'd bought that afternoon for his wife. Only half-drunk, he claimed.

"I am the egg man," said Mark. "Oo-coo-ca-choo."

"Me, I'm the walrus?" Pulitzer said. He remembered the Beatles song too.

"No," said Tasker. "We're the bingo swine. And eager, ma'm, to be of service. Here they come, boys, right on time."

Nearly every Saturday, about midway through the evening's bingo, two heifer-sized young women, sisters apparently, lumbered into the hall and took up their positions, always the same, at one of Pulitzer's two tables. They half-concentrated on the bingo and spent most of their time casting humid looks at the four collectors gathered at their table. The girls both seemed to be married because they wore wedding rings, but then they wore a lot of stuff—bracelets, gold studs through their nostrils, plus lots of other rings on their pudgy pink fingers—yet nothing deflated their steamy stares or the monstrously suggestive way they smoked their cigarettes. Their hair was lank and wet looking, their bodies pale. Pulitzer tried to imagine them at home, on some backwoods porch.

"Big Mike said if I get involved with any women I'm going to start using again," said Mark. It was hard to ignore the sisters' looks. "You think he's right?"

"If it was those two I think I'd get drunk first," said Tasker.

"How come I always imagine flies buzzing when I see them?"

"Can you imagine it?" said Mark. "I mean, what it might be like . . ."

"Lost forever," Tasker said. "I'd advise a scuba suit."

"I hate to admit it," said Pulitzer, "but he must be right."

"Who?"

"Big Mike. You know how he's always telling us, beware these meeting sluts? I mean what woman in her right mind is going to fall for a guy in rehab? Like he says, they must be even more fucked-up than we are."

"Maybe they hit bad times," said Tasker. "Maybe they were rich once, like me."

"I can't stand it," said Mark. "If we can't get involved with anyone, do we still get in trouble just for noticing them?"

"Like what? Wait, I got it. Flypaper. We tack a strip to the ceiling and then they'll always know where to sit. Underneath, you know?"

"That's disgusting," said Pulitzer. "What chauvinist talk."

"They don't need it anyway," said Mark. "They sit in the same place every week. They're not going anywhere."

"Look who's talking," Tasker said.

— ❈ —

"It's sometimes hard for me to stay away from the phone," wrote Pulitzer to his psychiatrist a few weeks later. "I can't pay for calls, which is a good deterrent, but I still wanted to let you know where I was and what I was up to. I feel badly I was drinking so much when I was seeing you, I might have gotten more out of it. I'm writing now as a sort of celebration, since as of this morning I've been sober sixty days. You gave me three objectives a couple of months ago and right now I'm two-for-three. I've stopped drinking and I'm about to be divorced. My long-suffering brother, the attorney, has been a big help with that.

"When I say that it's hard not to call people, I mean Rose or my kids. I talk to the kids twice a week about school and what they're doing and it seems sometimes that they're the only important things in my life. Last week I got my ex-wife on the line by mistake and she said something like, 'These kids don't feel like they have a father,' to which I said, 'No, they have a father who was in jail and now he's in a halfway house.' Halfway to what? I go to the beach sometimes on weekends with my pals from the house, and that afternoon I lay there in the sun as rigid as a stick, reviewing all my shortcomings as a father. One incident with my son seemed particularly reprehensible. This happened when he was six or seven and was playing soccer for the first time. My son didn't concentrate (in fact he was picking dandelions). The way I yelled at him afterward I can only associate with the most despicable behavior, as if my own identity was somehow mixed up with his performance. What's done is done, I guess. I can't wait to see them, which ought to be in a month or so if the court will let me leave California.

"As for Rose, I had a long talk with my brother and we agreed there was no point not to go ahead with the divorce. Just more money that I owe him. It's been hard for me not to call her (her apartment's only about a mile away from here) or go by and surprise her, even though that would violate the court order and I'd likely be arrested. How can I imagine at this point that she'd like to see me? Just because I'd like it to be so? Who can blame her, really? If you'll recall, I met her in Los Angeles when I was there on business, she was in the States on holiday from the Philippines, and we got married three weeks later. My drinking didn't help. My brother's convinced she did this just to get her green card, but I still have difficulty accepting that. The whole thing was a mistake, I married her on the rebound, and it was inappropriate from the start.

"I had a breakthrough of sorts on that, I guess, the other evening. There's a porch off our room here and I went out there on the balcony to smoke a cigarette. As I mentioned, it was evening and from the porch you can see the local K-Mart, which happens to be where Rose and I once had this terrific argument, there in the parking lot. The argument wasn't really important, it was about money as usual, but I remember realizing then, suddenly, what a drag all this must be for her, me unemployed and all, and that she really didn't, truly, want me around, that she'd gotten her own new group of friends. This was a cruel blow at the back of my knees, this picture of myself as no more than a pest. So I was out there smoking and I remembered that incident and I started to cry, just really feeling that rejection, I mean understanding it in a sober way. I didn't tell anyone this and I was alone there and I didn't even share it with my sponsor, which I'm supposed to do.

"My sponsor is a guy named Rob who's in his mid-sixties, and he's got a light touch, which is probably right for someone like me. Why this hostility to authority, I wonder? Rob used to drive a big rig but he had to retire (bad heart), and now mostly he just sponsors guys and goes to meetings. He was in and out of jail all his life and once broke a deputy's arm while resisting arrest. He's married to a nice black woman who's a nurse (his fourth, her third) and they're a pleasantly resolved couple. I'm supposed to have a sponsor and for me he's been good, about once every two weeks he just asks me what I'm up to, which is fine.

"Of course one feels sort of obvious here among your fellow drunks, all these old-timers who hang around the meetings and ask which step you're on, as if you were building a model airplane and just following directions. It's an unnatural state for drunks to be undrunk, so this place is kind of otherworldly. More people arrive and leave than actually stay and stick it out. Still, I have a good bunch of buddies with whom to chat and I draw some strength from that. I would not count among my friends a medical doctor who is one of my roommates. He is manic-depressive I guess, and gobbles handfuls of Lithium like Chiclets but still seems on edge. He and his wife are broke and while I sympathize in theory, I've discovered that he occasionally steals a one or a five from my wallet when I leave our room to take a shower. Why not simply ask? Another fellow who was here is a crack addict who tried to leap off a highway overpass when stoned. There was a big newspaper story on this that he carries carefully folded in his wallet. He told me in private about his numerous visitations with extraterrestrials. While it was fascinating to hear about their food-gathering techniques, I'd submit that the prognosis for this fellow might not be very good.

"I have been out several times here with friends from the house to bars, where we drink Cokes and shoot pool and look at women. Everyone seems afraid that sober they will lose all social life, so this has been an important test for us, and one I'm pleased to report that I survived.

"I have written apologetic letters to those people I most offended in an effort to make amends and the responses have been favorable, save one business colleague who told me to get fucked, on company letterhead no less.

"Why did I drink? This is a question that has no answer because it's so complex, a riddle from the sphinx. The only answer is, because I'm an alcoholic. What else? My parents' early death? Troubles that accumulated and grew till they seemed like the ache of an illness? Not to feel, to feel too much, to feel somewhat less? As I'm sure you know, at a certain point physiology takes over. My liver is perhaps less than county-size at present, a big improvement.

"As ordered by the court I have been attending a drunk-driving class and a weekly session on domestic violence. There is little to say about either of these except that the counselors try their best and are met with a wall of hostile faces. Thankless jobs for both. I will be able to drive again in a few weeks upon completion of that course.

"I have been drawing up time lines or chronologies of my life, thinking that if I recognized my problems I might solve them, or at least create an atmosphere of solution. Having gotten to the present day, I usually end up staring at the paper. At least I realize the problem is me and nothing else. Learning how not to drink is like an act of impersonation performed from dawn to dusk. Can I, can I? Perhaps my brush with death has claimed for me a certain serenity. I would like to begin a new life and be content with the effort, yet the question remains, can I reform this bone and fat and muscle to suit a new world I have yet to enter?"

— ❈ —

Three weeks later Pulitzer got his wish. On a Thursday morning he appeared before the judge in a borrowed suit and tie, and was given permission to leave the state. The judge recognized Volunteers and applauded the facility. At Pulitzer's request, he also deferred for six months Pulitzer's payment of his fines, allowing the defendant time to get back on his feet.

When he returned to the house Pulitzer commenced his preparations. He called Greyhound, then his brother, and his sponsor. Rob, his sponsor, wanted to drive Pulitzer to the bus depot on Sunday morning. "Afraid I'll drink?" chided Pulitzer. "No," said Rob, "the trip's expensive and I figured you could use a lift. True?"

"Absolutely," Pulitzer said.

"You got money for the ticket?"

"Just. I'd been anticipating it."

Then Pulitzer called his kids. Clark and Marcie were clearly pleased, though mystified by Pulitzer's mode of travel. "Bus?" Clark said. "What about your car?" He paused. "I guess they couldn't fix it."

"How many days across, Dad?" said Marcie, who had picked up on the other line.

"Five, something like that. I'm going to borrow your uncle's car and then I'll be down to pick you up for the weekend. Your uncle's invited us to stay at his place."

"Cool," Marcie said. "Dad, you rule."

That gave Pulitzer Friday and Saturday to kill before he left. He rather avoided Big Mike, because, frankly, he didn't know what to say. But Big Mike caught up with him on Saturday night just as bingo was beginning.

"You owe me fifty bucks," Mike said. "Your last week's rent. So you're leaving, are you?"

"I am, tomorrow morning. I'm afraid I'll have to mail you a check."

"If you do you'll be the first one." Mike held out his hand. "Good luck, Pulitzer."

That night was Pulitzer's final stint as a collector with his fellow swine-men, and a festive mood prevailed. Tips were, however, modest. The flypaper sisters appeared as usual in midgame, in matching jogging suits. It was a warm evening and there was perspiration on the women's foreheads and above their lips.

After the game was over, the collectors had to stay on to fold chairs and wipe down all the tables. Pulitzer was wringing out a rag into a bucket of soapy water when Mark, Dennis, and Tasker approached.

"Going-away gift," Tasker said. He held out a twenty. "It's our tips. We pooled them."

"No," Pulitzer said. "I can't."

"Take it," said Tasker. "Anyway, what can you do with twenty bucks?"

Later, in his bunk at Volunteers for the last time, Pulitzer contemplated Tasker's question. He was touched, no question, by their gesture. The twenty was safely in his wallet, in the bureau drawer. And at some point, as he lay there, it occurred to him what to do. The twenty would be with him tomorrow on the bus. In a year maybe, it could still be in his wallet. Old farts did things like that, didn't they? Pulitzer's father had carried a two-dollar bill until he died. If Pulitzer was lucky and lived to fifty, perhaps the bill would still be there. It was twenty dollars, and you never knew when you might need it.

# The Goodman Keilworth 1938

Even to mention it is wrong, but I have to. It was such an unusual request, come via fax from Bangkok, on letterhead from the Royal House of Chakri: find the Keilworth B-flat clarinet Benny Goodman played in his 1938 Carnegie Hall debut. But that's my business. You want the shoes Paul McCartney wasn't wearing on the cover of *Abbey Road*, the piano bench Gershwin used when he composed "Rhapsody in Blue?" Call me. Though if you're looking for knickknacks to fill up the Hard Rock Café, try elsewhere, please—I only deal in relics.

Chatichai represents the House of Chakri. From his fax, and the letter and bank draft that followed, I knew he was no factotum—he was emissary to the King. A few weeks later, when he happened to be in town, he phoned—could he come by to see how our search was progressing? Of course, I said, I'm on the fourth floor, you have to climb.

He was a smallish man, distinguished-looking, toffee-skinned, with close-cropped gray hair. Wearing a blue pinstripe suit. He was slightly winded from his ascent, though, so I let him look around: my reference books, my cabinets, the walk-in safe. Documents piled all around me.

"It's a difficult instrument to find," I said. "What about a B-flat played by Artie Shaw instead?"

"Oh, no," said Chatichai, seeming shocked. "That wouldn't do at all."

Let me tell you, the harder it is to find a thing, the more determined people can become. Still, it's not my business to know why people want a thing; they want it because they want it, and it's my job to help.

"There's the clarinet Goodman played at the Palomar Ballroom," I said, referring to the musician's famous California gig in 1936. "It's available," I added.

"I'm afraid not," said Chatichai.

The clarinet Goodman played in Carnegie Hall was a Keilworth, hand-made in Berlin in 1924. Goodman played it with a Beechler mouthpiece. That concert, too, had marked a milestone in Swing. It was one of the most famous performances Goodman ever gave, and it lent legitimacy to a whole new brand of music. Goodman died in 1986. To the end, he was still doing scales every morning before breakfast. His rimless glasses were gone by then, replaced by modern horn-rims, yet he still had that slightly quizzical look, like a surprised grocery clerk.

"You have to understand," said Chatichai. "About this instrument the King is very keen."

"A King in love with Swing?"

Chatichai was not amused. "Please, let's not be disrespectful. King Bhumibol has ruled Thailand since 1946. He went to school in Switzerland, and as a young man he fell in love with Benny Goodman."

"I take it he also plays?"

"It's a little-known fact, but at one time he was probably the most accomplished clarinetist in all of Asia."

"I'm beginning to like this," I said. "The irony, I mean. Today, people are in love with everything that's royal—they'll buy anything from evening gowns to a slice of wedding cake. Now here's a real-life royal who loves a common man."

"Ah," said Chatichai. "It's that human touch that makes him so revered."

We shook hands before he departed. In fact, Chatichai clutched my entire arm—first my wrist, then my forearm, then the meaty part just above the elbow—as though it were a rope and he was pulling himself ashore. Was this a custom peculiar to Thais, or was he just trying to impress me with the urgency of our quest?

"Once you've located the clarinet—and I know you will—you can present it to the King in person."

— ❋ —

Of course, I can't tell you how I got it. Or where. Let's just say that certain people were contacted, an exchange was made. You can find anything if you know where to look.

Chatichai arranged our meeting. Thai Consulate, Friday evening, eight o'clock two weeks hence. I took the clarinet uptown with me in a taxi. This time, Chatichai's pinstripe was a muted gray. He smiled, grabbed my fingers in the foyer. "The King is very pleased."

Bhumibol awaited us on the second floor in a salon. He was standing at the far end of the room, silhouetted by the window. All the windows had been thrown open, letting in the twilight breeze. A table with a bright light above had already been prepared. On a white cloth, several reeds were aligned beside a Beechler mouthpiece.

Chatichai approached the King, and after a moment Bhumibol came over. He was a tall, caramel-colored man in a dark business suit. Thinning hair and glasses, utterly composed. His hands were clasped behind him—he was a presence in the room.

Chatichai nodded me over to the table. "The Goodman Keilworth," I announced, opening the case before I withdrew.

Bhumibol approached the table. For a long while he just stood there, looking down. It was a beautiful instrument, it was! The plush lining of the case looked rather chewed, but the clarinet itself was perfect, and I felt proud—all the stops still had their exquisite action! Bhumibol held this attitude so long I began to notice shadows darkening the room. Then he turned and thanked me quietly in English, and Chatichai saw me down.

Outside, it was a balmy summer evening with little traffic. City lights were beginning to come on. I began to make my way down the sidewalk, toward the avenue, when suddenly, above me, I heard the King of Thailand playing scales. Through the leafy summer evening that lovely sound was my reward.

# The Girl from Blue Hawaii

E dward Allen Webber's first close-up of Manila was the faux marble floor in his bathroom at the Philippine Plaza, where he lay on his side doubled-up with stomach cramps. It was midnight somewhere when he'd arrived, and jet-lagged and dopey from his sixteen-hour flight, he'd ordered from room service an American-style hamburger and a local soup called *pansit molo*, which contained the offending peppers. Like a fool, he'd eaten them—little inch-long red fuckers that looked like the bloody incisors from some fire-eating beast—and they were pulsing now inside his stomach like pods of nuclear fuel.

Webber finally struggled to his feet, out of the bathroom and onto the bed by the phone. When the hotel doc appeared, he gave Webber paregoric and several liberal swigs of mefloquine. Like the other Filipinos Webber had seen thus far, the doctor was small, black-haired, and toffee-skinned, and seemed eager to please. He wore a white flaxen shirt they called a *barong* outside his slacks. "You are not to eat the peppers," the doctor told him. "They are simply to taste." Then he made Webber take down his trousers and he injected something into Webber's buttock. The effect was nearly instantaneous: a sort of frozen feeling from Webber's knees up through his abdomen, plus a massive erection, with which, at last, he went to sleep.

Eating those peppers his first night proved to be only one of Webber's many miscues. He was out of his element, culturally speaking, in Manila, though his displacement there was entirely intentional. He had taken leave from his law firm, where he was an associate, and if he had the time—that was the senior partner's phrase, anyway—he was going to check out a new plant site for one of the firm's investment clients. But why Manila? He and Jean, his departed wife, had vacationed together often in Europe, so for Webber that was out; instead he'd looked east, hoping for a change. He'd had a number of letters over the years from a college classmate who was living with his family in the Philippines, stationed at the U.S. Embassy as undersecretary for such-and-such affairs—the man had invited Webber numerous times to visit. Yet it was only after Webber had his ticket in hand that he learned by fax that the man had been transferred to Turkey. Well, what the fuck, he thought, he was going anyway. In Manila they spoke English, and money wasn't an issue. Jean had been a hot-shit lawyer herself, the youngest female vice president ever appointed to the SEC, and Webber was sole beneficiary to her life insurance. They had no children, and even if she'd lived they never would, since it was ovarian cancer that had killed her.

What Webber really wanted was for Jean to be alive. Jean, Jean, the chemo-queen, which is what she'd taken to calling herself, after the chemotherapy took her hair. Oh, how she'd diminished! Watching her sleep one night in the hospital, stick-thin and with a face the color of a pumpkin, Webber saw through his tears that she was curled in a ball at the edge of her bed like an animal that had struggled to the farthest end of its burrow.

"When is a person a healthy person?" Dr. Deitch had asked, repeating Webber's query. Dr. Deitch was the grief therapist Webber's law firm had referred him to back in Washington. Deitch was utterly hairless (no eyebrows, even), overweight, and pink. He was much prone to maxims and fond of quotes. "In order to be reborn, sometimes you have to die first." "Who said that?" asked Webber. "Deitch," said Deitch. "Sometimes it's life that provides the therapy, not the therapy." "Author?" Webber asked. "Freud," said the doctor, sighing in deference to the master.

That had been two months ago, four months after Jean's funeral. All that while Webber, seeking to bury himself too, had continued working. "The answer," Dr. Deitch had said, "is that the healthy person is a person who can love and work. Neither thing, right now, which you can do."

"Maybe I should take some time off, go away somewhere."

"Yes?"

"But what about the office?"

"From what you tell me, you're so distracted you're just making yourself a nuisance. So take a leave, get lost for a little while."

"Like where?"

"Better make it someplace far away. You don't like this world very much right now, so try another. Meet a woman, help you get over things. Someday you'll look back and see that every life has its rough spots. I know that sounds cruel, but there'll come a time, I hope, when you'll see it that way too. Allowing yourself that first step is very important."

Thus Manila. Deitch might be a crackpot but for Webber there weren't many alternatives. As for the city, aside from the high-rise hotels and a few concrete government buildings, the whole place looked like it had been flattened by a typhoon—even the shantytowns Webber saw from his taxi were made of cardboard and corrugated tin.

After a drugged sleep, the next day Webber checked out the view from his balcony. There was blue sky and high humidity. Traffic sped past below on Roxas Boulevard, and there were freighters out beyond the seawall on Manila Bay. There was a keen sense of a strange life going on all around him, but of Webber having no obligation to take part in it.

Downstairs, the lobby was full of Arabs. Not sheiks or diplomats, but dark men in sunglasses with silk suits and expensive jewelry, business types. Webber took a seat and a hawk-nosed man with a chunky Rolex immediately sat down beside him.

"These people," he said, exasperated, indicating an entire race as he spread his hands. "They are never on time."

"What brings you to Manila?" Webber asked.

"I'm here to hire hospital staff, and clerks for a supermarket. Contract laborers. Filipino nurses are very good."

"Where will they go?"

"Saudi Arabia. Overseas workers, they're the chief source of foreign income for the Philippines. No oil." He smiled. "What business are you in?"

"None," said Webber. "I'm on holiday."

"First time here?"

"Yes."

Presently the man rose to his feet. "My colleague," he said, pointing as he looked across the lobby to a Filipino in crocodile slip-ons and a flowered shirt.

"A word of advice?" said the Arab.

"Shoot."

"The little women here, they screw superbly. They'll take good care of you."

Webber returned to his room, to shave and shower. Sex, in fact, had been largely absent from his thinking. Rather, it was very much on his mind that he wasn't giving it any thought. He should, shouldn't he? Something ought to happen, he felt. The last time he'd made love to Jean was some eight months ago, and the memory of it still filled him with sadness. Curled on her side in the hospital bed, Jean had sucked him off as he stood beside her. That was illicit and exciting, but still, this woman with the hungry mouth, his wife, was dying.

"You don't have to do this," Webber told her. "Please."

Jean felt his prick soften, and the look she'd given him was villainous. "I'm not doing it for you," she said. "I'm doing it for me." Then she made Webber come and drank him down like an elixir, and afterwards turned away from him on her side and wept. It was very nearly Webber's last contact with her, with Jean as a human being, because as the days dragged on she retreated deeper and deeper into the narcotic stupor of her nonself, this dwindling nonperson who was mortally ill. Without consulting him, she'd made arrangements for her body to be cremated, so afterwards there had been nothing save an anonymous black urn for Webber to mourn. Where had she gone? Webber tried talking to her, talked to her as he remembered her, discussed with Jean what she might want him to do in this new solitary life of his. They hadn't, in fact, discussed it. "Just try to live," Dr. Deitch had advised him, trying to be helpful. "At dawn, pray for dark. In the dark, pray for dawn."

OK, Webber thought, sure thing. But what help was that?

— ✳ —

At dusk, he took a taxi from the Plaza over to Ermita to a bar called Blue Hawaii. It was a warm breezy evening and traffic on Roxas Boulevard was bad, so he sat watching it get dark as the neon signs came on. The air was foul with exhaust fumes.

"Cockfight tonight," said the driver. "Over Taft Avenue."

Thus the traffic jam. Half the city seemed to be named after

Americans—the rich vanished lords with their money and their displaced military. Webber watched a street vendor in flip-flops dodge between cars and jeepnies and buses, selling from a tray he wore on a halter hung around his neck. Webber's driver signaled him over, bought a single Marlboro cigarette, and waited while the vendor lit it with an imitation Zippo.

Ermita had a carnival atmosphere, the street jammed with taxis and music blasting from the clubs. Boys scampered about hawking cigarettes and candy. Inside, Blue Hawaii had a low ceiling and a raised stage where women danced. Webber took a seat at the bar and ordered a beer. The music on the sound system was Pinoy rock—Filipino versions of American hits. The girl sitting next to Webber had orchids in her hair and some sort of nasal obstruction, which caused her mouth to hang open like a trout's. She was wearing a sleeveless kimono and was smoking a cigarette, and every time she caught Webber's eye she stopped to sigh ostentatiously, as if she were already burning with desire for him.

"Remember me?" the woman said.

"No."

"I think we met before. You want to buy me Coke?"

"No, thanks."

"You don't like girls?"

"Girls are fine."

"You homosexual, you're in the wrong place," she said. Then she plopped down off her stool and went back to a corner, where she replayed their conversation to one of her girlfriends. Webber flushed under their amused, brazen glances.

Presently a door opened in the back of the bar and there was a tumult in Webber's chest. Here now was a girl! She was tall and dark, wore a white jersey top and blue jeans, and was grave and beautiful. She displayed no interest in Webber, nor in any of the other tourists drinking at the bar— Americans, Australians, Germans. She didn't get up to walk the room in a restless, flagrant attempt to attract attention as the other women did. She didn't have to. She was entirely self-contained, and she was smashingly good-looking. When she gave her short hair a tug the play of muscles in her shoulders was exquisite.

The girl had turned her head away as he approached but now she looked up and offered Webber a minimalist smile. "You want to dance?" she asked.

Webber shook his head. "Talk, maybe."

"You want to buy me drink?"

"Sure."

She extended her hand. "You American?"

"Yes."

"I thought you either American or English."

"Which do you prefer?"

She shrugged. "Doesn't matter. Why were you staring at me?"

"Because you're the best-looking girl I've seen in here."

She was pleased all right but still had her suspicions. "I trust you, maybe then I make a big mistake. Maybe you like me because you have no other girlfriend."

"That's true," Webber said.

The girl changed the subject suddenly by standing up. "I have to work, make money. I have to dance now."

"You can't stay?"

She narrowed her eyes at him. "You want?"

"Sure," Webber said, laughing now, embarrassed.

She leaned in a little closer. "You understand, you have to pay my bar fine?"

"I understand," Webber said, a bit confused.

"I'm Tess." She offered her hand and made him shake it.

Tess returned to him five minutes later, having changed in the back somewhere into a pair of shorts, rose-colored flats, and a white blouse with a smudge of color. Over her shoulder she toted a bulky leather handbag. Webber ordered her an orange juice, for himself another beer. An air of goodwill encompassed them. They talked, though later Webber couldn't recall what about. He had the impression that he was charming and witty and interesting, and that his audience was unusually receptive.

Tess listened and rarely talked. Under the dark canopy of her short, curly hair, her high forehead narrowed downward to the wings of her eye sockets; her cheekbones were high-set and prominent, jutting inward toward her tip-tilted and practically bridgeless nose, which gave her an exotic, Siamese look.

"Maybe we should go now?" she said.

Webber paid and headed out the door with the girl on his arm. The sidewalk was crowded with touts and beggars. Women slept in doorways with two or three grubby infants, an empty cigar box before them for alms.

Back at the Plaza, high up on Webber's balcony, the nightscape spread out before them looked similarly impoverished: the sprawling city with its bleak, tiny tin-roofed houses and shabby high-rise flats. It was like the view from the plane, only passing overhead one had to wonder if it was worth coming down here.

At the moment, yes. Inside the room Tess kicked off her flats and used the toilet, and now they stood together on the balcony smelling the swampy salt breeze blow in off the bay. She leaned against Webber and yawned elaborately.

"You work tomorrow?" she asked.

"I don't work now. Just holiday."

"Lucky you."

"My wife died six months ago," he said, surprised that he'd admitted it.

They went inside and while Tess showered, Webber undressed and drowsed beneath the covers. When Tess came out she was wrapped in a white towel, all thin brown legs and arms. She sat on the side of the bed for a moment looking down at him, alert, but not unlike some placid friendly dog. Then she reached over and snapped off the lamp, and slipped out of her towel and slid under the sheets beside him. Finally, with his fingers Webber felt down her back, felt her skin warm and still moist from her shower. His heart was going like crazy but he made no further move to touch her.

If she was a seasoned professional she hadn't learned yet the art of waking up in a hotel room, because the next morning Tess started up with a violent jerk, then lay tense and rigid beside him. At last she relaxed and with a groan sat up, found the towel on the floor, and wrapping it loosely around herself crossed to the bathroom. She looked at herself in the mirror, first taking a general view of herself and then, thrusting her chin out, a more detailed one of her face. Then she showered and came out again, found her handbag on the chair, and sat down on the bed beside him.

Webber watched as she took out her compact and a jar of cream, then fiddled with the compact on the pillow until the mirror reflected her face. She did up her towel again more securely and began to work the cream into her face and arms. Occasionally she would lean back like an artist from her easel and judge how her work was progressing.

"How old are you?" he asked.

"Twenty-six."

"From Manila?"

"Where did you meet me?"

"I know," he said. "But maybe you didn't always live here."

"Maybe not." She paused to look him over. "My family's down south."

"So you're alone?"

Tess looked over toward the balcony. "Not this minute," she teased.

Webber watched her while she combed her hair. Then she gathered up her underwear from the chair and slipped into her panties, keeping the towel around her until they were hoisted. With her back to him, she took off the towel and then slipped on her bra, squirming like an eel to get her arms through the straps.

"I have another job too," she said. "Not just dancer. Sometimes I work in the office, do secretarial."

"Oh?" he said, rather doubting her.

Tess sat down again and leaned over and kissed Webber on the forehead. "Maybe tonight you want to take me to dinner?"

"I'd love to," Webber said.

While he showered, Tess ordered for them a room service breakfast. When he returned there was fresh mango juice and coffee and toast on a tray. Tess put marmalade on one slice, honey on the other, then handed the slices to him. The movement of her hands was fluid and graceful, the perfect little hostess.

In the afternoon they took a taxi over to Fort Santiago, the old Spanish bastion defending the original city. Filipinos had been, over the centuries, a subservient folk: to the Spanish, the Americans, the Japanese. Tess, too, seemed dependent on the kindness of strangers. In the taxi, Webber wondered for a moment if she really liked him, or if she was just taking advantage before he moved on. Moved on to what? The truth was, Webber wasn't much thinking, because for him thinking hadn't paid off the past few months. "All I want is to take care of someone," Tess had said that morning in their room. "All I want is someone I can look after, who wants to look after me." Had anyone ever put the case to him so bluntly? Did she sense that Webber was someone she could trust? After she'd said that she just looked at him, as accustomed, in all likelihood, to rejection as acceptance.

Fort Santiago was on the Pasig River, not far from Malacanang Palace, which had once been filled with Imelda Marcos's shoes. There was a Spanish cathedral there, in Intramuros: the stones in its floor had come over as ballast in the hulls of old galleons. From the walls of the fort they overlooked the vast Tondo slums.

"Let's have a look," said Webber, pointing.

Tess was shocked.

"I'm a tourist," he said. "Come on."

There were people in Tondo barely living on the brink of existence. Houses lining the street were made of packing cases and cardboard, where entire families lived in places no bigger than a kennel. Even the piled trash hadn't the dense, bulky quality of rich American dumps, but looked picked over, sifted, like mountains of confetti. The place was unsewered and baking in the sun. At a *sari sari* shop on the corner everything was sold on a *tingi*, or piece-by-piece, basis: individual cloves, cigarettes, and sheets of writing paper could be purchased.

Afterward, riding back to the Plaza in a taxi, Webber realized that his little tour had been a bad mistake. Having come from poverty, no doubt Tess associated these places with her own stricken past, and to her his ignorance must seem clumsy.

"Don't ever ask me to take you to a place like that again," she said, once they were back in their room.

"I'm sorry."

"The Philippines is a beautiful country. Why do you want to look at filth like that? Those people there, they're too stupid to work."

"Stupid?" Webber was shocked by her lack of compassion. "Doesn't anyone try to help them?"

"Why?" she said defiantly. "Anyway, it's none of your business. This isn't your country and it never will be. Just don't take me there to rub dirt in my face."

"Jesus," Webber said, stung. "I'm sorry."

"Forget it," said Tess, "I'm going to shower. Afterward maybe we'll make love."

Startled, Webber said, " I guess we shouldn't waste any time, then."

"What do you mean? I'm hot and dirty."

"Me, too," he said. "But maybe now I'm a little too distracted for fucking."

Tess didn't care for that word. "If you don't want me to stay here then just tell me. If I stay here maybe we'll make love. It's what people do, you know? Or maybe you can just sit here on the bed now and think. Think of what? Is there something about me that you don't find attractive?"

By now she had slipped off her shoes and presented her back to him so he could unzip her dress. She held her hair up from the zipper and the muscles in her neck and shoulders were perfect. She snaked her hand back into Webber's lap.

"Shower first?" she mumbled. "Or not?"

Tess pulled the dress over her head and tossed her bra and underpants on the floor. On her belly, she turned and watched as Webber disrobed behind her. He kissed her then, on the back, and nibbled at her neck. Tess moaned and drew up her legs beneath her. She reached down and guided him into her, then lowered her shoulders and wriggled her backside as she pushed herself against him, impaling herself with a long deep-throated moan. By that time, of course, Webber had climaxed already.

— ✳ —

They were good together. Tess was patient and pleasant and adept at taking care of him, and for Webber it was easy to surrender to her attentions. They talked, though the questions she asked—what job his ex-wife had, did they have any children?—mostly concerned life in the States, which Tess imagined as a vast palace of skyscrapers and shopping malls, where one was likely to run into Sly Stallone or Cindy Crawford. Her lack of sophistication didn't trouble her and charmed him. She had a mother and a sister in the provinces, she said, and had graduated from a junior college in Manila. A boyfriend? "Not anymore," she said, looking shyly away. A moment later she gave Webber her most radiant smile. "Maybe today," she said, "if you're going to be my new boyfriend."

They spent an inordinate amount of time in bed together. Tess was wholly uninhibited about her body, her breasts smallish and thick-nippled and sensitive. Webber made love to her, stupidly, without condoms, and sucking at her small, nearly hairless sex, his mouth filled with something syrupy like sap, and he wanted more.

In short order, there was the issue of money. Once she'd decided to stay, it cost Webber two hundred dollars to buy her out for the week from Blue

Hawaii, which was rather unpleasantly like renting a car. Then there was the matter of her debts, for a single room in Mabini on which she was behind, and a loan she had from a girlfriend. Also, when they went out together, it was mostly for shopping. A native-carved chess set and a cotton *barong* for him, two dresses, skirts, blouses, and jewelry for Tess. Not gold, but bracelets and amulets made from coral or the skins of lizards. At home, in their room at the Plaza, in her bare feet Tess modeled her new clothes.

Each time when Tess left the room on some errand, a wad of pesos stuffed into her purse, Webber worried that this view of her, departing, might be his last. What could she see in him, after all, but a bankroll? Sitting on the balcony, waiting for her, as he watched the day fade he felt a familiar despondency settle over him. Behind the mountains of Bataan the sky darkened and the freighters began to twinkle with light. Then along the crescent of the bay all the street lamps suddenly came on. It was easy, wasn't it, just breathing in, then out? When the knock on the door came, at last, it was only Tess returning.

None of which could be explained easily to Jean, if she had been alive to listen. Jean, Jean in her dark vessel back in their Washington apartment, who wasn't there for Webber—and now he had to question whether she ever had been. What would she think, or say? Whenever his union with Tess struck him as incongruous, which it did frequently, Webber wondered if it wasn't due to his own desperation, his newfound taste for the absurd. If there were other Americans around (and there weren't many), would that inhibit him with Tess? Of course the differences between the two of them could be pretty exhilarating, but then Webber wasn't an anthropologist— Tess came from somewhere and so did he.

Still, in the course of paying for her favors he allowed himself to believe that her feelings for him were a lot more than a delusion, and he was happy. Sure, she was a primitive and lived deeply—or maybe just closer to the surface. But Tess had reawakened something in him and for that Webber was immensely grateful. "Bitch," he thought. "My wife was a bitch to leave me." Let's face it, he thought, what thing, other than her dying, could have propelled him into *this* relationship? He hated Jean for dying. But at least now he was making an effort to cast off his piled-up past for this remote idyll where he could be someone different.

As for Tess, she withheld much and in a funny way seemed to resent the intimacy of Webber knowing her secrets, as though that might lock her in somehow, into an identity she couldn't bluff her way out of. Yet she confounded him by showing him how unhappy he had been in the final days of his marriage—and how foolish it was for him to mourn a woman who was no longer alive.

— ❋ —

After two days Tess's husband showed up at the Plaza. Leaving the lobby one evening for a walk, Webber noticed some Filipinos hanging out around the entrance to the hotel. He thought they stared even more than the locals usually stared at him—they all assumed he had lots of money. Then, coming back later at dusk, he thought he heard someone following him but shrugged it off.

The next night when he returned to the Plaza he found their room in utter darkness and Tess crouched in a corner, weeping. It took Webber half an hour to get any sense out of her, but when he'd heard her story he was frightened for her too. If it had been entirely clear to him what was going on it might not have ended so badly.

The next morning the same Filipinos were waiting for him at the entrance to the hotel—three of them. They said something to him in Tagalog, the native language. No one touched him. "Money you got?" one said in English. "Go away now," said another. Webber understood that much. They let him go then and walked off, joking grimly.

Tess was weeping again when Webber got back to the room. These people had been pushing notes under their door for the past two days, apparently. Tess showed Webber the scraps of paper with their inky messages but was too upset to translate.

"Tess," he said. "You've got to explain."

She turned her head, thrusting her hand away and refusing to answer.

"He's my husband," she said sobbing, finally. "Not those boys in the street, but another. Those are his friends. He's the one sending the letters. I married him five years ago and now he wants my money. He's threatening my daughter."

"Your daughter?"

"Yes."

"You're married?"

"Yes."

Webber felt stunned for a moment, then foolish. "So you lied to me all along?" In his own ears his question sounded petulant and stupid.

"Of course I lied to you."

"But why?"

"You want to go with me if I'm married? If I have a husband and a baby?"

"Just because he says so, you don't have to do what he wants."

"He threatens to take Ja–Ja, or hurt her."

"Ja–Ja?"

"My baby, she's two."

"We'll get her back and we can leave here."

"Cannot."

"Why not?"

Tess wouldn't, or couldn't, answer.

"Didn't you know something like this might happen?"

Tess was silent.

"You set me up," Webber said, finally.

Tess stretched out on the floor, regarding him with narrowed eyes. For Webber it was doubly disquieting: her look was far from amiable, and all access to her was now denied. Sure, she had lied to him—what difference, really, did that make? Couldn't she see that he loved her? Or did this paradise, too, have to vanish?

A sensible man might have called it a day. Just packed up and left, looking back later on his Philippine adventure as one protracted miscue. But not Webber. Because he was made of sterner stuff? He'd been in the Philippines just a week. Seven days of bliss and betrayal.

The final insult came when Webber returned the next afternoon and found the room they'd shared picked clean. No suitcases, no clothing in the closet. Also the two or three hundred in cash that he'd left behind in his wallet, which she'd taken. According to the manager at the Plaza, Tess had come down with the suitcases that afternoon, then climbed into a taxi, and that was the last time anyone had seen her.

Upstairs the room was empty, save what he remembered had happened there. Webber felt sick and squatted on the floor. To know that Tess was alive somewhere and breathing the same air was maddening.

Fleeced, ensnared, and swindled. It happened all the time to Americans. Innocents abroad. For Tess, wasn't it degrading to be the one to have to do it? Apparently the men in her life were all swine. He remembered her mouth, tight and serious as the wound from an arrowhead.

"Grief isn't an event, it's a process." So said Dr. Deitch, his head as hairless and obtrusive as a thumb. "In order to get over things, sometimes it's necessary to interpose between the event itself and your future life . . . some other thing."

So then, was this some other thing?

— ✳ —

Webber spent the next few days in a solitude of sun and sea. Home was a one-room tourist cabin he'd moved to from the Plaza, at the end of a lane of crushed shells lined by frangipani trees, which filled the air with their sweet scent. There was a bed, a wicker table, and a rattan chair. He had wired the States for more money and kept it in an empty soda can. At night geckos crawled across the walls chirping, but he soon got used to them.

Days he spent at the beach or fishing. After a day of swimming the beach grew dull, and the next morning he rented a crude fifteen-foot *bangka*, a sort of canoe with pontoons to give it stability. With the help of a push pole he could skid the boat across the shallow lagoons at high tide. He investigated the small harbors, sticking close to shore. Each day dawned hot and clear, then in mid-afternoon there was a tropical shower. With a crude line and shrimp bait he caught small black fish, which he unhooked and threw back in. One hot, calm morning he hooked a marlin in shallow water and was profoundly shocked when it hurtled out of the water by the bow of his boat, twisting its powerful body as it threw his line. Afterwards he counted a hundred different shades of blue in the still water.

— ✳ —

That afternoon he found a note stuck under his cabin door. It was a thin envelope and inside was a letter written in a looping childish hand. It was from Tess, and as he read on her matter-of-fact voice began to speak to him: "How are you, same here with me. I'm alone again with Ja-Ja in

Lubao. Your new address I got from the Plaza. This is a hard letter for me
to write. I'm so sorry to you if I wasn't always truthful. Still, if you can spare
it I could use your help. I would like to see you. Just show my address and
any taxi can take you where I live."

The nerve! Yet should any of this surprise him, in a country he didn't,
and couldn't, know? Somehow he could not, and would not, refuse her.

Lubao was no more than a crossroads on the outskirts of town. It was a
dismal district, all ditch and stagnant lagoon. There were shacks where children poked through piles of garbage along the roadside with sticks. The
driver pulled up to Tess's place—a tin shack with two or three similar ones
next door—and Webber climbed out of the taxi. A nondescript dog loped
around the corner and barked, then stared good-naturedly. Feeling at the
end of something, Webber took a deep breath and approached the building.

There was no proper door so he rapped on the plywood panel. From
inside there was a rush and a shuffle, and then the panel opened.

Same height, wire-rimmed glasses. Same black, olive-tree hair. For some
reason, her head looked smaller and oddly misshapen. She wore a choco-
late-colored sleeveless dress and pink slippers with little pompoms that
looked well chewed.

"My God," Tess said. "It's you, Webber. Come in." She flattened her back
against the plywood panel and did her best to let him pass without touch-
ing her, then pulled the door closed, and followed Webber into the all-pur-
pose room.

"My neighbor, he's working," she said, pointing, inviting Webber's gaze
to follow out the open back of the room—it appeared to be her bedroom,
kitchen, and laundry combined—to a primitive vista where a Filipino was
caulking the hull of a boat with tar.

"Your husband?" Webber asked.

"No, the owner of this house. My neighbor. I'm tenant only."

Tess stood in the middle of the slanting, linoleum-floored room and
made familiar Siamese gestures with her wrists and hands, offering Webber
either a canvas chair or the couch, which at night must be her bed. Webber
chose the chair, Tess the couch. How diminished, her circumstances! But
then, hadn't their life together at the Plaza always been more his than hers?
There was a makeshift cardboard closet over Tess's shoulder, and inside it
Webber could see the dresses he had bought her, mocking him.

"You left quickly enough," he said.

Tess's eyebrows puckered. "I had to. I'm sorry."

"Where's your husband?"

"Gone again, that's our deal. He gets your money, and I get Ja-Ja."

"Where is she?" Webber asked.

"In the garden." Tess pointed outside again.

Webber looked out the back of the shabby room to where her neighbor was working on the boat. This was a garden? Indeed, there were some vegetables struggling in a rank corner of the yard. Ja-Ja, or what Webber took to be her, was sitting on the ground. Her hair was black and long.

"This was big trouble for you," said Tess. "Me, I have Ja-Ja back at least."

"Did they *make* you steal my money? I would have given it to you, you know."

Tess was stung. "I was too upset, and worried. Not thinking right. *They* got your money, not me. I have nothing."

Webber didn't know if he believed her—or if it mattered. She seemed a different person now, a little mother. Even her eyes, strangely spectacled, and her body hidden within the shapeless dress, seemed to suggest her complete removal from that girl he'd met back in Blue Hawaii, that girl who'd been so eager to please. Their tryst had been no more than a doomed extravagance.

"Webber." Tess said. "Edward. Alan. Webber." She had always liked to roll all those vowels together along her tongue. She was still vigorously beautiful, of course—despite her surroundings. Webber watched her close her sooty eyes and open her mouth, leaning back on the couch with one naked foot on the floor.

"If you want, we can make love right here," she said.

"No," he said, shocked. "I'm leaving this afternoon."

"You're a nice man, Webber. Can you forgive this dumb girl her mistake?"

Webber rose from the chair and handed her the envelope. There was, inside, a little less than twenty-five hundred dollars—what he'd had wired to him from Washington, less his modest expenses for the week. All along, he'd planned on giving it to her—if he could only find her. It wasn't, after all, a question of the money; it was easier to give it to her now than worry later on about how he'd behaved. And wasn't that the important thing? He loved her, in a way, just for giving him a hint of life—or for showing him that such a thing was possible.

"My God," she said. "You giving me all of this?"

Outside, the muddy mutt barked. The taxi driver was still waiting by the road. Webber crossed the yard and climbed in, and as the driver started up he looked back and waved to Tess standing in the doorway of her house. Then she disappeared as she pulled back the plywood panel—which was, years later, how Webber remembered it. The third-world adventure he had paid for was over, and now other things lay ahead.

# What I Know Now

So life sucks, so what. Still, since you forget things, what you remember about your old wives is mostly good, even the bad parts. When you don't have much else going for you, those memories can be lethal. I should know, I've been married three times.

Stacie was my first wife. She was dark and big-boned and slept fourteen hours a night. Anne was from Kansas and had a yen for kinky sex, but she got homesick for the prairie. Carrie once threatened to divorce me if I didn't carry an air-conditioner up four flights of stairs to our apartment, but we split up later anyway. Where were the good times, I wondered?

By omission, Stacie's father lied to me. When I asked him if I could marry his daughter, he scratched his jaw and said, "I guess she's OK." He didn't tell me about the pills and the suicide attempts, the years of therapy. When I landed my first real job, that evening we went out to a fancy restaurant to celebrate and Stacie got drunk and threw up at the table. Passive-aggressive, I guess. I had to put her in the back seat of our car, covering her with a blanket because it was winter.

I wanted things to be different. I didn't want the same meals over and over again, cleaning the house every weekend. No. I wanted cut flowers on the table, her wearing a beautiful dress, seeing a fantastic exhibit at the museum, blow jobs on the interstate. Going to Paris for her birthday—you know, wine, the Louvre, making out in the shadow of Notre Dame. Or was I asking for too much?

On the wall in my house I have a photograph of my second wife hanging above the table. I've been thinking about Anne for days. It's been a long time since I've seen her and that's a good thing, yet I think if she walked in here right now I'd marry her again in a second.

Anne went to Kansas State and got a doctorate in Russian history from the University of Chicago. In my picture of her she's wearing a pair of blue jean shorts and a sleeveless T-shirt. Also cowboy boots. She looks incredibly hot, but I still get this awkward feeling looking at the picture—I know I did something wrong, and the reminder of my guilt is deep and unpleasant. Still, when I look into Anne's eyes I want her back. I'd do anything to get her back. If she called me on the phone right now and asked me to, I'd drop to my knees and beg.

"Jake," she'd say. "Would you like to give us another try, sweetheart?"

I need her to want me. Then, once she says I can come to visit her, and later when she looks up from down there with those big blue eyes that drink you in—she's got this amazing mouth—I'll want to leave, and I won't want to see her or talk to her or listen to her voice on the phone ever again.

So tell me, what's that about? Is that love? How is it that you can care for someone so much and then despise her five minutes later? I admit it, women confuse me. It's either that or my reactions I don't understand. Maybe I'm a sprinter—I mean, some people can't go the distance no matter how hard they try.

Speaking of stamina, in college I was good, on the swimming team—I was a diver and made varsity at Michigan State four years out of four. I've still got thick hair and my skin, my body—they're decent, really. I mean, I'm not in bad shape for a thirty-five-year-old former athlete.

Despite my recent setback, which I'm coming to, I love women. I love having a girlfriend, a wife. All they ask of you is a normal degree of fidelity, and then they'll let you do whatever you want to them. Anything, almost. It's unbelievable.

After I'd been divorced for the third time it began to puzzle me that I hadn't learned more from my experience. Other men stayed married to the same women all their lives and could generalize in a helpful way about their habits; me, I'd been around a lot of women but didn't have much to say for it. Still, I love being in love. Those first weeks together, when the next morning you find a long hair of hers stuck to the sleeve of your jacket, and for the next ten minutes you're stoned, thinking about last night. When I'm in love I can smell the woman I'm in love with in a city two hundred miles away. Her perfume lingers, or the warm sunny smell of her shampoo. Memory fools you by bringing back these scents. I could fill a building with them.

— ✳ —

Sometimes, it seems like Jane, my most recent girlfriend, is the only person I've ever really loved. Jane knows me and, despite that, wants to be with me. She's a research chemist at the university, and rather quiet. Mousy, guys might say. She's got short brown hair, no kids. Believe it or not, her ex-husband's doing time for armed robbery.

The other evening we went to a party—mostly university people I know from work. The party was held in a refurbished power plant. There were guys carrying around trays of hors d'oeuvres, and an open bar. I was tired after a long day and annoyed with myself for bringing Jane because she didn't seem to know anyone.

We were standing around talking when Jane suddenly waved to this woman who was heading up to the bar. She was tall, with silky jet-black hair just above her shoulders and hanging around her face. She had on blue jeans and a maroon T-shirt, and had a high, tight athlete's ass, with those sharp hipbones you can feel underneath her bikini.

I wanted to get to meet her. "Janey," I said. "When you go to the bathroom can you check my messages at work? I'm worried about some stuff."

"OK," Jane said, and left. I hustled up to the bar and edged over to this new woman.

She had high cheekbones, all right. She looked like one of those pretty, sullen models you see in Calvin Klein ads. I don't know, I'm no expert on women's looks, but she was beautiful. No lie, I was already imagining our future together. Maybe she knew people in common with Jane—that's why she'd waved.

When Jane returned I tried to get back into the swing of things. If she'd noticed anything Jane didn't say. In fact, she was always quick to forgive me. Why? Maybe it's because I'm such a fantastic lover. I have to give myself that, at least.

By the time we left the liquor had begun to work on me. I kept grinding the tires into the curb as I tried to back out of the parking space. We went home to Jane's place and got undressed. I climbed into bed and shut my eyes and tried to sleep, except there was this woman, the woman with the black hair, walking around in my mind. I watched her walk up to the bartender, I saw her reach into the front pocket of her jeans to get some change, and I saw her round butt sticking out—I was so horny I couldn't believe it. Jesus, just her butt inside her jeans! I wanted to whack off.

Instead I fucked Jane. I didn't want to but I did. Any guy would do the same. Then the next morning over coffee, I asked her how she knew that woman, what her name was, where she worked. Now what? Was I all of a sudden on the prowl, ready for someone new? I mean, there was nothing wrong with Jane, she was good—she just didn't stir me.

A few days later we were having drinks in town after work, and that woman—Elana was her name—came in. It turned out she was a famous athlete, at least locally. She'd played soccer on the U.S. Olympic team. She'd played wing, and now she was coaching at the university. Jane knew her because some member of the chemistry department had some connection to the team.

"There's your friend," Jane teased. We both laughed. Jane waved hello again and offered Elana a seat. We talked about all the usual crap. Elana seemed like a pretty cool woman, very normal acting for a sort of celebrity. She had very pale, light-blue eyes. Maybe she was half Latin or something—her skin had this caramel hue. Her hair was thick and shiny and when she smiled her teeth were white and perfect. She was gorgeous! I realized then that I'd seen her around before on campus, at the field house.

Later that night we were lying in Jane's bed, and I was trying to picture what Elana's house might look like inside. I wondered what kind of stuff she liked to hang on her walls. Jane started kissing my neck, gently imploring me to get on top of her, and in my mind I saw Elana's butt again. She had on different slacks this time—tan khakis—and a faded denim shirt. You could tell she was very slim and in perfect shape. I was desperate to see her nipples. Were they fat or small? Gumdrops or little raisins? There I was, all horned out and at the same time feeling guilty, like I was thirteen years old again and someone had just caught me beating off. You know what I mean, we've all been there.

— ✳ —

We had this big fund drive going at the university. That's what I do: I try to get alumni and corporations to open up their wallets. I had to come up with a new annual giving theme. I wrote the direct mail letter, we presented it, and I personally got a high-five from the dean. He took us all out to a Chinese restaurant in town to celebrate. We had platters of spicy noodles and lots of cold beer. Believe me, I was feeling no pain.

The last place we visited was this campus bar. It was late and the place was thinning out. A few couples were dancing. I bought a pitcher of beer and wandered around with it in one hand and my mug in the other. I was in a high good humor and wanted to dance. I just kind of bounced around by myself for a while, then started dancing anyway, splashing beer around. When I looked into the corner at a table filled with people, Elana was sitting there.

She was seated in the middle of the crowd. The rest of the men and women were all good-looking and healthy and young—they were athletes, I could tell. They were all the kind of people I used to hang out with when I was on the swimming team. Elana seemed pretty intent on their conversation and didn't look around much. As I watched her I started to get into the music, doing a sliding move here and there. I kept my eyes on her and went up close to her table, and danced up and back and snapped my fingers. I yelled "Hey!" She nodded and gave a half wave, and then I shouted over to her, "You want to join me?" She motioned to me that she couldn't hear. I moved as close as I could and yelled the same thing again. She made a face and looked away; maybe she didn't understand me. I yelled again and she turned to the girl sitting next to her and laughed. Then I yelled, "You want to have a drink after your friends go home?" Elana was looking straight ahead.

— ❋ —

I woke up in bed with my coat and tie still on. It was Saturday afternoon. I took everything off. At the bar, I'd puked in the men's room—at least that came back to me. And when I'd gone over to try to talk to Elana I fell over a chair. I remembered someone calling me an asshole. I didn't remember how I'd gotten home.

I went into the kitchen and made some coffee. Afterward I lay on the living room floor and read the newspaper. Then I got up and went into the bathroom and looked in the mirror for a while. I vacuumed and did the dishes. I napped, then called Jane, and made some lame excuse about not seeing her. That night I tried to watch a movie on HBO but gave up. I listened to a Bob Dylan CD, drowsing on the sofa. Then I got up, went over to my desk, and sat down. It wasn't even midnight yet.

I started looking at that photograph on the wall again, the one of Anne in her cowboy boots. I remembered a night when we were in a hotel in Kansas City. It was two o'clock in the morning. Anne was wearing a pair of my knee-high dress socks and an old Michigan T-shirt, nothing else. She sipped her white wine. "You know," she said, "after I have two or three glasses of this stuff I like to be fucked from behind."

I went into the bathroom and brushed my teeth. The moment I came out Anne reached into my boxer shorts with her hand—into which she had already poured a liberal amount of Astroglide—and began to massage it in. The sudden sensation of the oil made me instantly erect. I watched as she positioned herself over the edge of the bed.

"Could you please take off my socks?" Anne asked, in a vulnerable voice that took me by surprise.

I reached over—amazed at her rapid shift to docility—and tugged her sock down.

"Now could you take off my T-shirt?" she said in the same submissive tone.

I pulled the T-shirt over her head and took off her other sock. Then I looked down and rubbed my hand lovingly over her gorgeous bottom, and licked my finger to moisten my favorite of her openings—though presently I discovered she'd taken care of that herself while I'd been in the bathroom.

She turned onto her stomach and carefully pulled me in. I felt like a giant hook. I tried not to touch anything except her ass, but after a few seconds we were grinding and I was rubbing against her hard. She got ridden down into the bedspread and was making sweet painful noises, whimpering. She let out a big shout when she came.

"It's well documented that Boris Yeltsin had a serious problem with alcohol in his early teens," she told me the next morning over breakfast. "Even when he was a kid the local KGB had a file on him a half-mile thick."

— ❀ —

Sunday morning I looked in the university directory and found out where Elana lived. I put on a clean shirt and pants, shaved, and started over in my car. I stopped on the way at a corner store and got the Sunday paper and a bouquet of flowers. In front of Elana's place I paused to check myself in the rearview mirror: I looked pale and swollen but well rested. I got out and walked around her house and up the steps to her back door.

I could hear somebody going around inside the kitchen, the refrigerator door slamming and water running. When I looked in the window I saw Elana standing behind the table looking at me. She was trying to figure out who I was. She opened the door and said something I couldn't make out, then stood there watching me.

"After the other night I've been going around apologizing," I said.

She held the door open, leaning halfway out. Her light-brown skin showed against her white T-shirt. She was wearing jogging shorts and the muscles on her legs were fabulous.

Elana told me to come in. I followed her inside and tried to get comfortable. Instead, I knocked over the dog's water dish. If there's such a thing as retribution, I was living it. I wondered if there was a chance my humiliation might make her like me more.

We started to talk. I reminded Elana about me yelling at her in the bar while she'd been with her friends. That didn't ring a bell. So I mentioned falling over the table. I said, "At least I didn't get sick on you." Then her memory of me came back and I handed her the flowers. She laughed and went and showed them to somebody in the other room, and another woman came out with her and we were introduced. Her name was Blue. I'd never seen her before. She was a skinny brunette with long hair, wearing a nightshirt. Elana asked me if I wanted coffee, and while she was making it Blue went behind her to toast some bread and placed her hand lightly on the small of Elana's back. They kissed, very lightly, on the lips. When Blue went from the toaster to the refrigerator, Elana's eyes followed her. Blue poured some coffee for herself, Elana handed her a spoon, and Blue went back to bed.

I told Elana that I'd gotten sick of acting like an idiot—there's no dignity in being such a pig. Then the conversation turned around and I told her what I do, writing promotional stuff for the university. I said the next time we needed a spokesperson for something I'd call her if she'd be willing. I said I'd been wanting to talk to her about a mailing we had in mind with a sports theme, and that we needed a famous athlete.

"In fact," I lied, "the dean wanted to know if you'd be willing to participate in this mailing we're cooking up right now."

"I don't know," she said.

"It's not really selling."

"Do I have to be on camera? I hate that."

"No," I said. "Maybe just your picture and a quote."

"Uh-huh," she said.

Then, because Elana was waiting for me to say more, I laughed. "Why don't I mail you a draft of the letter and then maybe we'll discuss it."

"Okay."

"That was your girlfriend I met, right?"

"Yeah," she said.

"It's a crazy thing," I said.

"What?"

"How long have you two been living together? Is she an athlete?"

"About three years," Elana said.

"Wow," I said.

"That's right," Elana said. "Wow."

I told her, "I could write a book on everything I don't know about women. Isn't it weird?"

"Maybe you should be going," Elana said.

"Right," I said. "You ought to come over to my place tonight and I'll give you my complete history."

"What?" she said.

"Never mind," I said.

"Right," she said. "Bye."

I went home, took a nap, and cooked my dinner. When Jane called and asked to come over I made an excuse about work and hung up. I turned on the TV and thought of Elana, images of her walking around her kitchen. So she was a lesbian, so what? What right did she have to such a happy life? Then I switched off the TV, because in my mind Elana had started doing this little dance in her smart, tight-fitting jeans. I went into the bathroom then and combed my hair back with gel and stared at myself in the mirror. After a while I noticed that I was holding my stomach in and pumping up my chest. When you come to think of it, that's how I spent a lot of my time at home.

— ❊ —

In fund-raising you have these really hectic times, and then the drive ends and you get bored shitless. Sometimes the administration starts letting the less experienced people go. I mean, people go out for lunch and they don't come back.

After work the next day I drove out to the mall. I walked into every store. A men's shop had some loose, blousy shirts on sale, with rounded cuffs and pleats on the shoulders. I looked around inside every shop. Finally I went down to the department store and got some new hair gel and a big jar of cream that's supposed to make you look tan. I paid with my credit card and the counter lady handed me the bag. Then, walking past the sportswear department, I got this idea.

When I got home I took a shower and shaved. I dried myself off with a towel, then used the tanning cream. When I was finished I put on my new bathing suit. My big ass barely fit inside the Speedo—it was red, white, and blue just like the flag. I ripped a hole in the seam trying to get the suit to straighten out. Then I sucked in my gut and had a look: not like my old diving days, but not too bad. I thought about jamming a pair of socks down my crotch but didn't do it. Then I pulled on a terrycloth robe and grabbed my wallet, and went out to the car.

Just as I was backing up headlights came up the driveway behind me. It was Jane. Now her car was in the way. She got out and spotted me and walked over. I rolled down my window and said, "Hey."

Jane bent down and looked in at me. It took a few seconds. Then she said, "Hey, Jake," scratching her upper lip. She was smiling, but her smile was weird.

I laughed. Neither of us could think of anything to say. "You taking up swimming?" she asked, finally.

"That's just where I was going," I said.

"Jake," she said, but it was more like a question. She looked in at me again. "I think you're lying," she said. Her voice was scratchy in her throat. She looked one last time, her hands on her knees, ducking down to the open window. "God," she said. "What's wrong with you? You look like you rolled in mud."

"I didn't do anything," I said.

"No, except we haven't seen each other in two weeks. Is that a message?"

"Get off it," I said. "Please."

Jane coughed and pulled a tissue from her pocket. "What am I doing?" she asked, and she stood up. Her hips turned toward the house and then toward her car, and she was gone.

At the entrance to the field house, cars drive up to drop people off and pick them up. I figured Elana worked out most evenings, and I wanted to be there when she came out. There are streetlights that make everything bright, so I stood off to the side where it was darker and out of people's way. I paced back and forth in my Speedo and my robe, checking each time the door opened to see if it was Elana coming out. I still had on the tanning cream and I guess I looked a little strange. Finally some basketball players came out, and at the same time a dean from school came out the other set of doors, carrying a gym bag. I'd forgotten about this possibility, that someone I knew might appear. This guy came down the sidewalk toward the parking lot, heading at me like a missile. I tried to figure out how I could avoid him, but there was no way so I took off at a run.

— ❀ —

The final phone call was pretty difficult. Elana didn't know what I was thinking.

"I mailed you that letter," I said.

"Who is this?" she asked. "Ben?"

"No, it's Jake. The guy about the fund-raising at the university."

"Oh, right," she said. "I'll bet you could write about anything."

"Thanks," I said.

We talked about some other stuff. Then I said, "Can I ask you something?"

"What?" she said.

"Is there any chance you could come over tonight and I could cook you dinner?" I figured if I just said it then something would happen, either way.

"This isn't about fund-raising, is it?" she said.

"I could make *tom yong kung*, it's a spicy Thai soup."

"I should have known you were just trying to hit on me."

"I'm not," I said, but she'd already hung up.

I didn't want to do anything with her. Just to hang around with Elana, the two of us sitting there together—she could even bring Blue along. Simple, no? I mean, isn't it obvious how I felt?

— ✳ —

Events happen in your life that can't be changed. In fact, afterwards you're not the same person anymore. You don't feel better, just different. Most of the time I just feel old.

It's been a while since Elana hung up on me. Lately it seems I can't get close to anyone without offending them. I keep trying to call Jane, but she has caller ID and won't pick up. Well, I dumped her, didn't I? I guess I'm getting what I deserve.

I started writing this confession a week ago, sitting here on the porch outside my house. I took some time off from the office. Not that I expect an epiphany—a small suggestion would be enough.

Across the road from my table is an apartment building with open balconies. It's morning now but at the proper time of day I can even see into the rooms. Nothing prepared me for the tall, fashionably dressed woman who seemed to appear out of nowhere and sat by herself on her balcony, her long blonde hair falling over her shoulders in loose curls. Her legs look extremely long from my vantage point. Her attitude is casual as she leans back and takes a long drag from her cigarette, then tosses it down into the yard. She appears across from me at the same time every day. This woman has noticed me, I know it. I can see already that beneath her calm exterior she is passionate, hardly able to control the need that must be driving her ever closer to me. And like her, I'm ready to fall in love again. Though I've been in love many times before, who's to say I won't be grateful? At least I'll know where I'm headed, that I'm into something I can understand.

# A Woman of Kansas

Beth had not yet accepted the queasiness in her stomach, her quickening pulse, and the dryness in her mouth that signaled the onset of an attack of anxiety. On the car seat beside her, her husband, Philip, thumbed out the disc in the CD player and commenced to fiddle with the radio, no doubt searching for a noontime financial report. Given their location—on Interstate 70 in western Kansas, about a hundred miles shy of Salina—it would have been a better bet to tune in for prices on soybeans and wheat, but it wasn't Philip's nature to be denied. His dawdling with the radio, not incidentally, had replaced one of her favorite CDs, Lucia Popp singing Strauss's *Four Last Songs*. The piece in question was called "Death and Transfiguration," an aching melody that the dwarf Billy Kwan had played for Mel Gibson in *The Year of Living Dangerously*. Beth and Philip had seen that movie together, in Lawrence, in 1983; Beth had been so taken with the music she'd remained in her seat after the film was over, until she could identify the piece in the credits. She had gone out the next day and purchased two copies of the album—one for herself, the other for her beloved friend Naomi.

"Do you mind, sweetheart?" Philip said.

"Not at all," Beth answered, partly because it wouldn't matter much longer and partly because her therapist at Menningers had emphasized to her the importance of giving up resistance to outside frustrations at the onset of an attack of anxiety, under the notion that you could sometimes starve outside impositions. For instance, Beth shouldn't have been driving at all—sitting with her eyes closed listening to her music probably would

103

have helped—but she drove to avoid having to talk to Philip. An additional problem for her was his car, an ostentatious black Jaguar that was so low-slung it made Beth feel like some dark scuttling bug about to be tromped on by a chasing semi. She preferred the higher vantage of her own ten-year-old Toyota, a functional sedan she and Naomi had used on their outings, which were somewhat famous in their town, Manhattan, the "little apple" of the Midwest, and home to Kansas State, where Philip lecturered in law.

Beth would be forty in three months. Philip was fifty-nine and eager to get on with life, a proposition about which Beth's feelings were distinctly mixed. It was late August and they had just been visiting Callie, their daughter, who was twenty and a sophomore at the Air Force Academy in Colorado Springs. The visit had been cut short by a quarrel between Callie and Philip. On the way home they were to spend the weekend in Emporia with Richard, Philip's brother, who was publisher there of one of the family's small newspapers.

The argument had been about Callie's selection of courses at the Academy, Philip having arrogantly assumed that his advice to her was singularly more valuable than her advisor's. "I love you, Mom, but I can't understand why you don't leave that big asshole," Callie said afterward. "He thinks he knows everything."

"He's your father, dear. Stop it."

"So what? He's still an impudent jerk." She and Callie had spent the morning walking in the hills above the campus. They had a good time, but then they always did. Callie was wearing a T-shirt and sweats, and looked far less formidable than she did in her cadet uniform. She had had her heart set on the Air Force Academy since junior high, and was as determined in her own way as her father. Now Callie seemed to feel that it was time for her to take on her mother's problems as well.

"People who love each other try to help each other, Mom. I want you to see why I'm saying this. Do something with your life, please? It's your turn now."

"Oh, sweetie," said Beth. If it weren't for Callie's sincerity—plus the familiarity of her argument—Beth might have been even more distressed. Later they kissed good-bye as they always did, with Beth's heart giving a quick wrench at separation.

A specific giddiness began to overtake her now as she recalled that farewell. Wasn't this the way she'd spent her life, raising a child and being wife to a successful attorney? You couldn't really fault Philip for being Philip, any more than you could fault Callie for being the same as she had been when she was three, a cantankerous and determined little girl with a sure sense of herself. The paradox, not lost on Beth, was that she had raised a very solid girl by giving Callie all her strength, yet Beth herself remained, somehow, quite passive.

"Goddamn prairie," Philip hissed, so loud Beth applied the brakes. How strange of him to say this, given that his whole life too had been spent in Kansas—aside from his years at Harvard and Harvard Law. To her, the whole legal profession seemed like a silly game to spend your life on, rather than the grave process with which Philip was totally obsessed. There was a cellular telephone on the walnut console between them in the front seat of the Jag, and Philip kept his hand perched on it, as if to throttle the thing should it spring to life. One of his associates was in Wichita that morning taking a deposition, and he was anxious.

Beth tried to contain her burgeoning anxiety by an act of will, reducing the fluttering quakefulness into a small box as she had been taught to do. There was a sign for a restaurant at the Quinter exit in ten miles and it was now just past one o'clock. Philip had given up looking for the stock market report and was whistling along to a Chubby Checker song he'd found on the radio, tapping with his right hand on the seat.

"I'm going to have to stop," Beth said. "I'm not feeling well." She stiffened at his possible reaction.

"Fine, sweetheart." he said, glancing at his watch.

Beth judged any further inquiry not worthwhile. She looked at Philip with a longing close to homesickness, since in many ways he was a good man, though recognizing this just made matters worse.

On the exit ramp Beth slowed the car. Philip's one concession to her when he bought the Jag had been the automatic transmission, so she could drive. At the top of the ramp there was a sign for Quinter, one macadam road heading east, while another gravel track led south. Beth sat for a moment and memorized the intersection. Then she turned right and eased the car into the rest stop. Across a gravel lot semis were parked with the muffled drone of their engines.

"I don't know why you always have to park so far away," Philip said. "I can never see the car from the restaurant."

"What's there to see?" Beth opened her door and pocketed the keys. "Do you think someone's going to steal it?"

"No."

"Well?" She stood for a moment holding her handbag. "Are you coming?"

"I'll be along in just a minute." He waved to her from the front seat.

Beth walked toward the restaurant. When she thought about it later she was surprised by how clear and cool her mind had felt, with every object, and the landscape itself, having the distinct, sharp-edged outlines like those found in a pattern book. The field of soybeans behind the restaurant looked luminous and lovely. Beth suddenly walked back toward the car, but Philip was on the phone, his clipped lawyer's voice saying, "And why was that?"

Beth entered the restaurant and walked directly past the counter to the bathrooms, noting as she did so that she was in luck—there was a back door with a screen, which was propped open, in the same narrow hallway that housed the ladies and the gents. In the bathroom stall she checked inside her handbag for certain items: Callie's Girl Scout compass, which she had sometimes used on her hikes with Naomi, and a small can of orange juice. In a Ziploc bag were her address book and her passport. It had been Naomi's notion that the act of taking your passport with you everywhere added drama to your life. They were both Kansas girls—Naomi was from Dodge, the daughter of an electrical contractor with a sixth-grade education—and though they rarely went anywhere that required an ID, now that Naomi was dead Beth kept her own passport with her always, like a talisman.

Beth also had inside the bag her father's flannel shirt. Curiously her father had liked Philip; perhaps this was foresight into the man he would become. Philip had been thirty-seven, Beth eighteen, when Philip had asked her father for Beth's hand. At the time, no one had been much bothered by the difference in their ages. "Why would you want to do a damn dumb thing like that?" her father had replied to Philip, though of course he'd been pleased. Philip's father owned newspapers all across Kansas and Oklahoma. Back then, Philip had been Beth's act of rebellion, a legal aid lawyer with political ambitions. She had gotten married in her sophomore year at Kansas State, and was pregnant with Callie when her mother was diagnosed with a brain tumor, and her dad had called Philip to bring her home.

Back in the stall Beth took out a metoprolol tablet, but put it back, preferring instead this itchy nervousness that was not at all unlike elation. Her heart was pounding so hard it actually hurt. She recalled from Janis Joplin's song the line about freedom being "just another word for nothing left to lose," and immediately forgave herself the banal thought—anyway, she disagreed with that defeatist sentiment, feeling she had much to gain. Then she took from her handbag the envelope and the photocopy of her Kansas driver's license that she had made that morning at the Ramada Inn in Colorado Springs. The note was simple enough: "My husband is abusive. Do not believe anything he says. I am with a friend in a black Jaguar driving west. Call my daughter." Below that she had added Callie's phone number, and on the outside of the envelope, "To the Highway Patrol." She closed the lid over the toilet and left the envelope on top.

Outside the hall was empty. Beth exited through the screen door, past a bucket and a mop that had been left there leaning against the wall. By now Philip would be inside, studying his menu. When Beth reached the corner of the building she stopped and peered around it, to where the Jag was waiting.

— ❊ —

Now Beth had to hurry. She recrossed the intersection at the top of the exit ramp for Quinter, but took instead the gravel two-lane heading south. Stones plinked loudly off the underside of the car. It had rained briefly that morning, which was fortuitous, since it kept the dust raised by the Jag to a minimum.

A mile down the road her sense of disorientation suddenly became so excruciating that she had to stop the car. She promptly climbed out and fell to her knees, vomiting out her breakfast. Her dislocation was so intense she felt she couldn't balance herself on her hands and knees, and pushed her legs out behind her until she lay on her stomach. At eye level, she looked at the pitted gravel in the road, and heard as if from far away the steady thrumming of the Jaguar. Then she rolled over onto her back, seeing the sky that was overcast and liquid. She tried closing her eyes for a moment, but then she heard a siren and only gradually understood the sound, which came from back toward I-70 and the restaurant. The siren became louder, then stopped.

Beth scrambled to her feet and jumped into the Jag, and punched the car into gear. As she drove on an image came to her of Philip explaining himself to the police. She hoped they would telephone Callie despite his cagey lawyer's prattle. "She's having a nervous breakdown," she heard Philip say. "Her father and her best friend just died and she's been clinically depressed." But then Philip passed away and with a flick of her wrist Beth reinserted into the CD player Lucia Popp and the Strauss he had terminated. She let this play for a moment before she turned down the volume. She kept driving, noting that the passing fields smelled like newspapers that had been left out in the rain.

She was pulled back from her reverie by the sudden insistent beeping of the cell phone. How foolish: she should have thought of that. Of course it would be Philip calling her now in his panicked voice. She let the phone ring, but slowly braked the car to a stop. After a while the phone stopped beeping, but then rang again almost immediately. She pictured Philip in a phone booth as a highway patrolman looked on. When the phone wouldn't stop its racket she reached down and unplugged it, then tossed the handset into the back seat.

She drove onward through a sort of daze, then was startled by the loud concussion of a large stone against the underside of the Jag. The pain in her head that had commenced with the ringing of the phone had localized now toward the right side and within it Rapp, her dear friend, called to her, though she tried to ignore this strange phenomenon. Why Rapp, why now? Besides, she liked Ben Rapp very much: he was her neighbor, her confidant, and her friend. He had been Naomi's friend as well. For a brief period, perhaps, Beth had been in love with him.

This recognition jolted her but she continued to drive across the plains at good speed. She had gone south for fifteen miles, then due east on another gravel two-lane, ignoring the signs for Castle Rock. She no longer felt quite so afraid. Beth liked to drive in the country because she was essentially claustrophobic and driving made the world feel much larger; moving within a vast space also gave her the illusion of control. On the plains, sturdy upright things, like limestone fence posts, acquired an importance they rarely had in congested areas. Thus she disliked New York, where to see the sky you had to tilt your head back and squint, as though peeking through a keyhole.

Ben Rapp was from New York but rarely returned there. He was a professor of psychology at Kansas State, a Buddhist, and celibate. He was gruff and handsome, and completely bald. His wife, Sonia, taught third grade in the public schools when she wasn't actively depressive. Once, late one evening at a dinner party, he had confessed to Beth that most of his university colleagues were already corpses, life to them being a mere excuse for a paycheck. He and Beth shared this sort of cutting wit, which made them both somewhat mistrusted in university circles.

"You're willful," he advised her boozily. "You should be careful because you've lived your life with the kind of will that can later cause you lots of problems."

"I know it," Beth had said, though the statement had only brought forth the familiar feeling of an unpleasant truth. It had taken Rapp several years to help Beth see that Philip was at heart a ruthless fuck, albeit a well-educated one. Also a closet anti-Semite. Beth had invited Rapp and Sonia to a large dinner party and late in a rather dull evening Rapp had made an acid but very funny comment about the university president, which everyone had laughed at but Philip, to whom the man was an object of reverence. "Jesus, but you people can be smartasses," Philip had said, identifying Rapp as a member of a larger ethnic group. The whole table had become so quiet that Beth had plunged courageously ahead with a lame joke, though later she was furious for having let the incident pass unnoticed.

Rapp had grown up in Brooklyn but liked the small towns of the Midwest, though he also said he would have gone mad long ago without his trips to the Buddhist retreat he attended every summer. Then he noticed a hurt look pass across Beth's face before she could conceal it.

"What about me?" she said.

"Oh, your reading keeps you grounded. Plus your friends."

"That's not very much."

"It's enough. You're lucky."

It was rare that such self-pity crept into Rapp's voice. Naomi, their mutual friend, had only recently died, and she was much on their minds. "Maybe life is just a long preparation for something that never happens," Rapp had said. Then he added, "You're the smartest woman in Kansas, Beth. How come you married such a shit?"

"Hush, Rapp. Anyway, I don't need to be wounded, not since Naomi and Daddy died." Beth's hair was blonde streaked with brown: she hadn't cut it since Naomi died, and didn't know if she ever would.

"I only know you don't take care of yourself," Rapp answered, in apology. "You're utterly passive and you're delaying doing anything constructive with your life."

Those two deaths had marked the beginning of the end for her and Philip, though Beth didn't realize it at the time. She was conscious of her grief, but what made her weep was Philip's scorn for her emotions. Was there anything worse than losing your father, then your best friend? Her father was eighty-one when they called her one afternoon—his aneurysm had burst and he was in a coma. After that Beth had become so accustomed to weeping for him that it was a shock now to find that she was crying for herself. It had been around the time her father died that Naomi was diagnosed with lung cancer, inoperable. In four months she too was gone.

— ❋ —

All that was required of Beth presently was that she keep the car moving ahead in a straight line. From the occasional signs, she knew that the road she was following in an easterly direction paralleled the Smoky Hill River and the trail of the same name, which had taken settlers to the Denver goldfields long ago. At a silent junction of two roads she stopped the Jag and drank down her can of tepid orange juice. The sky above was overcast and looked like rain.

In the quiet of the crossing, Beth gradually became aware of the sound of a small airplane circling overhead. She listened for a moment calmly, but once she had identified the sound and it had fully entered her consciousness, she grew agitated and anxious. Why an airplane, why out here? She was suddenly, frantically convinced that the plane was the police, or the police and Philip, and that at any moment they would swoop down and land behind her on the gravel road. As the invisible plane droned on she floored the Jag, trying at the same time to keep in mind the position of the plane, though it was lost now in the cover of clouds. A mile down the road there was another junction and a sign for the Cedar Bluff reservoir, and Beth swung left, spraying gravel. She had begun to sob. As the car crested a small rise she saw the muddy lake spread out before her. She was nearly in the water when she braked the car, then grabbed her handbag, and jumped out.

She thought she heard the plane again, off somewhere in the middle distance. Without closing the door of the Jag she plunged ahead on foot down the hillside into a small thicket of trees. Presently she found herself against a row of cottonwoods and briars that grew across her path so she couldn't turn left or right. She stepped back for a better view and made out the top of another cottonwood. Then, as her breathing slowed, she was sure she heard flowing water. Suddenly she felt tears welling up again. She had expected to find a barnyard and a farmhouse out here someplace, though she hadn't been looking for them very hard.

Her watch said it had been over three hours since she'd left the restaurant on I-70, though that didn't seem possible. Millions of women merely leave their husbands, so why had she fled? Had Philip's authority over her been so unassailable? She swallowed with difficulty, wishing she had saved some of the orange juice, and then looked up at the sky and saw the approaching thunderheads, their edges tinged with silver. She sat down and had the sudden impulse to discuss her predicament with Naomi, but felt that the pain of it might loosen her grip. Callie was a better choice, though what would she say?

"Damn you, this was partly your idea. What do I do now?" Beth had an urge to be angry and petulant. "I'm sitting here in the dirt and I don't know what to do. I think your father or the police have a search plane out looking for me though I could be wrong. I wasn't prepared for this. There's a storm coming and it's going to rain."

"Jesus, Mom, you've got to toughen up. First of all, you're going to need something to eat. In the meantime, you better crawl inside and stay dry. You can always climb back into the car."

"No, thanks. I don't want to be inside that thing again."

"Be careful. And if you get desperate, don't forget why you're doing this. I know you and dad stopped caring about each other a long time ago, but still, why'd you hold on so long?"

"I had my friends, my books, I had you, and I had the house. And I had your Grandpa to look after. Anyway, why does a husband have to be the center of a woman's life? Naomi's husband used to say that lawyers were the worst creatures on earth."

"You miss her, don't you? And Grandpa?"

"More than I ever thought possible. Strangely, I couldn't do this if they were still alive. It was a pleasure to give so much to them because I loved them. Then they were gone and I had to do something else. Well, I did."

Beth signed off on this phantom conversation and looked up at the rolling thunderheads that had begun to rumble. She crawled farther into the thicket and looked up, seeing enough of the sky to know that it would still be wet inside in a hard rain. Then she recalled how, as a child on her grandparents' farm in Corona, in southeast Kansas, she had liked to make small caves in the dried corn that had been stacked in shocks. She felt this memory comprised her first bright idea of the day, and she crawled deeper inside and could see that she would be all right because there was a dense area above that blackened-out the sky.

The thunder deepened in volume and she looked up to see lightning shattering the sky, like a long arm with luminous veins. The thunder clap that followed had a sharp edge as if the sky were being ripped, and the wind came up suddenly so that the leaves on the cottonwoods were pale and flopping. Beth backed into the overhang of brush with a feeling that things were well in hand, though she paused for a moment thinking she should have hidden the car. A torrent of rain commenced around her. I had a child and lived with a man for almost twenty years, she thought. What happened to me? She marveled that she had no real idea how all that time had passed.

The driving rain spattered mud upward and formed puddles outside her little haven, but inside Beth was dry and cozy. With a smile she imagined Philip's umbrage when the police asked him if he'd abused his wife. Did he know who her friend was, or why they were traveling west? Beth was not a bitch, though, and she raised in her mind some of Philip's many good points: for example, the fact that he had taken Callie everywhere, from Disneyland to the Smithsonian to the Museum of Natural History in New York, and to Royals games in Kansas City. Surprisingly, Philip was still a relentless lover (like clockwork every evening before bed, after his sit-ups), but Beth had begun to suspect that this had less to do with anything he felt for her than with some odd notion he had of the proper regulation of his body's fluids. And she still could not forgive him for forcing himself on her the night her mother died.

Beth was only twenty then. They had been living in the country, the air-conditioner was broken, and her mother had stopped breathing that afternoon. Beth was weeping but Philip was insistent. "Then why come to bed naked?" he had whined to her afterward, in self-defense. "You know you're too provocative, to offer yourself to me like that."

"I wasn't offering," Beth answered.

There were so many times when she thought their relationship was over. Five years ago she had been taking graduate courses in psychology at K-State, volunteering in the evenings at the local center for battered women. "You're the stereotype of a social worker!" Philip yelled at her one night. "You go in there like you're healing the world, and you're just as screwed up as they are! You're really trying to heal yourself, Beth, and it's not working!"

Another time, leafing through a biography of the poet Anne Sexton in Whistler's, Beth's favorite bookshop in Kansas City, Philip had said, "Your life sounds a lot like hers. I mean, what with the tumultuous love life and the anxiety and all the neurotic behavior. Minus, of course," he added, "the booze and the poetry."

And they had just within the hour made love at the Raphael Hotel down on the Plaza, where they were staying for the weekend! Philip's comment was so hostile, on so many levels, that Beth wondered what was wrong with him. Was he angry that she didn't work, that she'd produced nothing but a child? Why did he disdain her so?

The rain had stopped. Beth scrambled out, skidding in the fresh mud. "Fuck," she yelled. How stupid she felt, suddenly, here in the sodden countryside. There was a sense that she was stuck in a children's story of ominous dimensions, like Dorothy in Oz, though Beth resented the clichéd association of Kansas with Dorothy and Toto and that film, as if that was all there was to Kansas. She scrambled on her hands and knees out of the thicket toward what she thought of as the distant water. The thicket, though, had blinded her, because the reservoir was actually less than a dozen feet distant and she suddenly catapulted down the slick, muddy bank into the sluggish water. Then Beth was in the water and she came up knee-deep and laughing. It was cold! Suddenly she slipped off her blouse, jeans, panties, and bra, tossing her clothing on the bank.

Now she did not feel remotely sorry for herself, which there had been too much of earlier. Rapp had a theory that self-pity was the most injurious emotion to mental health. Naked, Beth felt more than a twinge of desire for him after his image shifted up from the muddy water. She felt quite free to think about making love to him because she knew it would never happen, since sex with him would break the etiquette of their friendship.

It was so strange to stand here naked, feeling the cool water purl down her body, with just enough light in the fading sky to make her legs and her tummy look slightly golden. If Naomi had been here she would have been sitting on the bank of the reservoir, watching and smoking one of the cigarettes that had killed her. It had been Naomi's nature to defy everything.

What a good-looking woman she had been, with that jet-black hair prematurely streaked with silver! Right up until the last day she had said she had no regrets about dying, but on the last day of all she joked, "I'm not so sure this is a good idea." Then her eyes had brimmed with tears.

Beth walked out of the water and up the slippery bank, and wasn't thinking about anything in particular when Rapp arrived again. A few days before the trip to Colorado Springs she had met him downtown one afternoon for lunch. "What would you think if I told you I was leaving Philip?" she had said, when they were settled at their table.

"I'd think you were smart, but I won't say any more. When did this occur to you?"

"About ten years ago. Why won't you tell me anything?"

"Because I've seen so many divorces in this town and outside advice generally confuses the issue. Plus, there's a chance I might screw up your one shot at freedom."

"I understand," she said. Then she hesitated, feeling foolish.

"Well, let's have it," Rapp said.

"I want to evoke life, to experience things. Philip wants to dominate. Is that too simple-headed?"

"No, I think it's quite exact."

"It's taken me twenty years to figure all this out. Or for Philip to grow into the definition. You know, I was just a girl when we were married. I know that sounds corny."

"When are you going to do it? Where will you go?"

"I don't know."

"Some small town in Kansas, I'll bet. There are lots of nice places over the years that you've said you'd like to live in."

"Wamego, maybe," Beth said.

"Ah," said Rapp. "I'd always look those places up on the map after you mentioned them and think it over, think about living there." Rapp was suddenly nervous with this admission and looked at his watch. It was then that Beth understood how much he cared for her, and how desperately unhappy he was with Sonia. They sat in silence for a few minutes while they waited for the bill, Beth's heart swelling in her throat. She wondered if Rapp's defeated air might be due to that fiftyish sense of disappointment people feel before getting into the next phase of life, when they're simply glad to be alive. Together they left the restaurant and when they reached her Toyota Rapp hugged her and rushed off.

Now a strange thing happened. Beth had emerged from the water after her inadvertent dip and was standing on the bank of the reservoir letting the cool air blow her dry. Then she saw the Jaguar. One door was open and the car's long black hood was beaded with rain. Oh, how she loathed it! Not just driving it, or riding in it with Philip, but its obscene presence out here on the plains. The car was parked on a steep incline, its nose just above the water. "Fuck it," Beth said. Then she walked over, reached in and turned on the ignition, and with a deft punch popped the car's transmission out of gear and hopped away. She stood back and watched as the Jag rolled forward, crunching gravel. It crept slowly down the bank and submerged itself in the reservoir with an understated gurgle. How British! Beth chuckled, as the car sank out of sight.

— ❀ —

*And what a merry fix you're in now, my dear.* Having dispatched the car Beth realized she'd further complicated what hadn't been much of a plan to begin with. She was dry now and from her bag she removed her father's flannel shirt and put it on. Then she set about gathering small twigs and patches of reedy grass, whatever was under the trees or brush that was still dry and hadn't been dampened by the rain. The moist ground was like clay beneath her feet. If she could get a small fire going she could dry her clothes and wouldn't miss a flashlight so much, because now it was almost dark. *If you're going to leave your husband and dump his car in the lake, take a flashlight.*

The sun had pretty well set and Beth made her way down the bank of the reservoir searching for more wood. Luckily there were matches in her purse, Beth having always carried extras for Naomi. At last she managed to get a small mound of brush on fire, which she fed. When it was big enough and roaring then she could set her damp clothes nearby on sticks to dry. She realized that she was hungry, but it was not something she wanted to preoccupy her mind. She was not frightened especially, because what more could happen to her?

When and if she emerged from her adventure, her friends and acquaintances back in Manhattan were bound to prate "nervous breakdown" or "depression" during countless phone calls and at university cocktail parties.

Now throw in the car to enliven their discussions. In her case the proba-
ble causes of distress would be pretty obvious—the deaths of Naomi and
her father, plus Callie gone—but quite stupidly her marriage would not be
questioned. More than age, most of the women she knew seemed to be
fighting a malaise of fatigue and dislocation. When all of this was over she
intended to live in an apartment or a small house on the far edge of a town.
She would find a job in a bookstore or a restaurant, something temporary
where she could make herself useful, a sense of herself that she had lost
since Callie had gone away and her father had died.

She kept the loose fire going and with larger sticks soon had a modest
blaze. It was dark now and the flames flickered off her calves and thighs.
She pushed several long sticks into the ground by the fire, then set her jeans
and shirt and underwear out to dry.

Why had they let her marry so young? Because of her unusual life history and the absence of a career, Beth had few professional acquaintances
and almost no experience with the sort of mundane camaraderie that
makes up the common social staple of the workaday world. It sometimes
seemed to her that her baseline emotional life had consisted mainly of
going from one loud mess to another. Events had clustered themselves
about her life at the ages of nineteen and thirty-nine, on the cusp of turning twenty and now, forty: she had been married at nineteen and her
mother had died when she was twenty; then her father and Naomi had
died within this year.

The sun was fully down now and a warm wind had picked up. Beth had
finished drying her jeans and was dressed, standing by the fire. What she felt
now was a prairie wind, which didn't falter; it was strong and steady and like
no other wind in the world, the kind that howled through door frames at
night and was said to have driven the pioneer women mad—though that
probably had more to do with the isolation of a prairie life. Presently Beth
fixed her eyes on the bright moon that had just risen. Goddamn it but her
mind was so exhausted with trying to hold the world together, tired of
being the living glue for herself, as if she let go, great pieces of her would
shatter all over! Beth wanted to see the light of a farmhouse or hear a dog
bark, but there was nothing but the wind. How wonderful it would be to
have a dog here with her now, for protection and company! Presently she
curled up on her side by the fire, then rejected the position and stretched
out on her back until there were satisfying bone crackles in her knees.

The truth was, lighting off like this was something she had always liked to do, having learned it from her father. Since, as a nurse, her mother had worked most weekend nights at the hospital, when Beth was a girl of seven or eight, on Saturdays her father would take off with her—always on a whim—to her grandparents' in southeast Kansas. What Beth remembered mostly and what seemed to be her father's principal form of pleasure in the trips were the long unhurried drives on two-lane country roads, and the leisurely stops for beer and soda at roadhouses along the way. Sometimes her father would wave her into a place when she was waiting outside for him in the car, and the waitress would give her a maraschino cherry and fuss over her golden hair. Her father had always spoiled her and hers had been, in all, a merry childhood.

And who was it, who said that prairie girls didn't grow up to be resourceful? Beth tried to recall who had suggested that good-naturedly to her, and quite suddenly a blush rose to her face as she remembered Seth, her single indiscretion, which was an unforgivable mistake and constituted her only real secret from Philip.

Seth was a friend of Rapp's, who had passed through town on his way back east from his stint at a rehab in California. He had stayed with Ben and Sonia for just one night. Beth had picked him up at Menningers in Topeka as a favor to Rapp, saving him the drive since she had an appointment there herself that morning. Seth had a compressed vertebra in his neck and had stopped at Menningers to see a specialist; as for Beth, she regularly saw a therapist there to try to conquer her anxiety. It was odd, yet remembering Seth, Beth suddenly saw Rapp's hand in this part of her life, too. Seth was a boyhood friend of Rapp's, a correspondent for *The New York Times*, and was entirely candid about his fall from grace and his descent into booze and self-pity, which he reported on with a clarity no doubt refined at his rehab in California. On the way back to Manhattan in her car, Seth had told her about his wife and his children; he became quite sad and told her so. His first wife had hurt him deeply, with lies and infidelity, then the prolonged assault of divorce for the rest of his life, denying him his children but for the scant time allowed by the court, and telling his children that he was the adulterer, the liar, and taking the house and most of everything else. He would never marry again. He would never live again with a woman.

When they reached Beth's house she invited Seth inside for iced tea.

Seth was immensely attractive to her, but what was most attractive was his sense of failure, his struggle. Presently Beth's iced tea was nearly gone. They had lapsed into silence on the porch when Seth looked at her rather strangely.

"I haven't talked like this to a woman in a long time."

"So?"

"I'm sorry."

"There's nothing to be sorry for."

"Then how come all I can think about is making love to you?"

"I don't believe that," Beth said. "You're teasing me." Then she blushed deeply, unable to look into his eyes, at the same time shocked with herself as she calculated the number of hours they might have until Philip returned from Kansas City.

"I'm not teasing you," he said.

To break the mood Beth went into the kitchen and ate a piece of fruit. She was about to ask Seth if he would like a plum when he suddenly kissed her, her mouth still full of the sweet juice of the plum, and then he tore open her blouse and bra and slathered her nipples with the juice. Then they made love on the floor. Beth might have thought that was the end of it, but they also made love in the dining room, this time as Seth lay on his back and she rode his mouth to noisy ecstasy.

Afterwards she closed her eyes, said, "Oh, well," and then her ears began to buzz. She was embarrassed at her excitement. They stood in the kitchen apologizing to each other, until he pinched her bottom and whispered, "I'm ready whenever you are," and laughed. Before Philip came home Seth departed rather sheepishly for Rapp's, and she never saw him again. She hoped she had been good for him. He had left the next morning, by bus, and had sent to her enroute to New York a silly postcard from Iowa—a photo of an outsized pig. She heard from Rapp that within a week of returning to New York Seth had been posted to Brussels to cover NATO and the EEC. The experience with him had left her feeling slightly used, and had the net effect of putting her off adultery as a solution. Even then, the lines between her and Philip had been more clearly drawn than she had known, and that was why at present she lay on her side in a cottonwood thicket staring at a fire, alone.

Beth pulled her father's flannel shirt about her to ward off a slight chill. He had been a difficult man, her father, tending to be taciturn and a natural cynic, but the months while her mother had been dying had been hard on him. Once Beth had come upon him crying in a tavern across the street from the hospital, after the doctor had told him that her mother would die now any day. Despite the pressures of his late hours at the newspaper, the year before he had driven her over to Manhattan to enter college. He had become quite upset when he dropped her off at her freshman dorm, and they had talked with an intimacy previously unknown to them about her mother. Her father nearly begged her to come home as often as possible, for his sake. The year before, amidst a terrible racket inside their house, Beth had descended from the second floor to the living room where she found her mother screaming and rolling about hysterically on the carpet. Some time after that her mother went away to Menningers for a month to cure her depression, but within a year she would be diagnosed with her tumor and she would die. It had been an unnerving moment for Beth, when her father chose to discuss matters like this with her in the car—he seemed not quite her father but an intimate. But why had he waited until then to try to become close, a time when it was no longer really possible?

Beth suddenly understood in a rush that she had been abandoned by her mother, then by Philip, by Callie and Naomi and her father, and that only being abandoned by Callie was truly predictable. Philip had disfigured himself beyond recognition and bore little resemblance to the man she in innocence had loved. Naomi had been plucked off the earth at thirty-eight. Dying, her father had smelled sharply of ammonia, though it was true what they said about the moment of death, for when his heart had stopped his old body had developed an erection. Beth was so embarrassed for him! At that moment she had become the last mother he would ever have. *Oh, Daddy*, Beth thought now. *Don't worry, I'm doing fine. I miss you, Daddy.*

Beth opened her eyes and froze then, startled by a movement to her left. For a moment she thought it might be a wolf or a coyote, but it was just a prairie dog, the same kind that had made her grandfather put a chicken wire fence around his hen house. The prairie dog studied Beth from half-a-dozen feet away across the fire, then sat down on its hind legs, its ears alertly erect and its nose trying to determine if Beth presented any danger. Around its ears on the pointed lobes ticks dotted the flesh, gorged with blood. Beth and the prairie dog stared at each other so long that she didn't notice that the wind had stopped. Then the dog's ears stiffened for an instant at some sound from the direction of the reservoir, and after a moment he got up and loped off.

— ✳ —

"The next day was the most difficult of all," Beth wrote Rapp two weeks later. "At first light there were more birds than I had ever heard before, the meadowlarks and wrens all fluttering through the branches of the cottonwoods by the lake. I gathered up my bag and scrambled out. I was hungry and wanted to get moving.

"About a mile down the road there was a field of soybeans and I could see a pickup truck. I watched as an old man got out of the truck and turned off an irrigation sprinkler in a field across the road, which was tinged orange by the rising sun and glistened. I followed his truck down the gravel road to a barn where there was a field with pigs under a low-slung shed, and I went into the yard where the old man was just coming out of the barn. He looked at me, startled, then asked if he could be of any help.

"I think I told him I'd been misplaced, but that I would love a cup of coffee and something to eat. It seems he recognized me as the woman he had heard about the night before on his TV. I had no idea I'd become a celebrity! The old man wondered where my car was, and I told him I'd spent the night in the woods by the reservoir and that the car was lost. Then I started crying. The old fellow came over to me and put his arm around my shoulder, then led me over to the house where I had some coffee. Then I told him I had some calls to make, could I use his telephone?

"Callie arrived in about two hours from Hays in a police car with a highway patrolman who talked farm prices with the farmer, while Callie and I sat on a porch swing out front. The highway patrolman had given her a lift to Brownell, which was the first I'd heard of the town where we were. Callie kept repeating to me how she never thought I would have the courage to do this, and hadn't I done it in dramatic fashion!

"I asked her how her dad was and she told me that he'd survive. She said he was unhappy but that she thought he'd be fine. Apparently he had told the police I was a patient at Menningers and that I was having a nervous breakdown! Luckily, they listened to Callie instead. I wondered then, at what point does the daughter become the mother?

"Later I spent an hour talking with Philip in his room at the Best

Western in Hays, while Callie waited outside in the car. How he had become this person I loathed, through what transformation I really couldn't say, only that the process was complete and could not be reversed. Philip wanted to put any major decisions off until I had come to my senses, which is precisely what I'd thought he would say. He hoped somehow that we could carry on. I told him I didn't think we had anything left to carry on with, which was a very painful thing to say but was also the truth. Then Philip wanted to know who I was in love with. When he asked me for the details, he leveled his eyes at me, then turned away as if he feared some kind of blow.

"I told him those kind of things had never happened, that he had always been enough for me, that I had been faithful to him always, and that knowledge seemed to cheer him. I apologized to him about his Jaguar, his briefcase, and his suitcase full of clothes, all lost in the lake. He was wearing the same blue oxford-cloth shirt and brown corduroy slacks that he'd had on when we first left Colorado.

"Now that I was being pleasant he asked me if I had any idea how embarrassing all this was for him, and he began to berate me for shaming him, and wondered why our marriage had to end with such a loud dramatic flourish. I had begun to crave the safety of my little campsite by the reservoir, and maybe Philip could see now that he was frightening me with his bullying. What he didn't see, of course, was my grief: for him, for the two of us, my helplessness and sorrow and my dread. I got up and hugged him anyway, but then I had to go. I told him we would talk it all over again in November.

"Rapp, I hope you will understand that my misadventures comprise less some kind of feminist anthem than my own personal struggle against long odds, and that poor Philip was a victim also. Everyone was pushing me, you and Callie included, and doing what I did was the only way to save myself from the melancholy my life had become.

"Callie and I were back on the interstate in a few minutes, and before long she had me laughing like a schoolgirl. God, that girl is wonderful! I don't understand it, Rapp, but can you see this beautiful young woman flying a jet plane? Thank you, Rapp, for being my best friend. I love you, Rapp."

— ❋ —

Six weeks later Beth was settled in a small frame house she had rented in Wamego, which was somewhat famous as the birthplace of Walter Chrysler, the industrialist. Beth's house had a swing on the front porch and flowerbeds by the steps, and a small plot for vegetables in back. Though she didn't need to work, she had taken a job, waitressing part-time at Wamego's only restaurant. When she'd applied, she'd told the owners she could work for them only three or four hours each day. They were an elderly couple and very kind, and had looked at her, frankly puzzled. No doubt they assumed Beth was in the midst of some kind of recovery, and she had watched as a nod of silent agreement passed between them.

Beth liked the pleasing simplicity of bringing people food and watching them eat. Also she liked the clean country smell of her uniforms, which she ironed every morning in the living room of her house. It was a start, and nothing more. In the afternoons when she returned home from work she wrote letters, or drank a glass of white wine and played the music of Joan Baez and Mary-Chapin Carpenter. She received letters regularly from Callie and Rapp and, surprisingly, from Seth, who had heard of her adventures through Rapp and who wrote to say that he was leaving Brussels to be posted back to the States, to Washington—would it be all right if he came to visit her?

Beth kept her hours: she clocked in, clocked out, and ate, and read. She felt a little lost but then supposed without anxiety that it was the natural condition of her life. In fact, she could not imagine being any happier—and knew that she was less lost now than before her damp night by the reservoir. Wamego was a lovely place, of white-sided wooden houses under leafy trees, a tiny town scattered across two purple hills. Beth did not envy anyone, and for the first time felt she was unique—not better, just herself—and that was all she needed now to make a start.

# *An Erawan Monkey*

Richard Kessler finally caught up with his brother, Wayne, in the basement-level coffee shop of the Dusit Thani Hotel in Bangkok. Richard had already explained himself, with great difficulty, to the patient Thai clerk in the lobby, and he'd gone upstairs himself to check Wayne's room, where no one answered. Still toting his small carry-on duffel bag—he'd only packed one change of clothing and his toilet kit—Richard was patrolling the Dusit's numerous bars and restaurants when at last he found Wayne, who was sitting alone in a banquette in a dark corner of the low-ceilinged, uncrowded coffee shop. By now it was late afternoon, and the Dusit Thani was the fourth hotel Richard had searched since arriving at Dong Muang Airport that morning from San Francisco. He'd already endured one of Bangkok's monsoon rains on the way into town, and his taxi had gotten stuck in traffic for an hour. He hadn't been able to get out of the cab because he didn't know where to go. He knew Bangkok was a city bisected by the Chao Phya River, but that was all, and he hadn't counted on the incredible heat, or all the diesel fumes and congestion, to say nothing of the surreal architecture—golden-spired temples, office towers built like Palladian palaces, and department stores with marble columns like the Parthenon. Nothing in Bangkok was what it appeared to be.

Richard had tracked Wayne this far thanks to American Express, which is how Wayne had purchased his ticket. Admittedly, they'd been reluctant to disclose details until Richard had explained that Wayne was manic-depressive and also alcoholic, with a history of impulsive and sometimes self destructive travel. "When I drink I break out in spots," Wayne liked to say. "Cleveland,

Kansas City, Seattle. The urge to move just comes over me." This was the first time Wayne had actually fled overseas, though, and it was Richard's fear that this meant his brother had no intention of returning—that he'd at last gone just far enough to make it impossible for anyone to retrieve him.

But now Richard doubted that scenario. Wayne was wearing a bright emerald green short-sleeved shirt, clearly new, and before him on the table amidst the gleaming silverware was a plate of untouched rice and a congealed dish of some kind of curry. There was also coffee, water, and Wayne's drink, which was empty. Wayne was thirty-three, two years younger than Richard, though he looked older. He was clean-shaven and had piercing blue eyes. Wayne had either showered recently or was sweating profusely, because his black hair was slicked back and gleaming, with a part over his right eye so emphatic it might have been cut there with a razor.

"Dickie," Wayne said, when he saw Richard approaching. "Sit down, kid. How good it is to see you."

"This time you've really done it," Richard said, sliding into the banquette. He dropped his duffel bag on the floor. "You're a crazy fuck, you know that?"

"I do," Wayne said, smiling vaguely. "I most certainly do."

"You have any idea how worried it makes people, you going off like this? Like your mother?"

"Tell me," said Wayne.

Richard looked at him closely across the table. Wayne was sweating, all right, in bullets. He also exuded a sort of copper-scent that seemed distinctly unhealthy—the toxic scent of adrenaline. Richard drew back. He was tired, jet-lagged, and exhausted, and for the moment it just felt good to sit down.

"I'm waiting," Wayne said.

"Gloria called me two or three nights ago," said Richard, referring to their sixty-eight-year-old adoptive mother, who was a widow and seemed to spend most of her time on the telephone in her condo on Marco Island high above the Gulf. "I can't remember exactly. I mean, when you didn't answer she knew."

"Did she?" Wayne said, softening slightly. "She likes to call every day to remind me to take my meds."

"Are you?" Richard asked.

"What?"

"Taking your lithium, damn it."

Wayne rattled the ice cubes in his depleted drink. He deeply resented the question and clearly had no intention of providing Richard with an answer.

"So how do you like Bangkok?" Wayne asked.

"I have no idea. How long have you been here, anyway?"

"Four, five days. Maybe six. I haven't been sleeping well. Did you go up already and search my room?"

"I knocked," Richard said. "You weren't there."

"It's a nice room," Wayne said. "And don't ask me, like who's going to pay for it." He held his empty glass up and gestured with raised eyebrows at a passing waitress, a dainty, dark-faced woman who wore a powder-blue silk suit with a red-and-gold embroidered sash over her shoulder. She took the glass and said something agreeable in singsong English. She was black-haired, with high cheekbones.

"So here you are," Wayne said. "In hog heaven."

"Meaning what?"

"Bangkok, the sex capital of the East."

"If I thought you were here for the women, Wayne, I'd take it as a good sign."

"Not me," Wayne said, offended. "This time I really think I'm onto something."

"Like what?"

The waitress reappeared and Wayne paused to accept his drink, taking the tumbler in both hands and bowing his head at the tiny woman. Vodka, straight up. It was pointless, of course, to ask how many. There was a stain-less-steel Med-Alert bracelet on Wayne's wrist, inscribed with the word "Bipolar."

"So how's Doreen?" Wayne asked.

"Doreen?"

"I thought you were married."

"Her name's Dorothy," Richard said, "and we're separated. Imagine, how easy that makes things for me, when Gloria wants me to go galli-vanting after you."

"Is it dark yet?" Wayne said, suddenly giddy.

"It might be," Richard responded. "I'm so jet-lagged it's hard to know." He looked down at his watch, which hadn't required elaborate resetting while he was in the air—there was a thirteen-hour difference from New

York. "It probably will be in another hour."

Wayne listened and then sipped his drink, paused, ran his tongue over his lower lip, and then drank down the rest. He returned the glass carefully to the table.

"We better scoot," he said. "I imagine you'll want a shower."

"I wouldn't mind something to eat too, if there's time."

"Later," Wayne said, as he slid out from the table. Richard saw that he was wearing a pair of cotton boxer shorts with a paisley design, and leather slippers with the Dusit Thani logo. He was paunchy, and his legs were thickly furred with hair. That was Wayne all right. He had the outcast's utter disregard for the niceties of convention.

"Don't hassle me," Wayne said, noting Richard's disapproval. "It's hot here," he said. Then he bent down and grabbed the canvas handle on Richard's duffel bag. "I'm really glad you're here, Dickie," he said. "I mean that. Just don't fight me on this thing, OK? It's my last chance, kid. Did you know Jesus Christ died when he was only thirty-three?"

"You're just sick, Wayne. I didn't come here to crucify you."

"You say that," Wayne said. Then suddenly he seemed to grow weary. He was holding Richard's duffel bag in front of him, in both hands, and he looked like the large nervous child who was about to be whisked off, by bus, to school, whom Richard recalled from his childhood. Wayne was still sweating but now there were tears in his eyes.

"I'm sorry," Richard said.

"Dickie, the place you're taking me has all the curative powers of Lourdes. The Erawan Temple, the shrine. Where do you think I've been every night since I got here? Evening's the best time for all the supplicants, and it gets crowded. If you really want to help me, then we can go upstairs and prepare."

"OK," Richard said.

Wayne had regained his composure. "Let's go then," he said, over his shoulder as he turned on his heel. "And Dickie, don't you think someone should pick up the bill?" With that Wayne went flip-flopping off toward the elevators.

— ❋ —

Wayne had a suite, actually, in the Dusit Thani, but either way it wasn't what Richard anticipated. First off, it was clean. There was a living room with a sofa, several chairs, and a writing desk, a refrigerator with a minibar, plus a television housed in a handsome teak cabinet with doors that slid out to conceal the set. Thick powder-blue carpeting led through an archway into another room where there was a king-sized bed facing another television, and a marble-floored bath. There were orchids in tiny vases on the bedside tables, and thick cotton towels in a fat pile by the gleaming sink. Obviously the maid had been in and cleaned up after him. On the bar was a gallon of duty-free vodka, and the writing table was piled high with Wayne's books—tour guides on Bangkok and Thailand, plus the *Mahabharata* and the *Ramayana* in deluxe leather editions, two copies of the *Bhagavadgita*, plus what looked like separate biographies of Vishnu, Shiva, and Brahma, which were stacked atop Wayne's indispensable *Physician's Desk Reference*, much bruised.

Wayne had dropped Richard's duffel bag on the coffee table and was slumped back on the sofa with his eyes closed. "Lumpini Park," he said, to no one in particular. The blinds in the room were fully open, and looking down from the window through the twilight, beyond the monotonously rotating cars in the traffic circle, past a plume-helmeted equestrian statue, Richard beheld the cool expanse of the park, indistinct beneath the palms in the gathering darkness. People in white shirts were strolling there across the grass.

"The Bangkok Sports Club's down there too," Wayne said. "We'll pass it on our way to Erawan."

"We're taking a car?"

"Walking, stupid," said Wayne. He had opened his eyes now and sat hunched forward on the couch. "How about that shower?" he said impatiently. "You'll have to forgive me, Dickie, but I'm just not in the mood now to play the perfect little host for you. I didn't exactly invite you, did I?"

Richard let it pass, instead gathering up his duffel bag and going into the other room to undress and shower. This was what—the fourth or fifth time he'd come after Wayne? It wouldn't have surprised him if, rather than a silk-shirted Wayne with his elaborate texts on Vishnu and Brahma, Richard had discovered his brother cowering in the corner of his room in some cheap hotel, amid broken glass and soiled bedclothes, his body smeared with his own excrement. That had happened other times, in past flipouts at airport hotels in San Mateo and Houston. They were depressing environs, of course, but Wayne seemed to wash up in such places when he was at the end of his tether. The fact was, there were just times when Wayne became so depressed and irritable—and finally so raving mad—that he had to throw away his meds, bolt town, and intoxicate himself so thoroughly as to extinguish his consciousness.

Both times, Richard had cleaned him up, doped him, and accompanied him home, to detox and then afterwards, to the farm. The farm? It was how Wayne referred, always disparagingly, to psychoanalysis, to Christianity, or group therapy—in short, to anything which in the cloak of aid strove to interpose itself between the bad Wayne and the good. Bad in this case was relative, but when you'd tried everything, just about, as Wayne had, whatever the next thing might be wasn't important. Work, theology, a new med? If it wasn't a better thing at least it was different, and new. If belief or contentment were like commodities to be bought in a store, then Wayne was searching for the one thing they just didn't carry. Years of pain and trouble, really. Frequent hospitalizations and a long succession of ineffective therapists. One of whom, quite recently, had diagnosed Wayne as having a temporal lobe ailment and suggested a radical surgical solution. No way. Desperation, it seemed to Richard, was the true engine of invention for Wayne. Hinduism? Well, why not? The only thing was, Wayne was intelligent and a passionate performer, but when he flagged and commenced to disbelieve himself there was usually all kinds of hell to pay. No, Richard didn't want to come on too heavy-handed. He had tried that in the old days and it hadn't worked. No, this time he was just going to listen.

Still, it hadn't always been so. Wayne had been all right until he was nineteen. Brilliant in high school, brilliant in early college. Prone to mood swings and hare-brained schemes and all-nighters, sometimes four-five-six days in a row. Then deflation, a profound sagging, and gloom, a loathing for everything on the earth, including himself. Still, in his early twenties he'd been a computer whiz, he took his lithium, got hired, and then had been quickly promoted by one of the big players on the Coast. Tustin, wasn't that the name of the town? Maybe it was the drinking, finally, that did him in. The truth was, Wayne hadn't worked regularly since he was twenty-five. He wasn't able to. Not mowing lawns, or washing cars, or loading furniture. He was a local eccentric who lived five minutes from the hospital. He hadn't been involved with a woman in any serious way since high school. He was a virgin, no doubt, gene-bitched and deluded. If he could bag groceries somewhere that in itself would be an accomplishment. Well done, Wayne. If Gloria didn't provide him with her credit cards and dote on him, then what would happen to him, what would he do? What then, stop or die?

The Wayne Richard found in the living room after his shower was a much-altered Wayne. He'd been drinking, that much was clear. The vodka was on the coffee table, along with an ice bucket and two empty glasses. Wayne had also changed into black baggy trousers and a black long-sleeved shirt, which was cut in safari-style and which he wore outside his slacks. He still wore the Dusit Thani's leather slippers though, which flip-flopped on his feet as he crossed and recrossed the room. Then he turned, stopped, and looked at Richard, giving Richard the impression that he had interrupted him in the midst of something exceedingly important.

"It was the trees," Wayne said. "Damn it. I should have seen that all along. Now everything makes perfect sense to me."

"What makes sense?"

Wayne glared at him, impatient and hateful. Wayne looked like lunatic Wayne. Ladies and gentlemen, fasten your seat belts.

"Let me just give you a little background," Wayne said, his voice thick with condescension and annoyance. "Just a little so you'll know what we're about. Who cares if we miss something exciting? Listen to me. So they decide to build this hotel. I mean, the government does. The Thai government. This all happened twenty or thirty years ago. Except there were a rash of construction accidents. A rash. This was when they were building the Erawan Hotel. I mean, it's not there now, it's gone. Now there's this monstrosity called the Grand Hyatt Erawan. Erawan was Brahma's three-headed elephant, but that's not the point. During construction of the first hotel they built a spirit house. A spirit house is a Thai shrine to ward off bad spirits. *San Phra Phrom*, it's called, in Thai. Pretty, huh? So they erected this spirit house, because when they commenced construction *they took down all the trees*. So now the spirits that lived in those trees, they had nowhere to go. They're deprived of their homes in an instant. So people get hurt, walls cave in, every day at the job site there are accidents. *Until they erect a spirit house*. Then everything is calm, cool, and collected. No accidents, and the hotel is completed ahead of schedule. Now it's a big place, a very big place, very, very famous in Thailand and the world. *San Phra Phrom*, the granter of wishes. Every night there are hundreds of supplicants, there are musicians and dancers on hand. All praying to the three-headed deity. *Phra Phrom*, the god of creation. To you, to me, he's just Brahma. And this shrine, this whole little Erawan industry, it sprouted up *because they cut down the trees.*"

"Wow," Richard said. "That's some story, Wayne."

"You see it now, Dickie, don't you?" Wayne approached Richard across the carpet. "Tell me, you do?"

"I do," said Richard, utterly confused now. "I think I see it."

Wayne put his arms out and gave Richard a great hug. Wayne was hot, damp, and boozy smelling, but it was a hug nonetheless. Richard patted Wayne's shoulder.

"We better be going," Wayne said as they pulled apart.

"One thing," Richard asked. "Where'd you hear about this thing in the States, this temple?"

A menacing grin suddenly captured Wayne's face. "*Di-onne*," he whispered. Then he broke into an uproarious laugh.

"Who?"

"*The Psychic Hotline*," Wayne explained, absentmindedly. He stopped laughing and was abruptly back in control.

— ❃ —

A doorman in a Burmese helmet and cream-colored uniform made way for them. Outside it was still hot, the air humid and suffocating. Cars stirred restlessly around the traffic circle in a haze of diesel exhaust. The brothers crossed at a light, waited, then crossed at another light, and plunged down an avenue. Talking to Wayne was out of the question. He was too preoccupied. Couples on small motorcycles whined past them on the street. There was an iron fence and, beyond it, a garden. Richard smelled flowers, jasmine perhaps. The whole city seemed damp and over-ripe. There were lots of people out walking, office workers with notebooks and small umbrellas waiting under lighted awnings for their buses. Up ahead, more lights, glowing in the distance. A sign with an arrow said, "Galleries Lafayette." The sidewalk quickly grew crowded.

"Gaysorn," Wayne said, pointing. "The ritzy shopping area. Across there, Ploenchit Road." Then suddenly, he made a left.

There was a tall wrought-iron fence, and at intervals white-washed stucco pillars. There was a wide entryway, and inside the Erawan shrine was crowded with people. In the center was a high altar, a series of steps, and then an ornate birdhouse-looking thing atop a thick post, which Richard took to be the spirit house. The crowd thickened, and before the shrine he could see people praying. The spirit house had a tall, whimsical roof and inside it was a small green statue of Brahma. On the ground and steps were garlands of jasmine, vases of roses, and incense sticks. The sights and smells and noises around Richard were uncommonly rich. No wonder Wayne liked it here. There was music, which seemed to come from a radio, whiny pipes, and staccato tom-toms. Women in gold, knee-length pants and elaborately brocaded jackets passed, barefoot, their heads made small beneath the elaborate pointy cones of their helmets. They wore brass amulets on their ankles, above feet that were flat and widely splay-toed. Dancers, classical dancers. They smiled at Richard and made pretty Siamese gestures with their hands, extending their long-nailed fingers like fans.

Among the flowers and incense on the altar were rows of small carved wooden elephants. Tourists passed by with cameras; they were not Americans. There was a man with an accordion, silently smoking a cigarette. Richard might have been mistaken, but was that Wayne's dark shirt among the kneeling supplicants? A lot of people simply seemed to be milling about. Along the edge of the grounds, against the iron fence, were more lavish garlands, bouquets of jasmine and orchids and roses. There was a not unpleasant hothouse aroma, as though fruit was ripening and rotting all around them. In another corner, a woman in a print dress carried a lame child. More incense, the burning tips glowing like cigarettes. Outside the fence, on the avenue, cars and taxis and trucks swooshed by, almost soundlessly. Wayne was nowhere in sight.

Richard looked for a place to sit down. He watched longingly as a space on the pavement by the wall opened up to him, then closed, as the crowd jostled and changed ranks. He was so tired now and disoriented it hardly mattered. He was here, in Bangkok, and the truth was, he didn't want to relocate Wayne just yet. Gloria would be happy, or at the least, relieved—Richard would have to call her. Poor Gloria. She and Hank, Richard's father, had been unable to have children and had chosen to adopt. Crazy Wayne and Richard were what they got. Now Hank was dead, Gloria was squandering what was left of his estate on Wayne, while Richard tried to keep the family business—select imported foods—afloat. He called it the family business, but he thought of it as Hank's, and now they were being taxed up the kazoo in a shrinking market. Was he, Richard, supposed to play out his destiny in a warehouse in Teaneck, New Jersey, fretting about anchovy paste and broken pallets and a forklift that wouldn't work?

Not that he didn't have his own share of troubles. Dorothy, his wife, had recently moved out and taken her own apartment. She was seeing someone named Vincent whom she described as sensitive and open—as though she had memorized a personal ad Vincent had written. Dorothy wanted children and Richard couldn't produce any.

My God! Here was Wayne enamored of Dionne Warwick, while his own wife was in love with some Jersey goon, some slick dude she'd met through an ad in the *Princeton Packet*. Chasing after Wayne was, perversely, for Richard a relief—it was always an adventure. Maybe they were all dysfunctional, since Gloria kept shelling out and Richard kept retrieving Wayne, who obstinately refused to get things together, not that he in the least had a choice. Richard was up to his neck. He was stalling.

Presently he surveyed the crowd moving about the shrine. If anything, now the grounds were even more completely packed. An English-looking woman passed, smoking a pipe. There were food vendors and a roving band of musicians. Richard stepped into the crowd, rather like a man leaping onto a moving carousel. Now, where was Wayne?

When Richard finally found him, his brother was deeply enmeshed in negotiation. It was in a far corner of the grounds, and a small crowd of Thais had gathered to watch. Wayne was gesturing at a small man in a black coat and a pink bow tie, on whose shoulder was perched a small rhesus monkey. It was an old monkey, with rheumy eyes and white whiskers on its chin. It was dressed in a dirty lime-green uniform, with gold epaulets and gold piping, and a bold red stripe down the leg of the pants. It looked like a Sgt. Pepper's uniform, complete with a small bellman's cap, which the monkey occasionally removed from its head, turning it over and offering it to the gathered Thais like a collection cup. A leather leash ran out of the back of its uniform to the wrist of the Thai gentleman in the bow tie.

The man seemed to have run out of patience with Wayne, who stood opposite him pop-eyed and expectant, covered with sweat. Wayne's hand was extended with a small wad of money.

The man in the pink bow tie said something in Thai that made the crowd titter.

"Come on, sir," Wayne said. "Make up your mind, please."

There was a pause while the man in the bow tie considered things. He was a performer, milking the situation for the crowd. How negotiations had even begun without benefit of a common language was a mystery to Richard, but it never paid to underestimate Wayne. And figuring out what Wayne wanted or didn't want, at any given moment, was generally pretty useless. Wayne was nuts, after all.

With considerable drama the bow-tied man at last plucked the wad of *baht* from Wayne's fingers. Then he pulled the monkey down off of his shoulder, held it under its arms like a baby, and kissed it on both cheeks. The crowd let out a long sigh and applauded. The man in the pink bow tie slipped the leash off his wrist and handed the monkey to Wayne. Someone in the crowd let out a squeal.

Wayne held the monkey to his chest like a proud child clutching a teddy bear. The animal itself looked deeply shaken, confused, turning its face first one way and then the other. When Richard approached, the monkey took off its jaunty cap and held it out to him. It smiled, though its rictus-grin was ugly. Its teeth were round-capped and yellow.

Richard said, "He does tricks, but I just haven't seen them?"

Wayne leveled at Richard his most furious stare. He was holding the forlorn-looking monkey like he might burp it at any moment.

"Have it your way, Wayne. Somehow you always do."

"You're not leaving," Wayne said. "You're my brother and I command you to stay with me."

"Was buying that thing really necessary?" Richard asked.

"Someone has to save it," Wayne said.

Presently both Wayne and the monkey gave Richard the most accusatory of glances. As for the monkey, after a moment, it blinked.

— ❋ —

While obviously old, the little monkey was also sick. That much had been determined in the elevator on the way back up to the suite. Wayne and Richard had reentered the Dusit Thani through an out-of-the-way door beneath the lobby, downstairs by the coffee shop where Richard had first discovered Wayne that afternoon—God, how many hours ago? Wayne had the monkey under the front of his black safari shirt, and crossing to the elevators, he might have been just another pop-eyed, potbellied tourist undone by Bangkok's heat. Wayne thumbed the button in the elevator and the car began to rise. There was a tight, anguished little chittering sound, and then a whimper from beneath his shirt. A moment later Wayne put a hand to his stomach, then suddenly removed it. "Shit," he said, and in fact he was covered with a wretched muddy liquid. The evening had taken such a bizarre twist now that even Richard had begun to see some humor in it.

Just now Wayne was washing off in the suite's bathroom and the monkey was resting on the sofa, its small whiskered head with the bellman's cap reposed against a sapphire-blue cushion. Richard had spread a towel beneath it in case of another accident. The monkey was trembling. From the air-conditioning? Richard wondered. More likely the little fellow had come to the end of his usefulness. What the man in the pink bow tie had gotten for him at the shrine were likely the last baht he would earn.

"How is the little fucker?" Wayne said. He had reappeared in the suite's living room and was bare-chested, patting himself dry with a towel. Half-naked, he resembled a thickly pelted bear, his chest, belly, and arms dense with black hair. Wayne threw the towel on a chair and went to the mini-bar and quickly fixed himself a drink. "He doesn't look too hot," he said. He stood looking down morosely, then put his glass on the coffee table and leaned down over the monkey, which hadn't moved. Then, on his knees, he gently pushed the monkey on its side, to draw off the dirty lime-green trousers. Beneath was the harness, still connected to the leash. "Oh no," Wayne groaned. "No, no, no." He was blubbering. The monkey's almost hairless rump, thighs, and abdomen were covered with ugly sores from the taut frame of the stiffly abrading harness. The monkey trembled and drew its hands up to its chin, like a child awaiting a beating.

"This is terrible," Richard said. He had witnessed that day from his taxi plenty of scenes of Bangkok's poverty and desolation, but the sight of this one now was truly miserable for him.

"The doc," Wayne croaked. He was weeping. "Call the house doc, Dickie."

"Maybe we ought to take him back," Richard said, soothingly. "He doesn't belong here, Wayne."

"Oh, no. No, no, no, no, no. Call the house doc. We're going to save the little bastard, Dickie. He needs us. I need him. He's my magic. Please."

After a moment Richard went over to the telephone on Wayne's table and called the front desk. Above the monkey's head on the pillow, on the side table, there was a bowl of fruit—mangos, bananas, jackfruit, and durian—and presently Wayne tried to interest the monkey in a small banana, which he carefully peeled and then drew up and down before the monkey's face like smelling salts. The monkey sniffed obligingly but didn't eat.

As he watched, Richard felt numb, mortally fatigued. Somehow, throughout the evening Wayne had kept the razor part in his thick hair, and as Richard beheld his inky crown he imagined the mottled scalp beneath, and he could almost see the dotted lines and tiny print labeling the region's of Wayne's brain—the errant synapses and, somewhere, the feral seat of all his misery. Wayne was truly wired now, and if it was true that he'd not slept for several days, then he was likely about to crash. Once he'd foundered, he'd be laid out in a sluggish black depression, insensible to any comfort or the reassurance of Richard's voice. Poor Wayne. That was the disease. Either the morgue or the lion's den, take your pick.

Presently Wayne dipped his finger into his drink and ran it over the monkey's lip. The monkey drew back its head and glared at him.

"He's getting it," Wayne said. "I can feel it. I can feel everything now. Even your resentment."

There was a knock on the suite's door and Richard got up to answer it. Standing in the hallway was the doctor, a diminutive Thai in gold aviator glasses and a scarlet polo shirt. His hands and feet were tiny.

"You're sick?" the doctor asked, entering the room. "I'm Sutachai, Dusit Thani house physician."

Richard closed the door. Inside the room, Dr. Sutachai placed his black medical bag on a chair, and then stood with his thumbs in the waistband of his slacks, surveying the scene judiciously.

"You sick?" he said to Wayne.

"It's our friend here," Wayne said, his voice breaking. He smiled up at Dr. Sutachai. "He's a little under the weather."

The doctor made to pick up his bag. His reluctance seemed entirely professional.

"Don't go," Wayne said. "I'll give you a hundred dollars to make him well." He was kneeling on the floor and morbidly stroking the monkey's leg. Given the chance, the monkey looked like it would gladly bite each of them, separately and severely.

"I'll give you five hundred," said Wayne. "Please?"

Dr. Sutachai peered over the coffee table at the small animal propped on the sofa. Then he reached down deftly and, with his index finger, turned Wayne's stainless steel Med-Alert bracelet over so he could read it.

"So, your two hands are full," he said to Richard. He gave Richard a nod, which suggested he understood, at least partly, the situation. "Let me have a look," he said.

"Bingo," Wayne exclaimed, and clapped.

Richard watched as Dr. Sutachai opened his bag, pulled on latex gloves, and then laid his aviator glasses on the coffee table. He drew his bag over, pushed up the gold-braided jacket, and with his stethoscope listened to the monkey's narrowly furred chest and back. He ran his fingers over the monkey's legs, gingerly, as though at any moment he expected the monkey to strike. Yet the monkey continued to gaze calmly upward. "Dehydration, malnutrition, fever," Dr. Sutachai pronounced. He dabbed at the sores on the monkey's hips with an iodine solution, making a brief sandpapery sound.

"Doesn't that hurt?" Richard asked.

Dr. Sutachai nodded as he squeezed unguent liberally from a tube onto a square of gauze, which he patted on the monkey's hips. Then he drew out a hypodermic needle and a cloudy vial of antibiotic, drew off some of the antibiotic, and injected it with great care into the monkey's rump. Surprisingly, the monkey didn't move. Then Dr. Sutachai removed his gloves with a snap and closed his bag. He remounted the gold glasses on his face and stood up.

"That might do something," he said to Richard. "I can't do more."

"Thank you."

"Old monkey," said Dr. Sutachai. "Better for you to get rid of." He waved Richard off as he backed toward the door. "It's all right," he said. "I can see myself out." Then he was gone.

Wayne had removed himself to an adjacent chair and seemed to be staring at the carpet with a bloated, screwy look. The monkey had closed its eyes and was resting peacefully.

"You remember our tree house?" Wayne said. "The one Hank built for us?"

"I do," said Richard.

"There were fitted windows with screens, and indoor-outdoor carpeting. And remember the telephone, that surplus Army thing he bought us with the two-hundred-foot cord, so we could call back to the house?"

"You used to ring up Gloria and ask her what she was making us for dinner."

"I know I did," Wayne said. He savored the memory for a moment before shifting gears. "I got that whole thing screwed up in my head. I mean, with the trees at the shrine. Them cutting down the trees, it was like when Hank sold the land, and those men came in and bulldozed our tree, and they didn't even bother to dismantle the tree house. Wow."

"I remember it," Richard said.

"Hank sold that land because I was sick."

"No," Richard said. "He sold it so he and Gloria could buy a condo in Florida and retire. And because someone made him an offer he couldn't refuse. He didn't expect to get cancer and die."

"It was the last time I was happy," Wayne said. "Sitting in that tree house in the afternoon. It's the last good thing I can remember. Before I went off. Before now," he said. "Before I became this *thing*."

"But weren't there other times?" Richard asked, rising to his feet.

"Hold me, Dickie," said Wayne. He stretched out his bearish arms. "Hold me, man. I'm just like a fucking house all collapsing inside."

Richard did as he was told. He held his brother tightly in his arms.

— ✳ —

Sunday morning in Bangkok was like a Sunday anywhere. There was hardly any traffic and the sidewalks were empty. There had been that Scandinavian fellow with the headband, a jogger, at whose floor the elevator had stopped when Richard was on his way down from the suite. It was what, eight o'clock? The Scandinavian had been so absorbed in his jogger's map from the hotel that he hadn't noticed Richard or his bundle. It must have rained during the night, because outside the air had cleared and the sidewalks around the hotel looked freshly scrubbed.

Wayne was still asleep, upstairs in the suite's bedroom amidst hurled pillows and tangled sheets. Richard had slept well, exhaustedly, on the bedroom floor with a simple cushion. What had happened, he supposed, was his fault, though whether it was himself or Wayne who had moved the bowl of fruit on top of the television, he couldn't quite remember. Regardless, the little monkey had evidently revived and stirred during the night. Perhaps it had tried to launch itself from a nearby chair to mount the cabinet for the fruit. Perhaps it had just fallen. Either way, the leather leash was still attached to the harness, and the whole thing had gotten hung up, entangled in the freely swinging door to the TV cabinet. God, it was a macabre way to start the day and it was better for Wayne not to see.

For Richard, it was like burying some aged hero. Maybe the uniform did that. But it was a disposal, to put it bluntly. What, Richard should call the front desk and ask for assistance, get the both of them chucked out? Instead, he took the pillowcase downstairs with him and wandered out into the new morning to the back of the hotel, where there were loading docks and dumpsters, amid the stink of moldering garbage. Fortunately, one of the dumpsters had been open and empty, and in went the monkey.

Back inside the suite, Richard called Gloria from the telephone in the living room. It was, he figured, nine o'clock Saturday evening, her time. After a few rings Gloria's answering machine came on. Richard said: "I'm in Bangkok, I'm with Wayne, everything's fine." He read the Dusit Thani's telephone number to her off the face of the phone. "Call me," he said. "I'll let you know when we're returning." He put the phone down and thought for a minute, of anyone else he'd like to call. Then he went to the tall cabinet and turned on the television. He heard Wayne groan from the other room.

There wasn't much to choose from on the TV. Some religious program in Thai, evidently an outdoor Buddhist rite. A familiar American rerun, then another. It was true: military might no longer mattered, because America was taking the world over with *Baywatch* and *Bonanza*. Richard heard, from the next room, Wayne cough and growl. His brother, the both of them from seedless parents sprung. Now it seemed certain to him that no one would provide grandchildren to grace Gloria's final years. Their line was running out. Richard's eyes blurred with tears.

Again he changed the channel. A game show, in Thai. Next a soccer match. Two teams were arrayed at midfield as music played. Richard thumbed up the volume. The camera panned the French flag, then the Stars and Stripes. America versus France. Richard recognized the familiar strains of "The Marseillaise" from his days of grade school French. He pushed the volume even higher.

"*Allons enfants de la patrie,*" he sang, nearly bellowing, "*Le jour de gloire est arrivé.*" Then, knowing he'd forgotten the rest of the anthem, he brushed the tears from his face and banged the door open, blasting into Wayne's room.

# The Field Desk

If my late wife, Margaret, were to draw up a list of my shortcomings, as she sometimes did after we had argued, chief among them would be the certain emotional reticence with which I've approached things, and my failure to demonstrate to her concretely an abiding interest in our family. I don't mean by this our three sons, who are all grown now and married and with whom I remain on good terms. No, what I mean to say is that during Margaret's lifetime I failed to share with her her passionate interest in our forebears, my ancestors principally, whose lives in the early days of this country were of note. To those charges I plead guilty on both counts, though I believe the mild stroke I suffered four years ago has helped cure me somewhat of my withdrawn aspect, and the relative leisure of my retirement (long resisted and likewise stroke-provoked) now provides me the opportunity to renew my acquaintance with the illustrious dead. Why not, since I'll soon be among them?

Correction. My own career was never illustrious. I was a surgeon, and I dare say a good one, from the time the Japanese attacked Pearl Harbor to the waning days of the Reagan administration. In the long days of this medical tenure I observed two intertwined developments: an increasing narrowness of expertise among my surgical colleagues and a corresponding compound growth in their vulnerability to malpractice suits. The men have changed too. They are even more highly educated, more expertly trained, yet somehow—perhaps because they're all made rich so quickly—they seem to me slightly off-center, ethically. They don't share my memories, but then how could they? To them, I'm just an old-hand burping and farting away in his decrepitude. My father was also a surgeon in this town and I can remember in the later 1930s (I was ten or so then) his being fetched during a terrible blizzard by a neighbor in a horse-drawn sleigh, and being driven to a patient's house out in the country, where he performed, on their kitchen table, an emergency appendectomy. Whether he billed promptly for this service, I don't know.

I was a thoracic surgeon, and if one's working days are thus occupied with the human torso—from shoulder to shoulder and neck to genitals— then life takes on a certain compactness and requires immense concentration, the responsibility of it, which left little time for the more robust emotional proclamations Margaret seemed to pine for. After my little stroke, when she had nursed me back to health and I had capitulated to my retirement, when, in short, what she had wished for at last seemed within her grasp—namely a shared old age made rich by our sons and their wives and our grandchildren—Margaret died. A massive coronary thrombosis, in her sleep. In four different houses for forty-six years we had shared the same bed, and I awoke that morning to a bright winter sun streaming through our bedroom windows, and Margaret chill beside me. Some two hundred people attended the funeral, so I'm told.

More than anything, I was angry at her for deserting me. It was akin to a decapitation: I saw only blackness and felt that every soft thing was gone from my life. During the funeral I wept, in long choking sobs, which my small stroke and old age and grief had conspired to permit me. It's a well-known fact that stroke victims often experience a strange emotional acuity and are prone to tears at odd times, something I'd discovered myself with Margaret one afternoon behind the public library in town. The stroke itself had clouded my vision, coating everything in a sort of furry black fuzz. There was a monstrous headache, and raising even one finger had been like lifting a heavy log. But I was lucky, a slight speech impairment and the stiffness down one side soon abated, and I'm kept mobile these days with my blood-thinning drugs.

The afternoon in question was some four months after my incident, and Margaret had driven us downtown to the library—a book drive was on. It was there that I discovered my newfound and quite childlike emotions. The backyard of my father's house, where I grew up, stood opposite the library parking lot in an adjacent alley, but rather than a paved-over lot with an old brick garage covered with spray-painted graffiti, I saw instead the backyard of my boyhood with its tall grass and the ducks and chickens and the dog—Tex!—I had played with, and I began to blubber away like some old fool. Margaret found my tears endearing, and it was as though my stroke—that slight blockage within my head—had allowed me, finally, to be more like her, or more like the husband she had always wanted. Those endearments are a tender memory for me today. I spend my time now in useful retirement, though what, exactly, is useful about an old man grunting to himself as he staggers from room to room remains a mystery.

The house is eerily silent and so I've attacked the silence, leaving a radio on in the bedroom, the television on in the living room, as if in my transit through the house I might draw some secret strength from their emanations. True, sometimes I find myself in a room with no memory of how I got there, or I climb the steps to the attic and once I arrive there have forgotten why I made the trip. I counter these insults by accumulating and surrounding myself with useful items: power saws, electric screwdrivers, a fine set of burnished steel socket wrenches, all from Sears. When I enter the tool department there a hush comes over my arteries, a calmness, as if I had stepped into the sacristy of a church. I am a man whose hands have always been busy, and I grow restless and despondent if they're slack. Luckily this house, with its worn latches and jambs that need planing, continues to require my attention, these projects my defense against our mutual disintegration.

On rainy days and in my spare time I've become much enamored of the family heirlooms Margaret herself spent so much time researching and treasuring. This, too, I think, would make her happy; she would laugh at me in that sharp, affectionate way of hers, as if at last I had come to my senses. For her, these relics seemed almost like religious artifacts; there was something nearly Confucian in her awe at handling them. Sorted and labeled, these things she reposed in an eighteenth-century field desk, also known as a lap box, though the notion of actually opening the thing and setting up the fold-out writing surface to compose a missive with quill and bottled ink is as foreign to me as today's computer-lapped executives, seen on television, firing off their deal-clenching missives as they surge moonward in the seat of a 747. The desk is made of a sturdy buff mahogany, the nifty fitted innards—for there are compartments for writing supplies, sealing wax, a blotter—are of darkly stained pine.

In size the desk is rather like a pushed-down picnic basket, with the real treasures also safely inside. There's a letter, dated 1736 on crude parchment, from Fort Halifax concerning the reenforcement of the British garrison there (five soldiers additional); the rules of incorporation for the Committee of Safety, also on parchment and dated 1775, for the executive group that ran this town and the surrounding county during the Revolution; on ruled notebook paper an order dated June 28, 1863, granting the recipient command of certain home militia, and containing the urgent suggestion that the Confederate advance be halted at Wright's Ferry, on the far side of the Susquehanna River, even if it meant having to burn the bridge. And so on. With these sacred documents was a leather volume my father referred to dismissively as the "herd" book, put together by some distant cousin from Virginia, a dilettante he didn't altogether approve of, which traced various family lines in an almost incomprehensible fashion from their arrival in Barbados in 1720, then onward to old Philadelphia, each of them from cradle to grave. More than once I lost the thread of the narrative, and I'll admit too that I occasionally fell asleep, with all these doctors (yawn) and lawyers going about their civic duties in centuries past with such a high sense of mission (I'm past president of the County Medical Society here, I'll note).

Yet in following this parade of family legends only one man fully caught my interest, that fellow who as a lad wrote the letter from Fort Halifax, who served as a captain in the French and Indian War and a colonel against the British, who was captured at the Battle of Long Island, interred on a British prison ship anchored in the Hudson River (where he cooked and consumed his leather breeches), who afterward served in the Continental Congress, and who, having sired one family and buried his first wife (cause of death: fever), in his old age married a second time, a childless union to a mulatto beauty from Barbados. This marriage struck me as something utterly unique, unfamily-like in its flaunting of social convention. How brazen, how hopeful! He died, I read, in a paroxysm of laughter (pulmonary edema), in bed at the age of eighty-five. What a life!

I have always been a good neighbor. By this I mean polite, friendly, not nosy. I have watched in recent years old Mr. Snoke, the retired building contractor, our neighbor across the street and himself a widower, slowly deteriorate, his stride become a shuffle, his house shabby and his yard full of black, twisted branches. One afternoon, as I sat in my study reading about my ancestors' adventures, an ambulance appeared in his drive.

Nothing happened for so long I grew weary of spying, but then two atten-
dants emerged with a wheeled gurney, upon it the sheet-draped form of
old Snoke, who, I later read, was four years my junior when he died. A
week later a red For Sale sign was stabbed into the lawn, the branches gathered, and then a heavy truck arrived and deposited a metal-hulled dumpster outside Snoke's garage. On weekends, from my window, I could see his
middle-aged son and daughter, who live away, depositing box after box
into the dumpster, heaving away with stern abandon old books, old papers,
clothing, who knows what. It struck me as ostentatiously disrespectful, this
purging of their father and the artifacts of his life. Later the truck returned
and hauled away the heavy dumpster. So this was death, I thought. As a
physician, of course, I've seen it all, but the sudden departure of a patient
from a hospital bed in intensive care is, by comparison, a regretful clinical
occurrence. One doesn't see the empty house or worry about the trashing
of its contents. What, I ask, of dignity?

All this I offer as a preamble to the visit my third son and his new
wife—his second—recently paid me here at home.

— ✺ —

Dan is six foot-two, and at thirty-four is young to be a lieutenant com-
mander in the Navy, but even as a boy he was prematurely self-possessed,
with an unmistakable air of authority. He was born to me and Margaret
relatively late, and I especially admire in him the calm manner in which he
deflects his older brothers' comments when our family discussions turn
political, when Michael, the oldest, who is a lawyer in New York, or John,
a biology professor at Amherst, commence to rant about our foreign poli-
cy or the shortcomings of the military. Dan went to the Naval Academy
and has the attitude of a mature man with work to do, who understands
that sometimes opinions don't count. Why he took to a military career I'm
not certain, but it's clear he intends to make it his life. He has a careful and
pleasant way of exerting himself when his older brothers commence to
needle him, and I wish Margaret could see them thus, these dissenting
adults with thinning hair, our three sons with their three wives and five
grandchildren between them.

Margaret and I agreed that introducing Dan to Becky, his first wife, was
probably our mistake. Becky's father was a surgical colleague of mine, in

Baltimore, and that she and Dan should marry seemed so right what with similar upbringings and friends in common. It wasn't long before things went very wrong, and though I regret the loss of Becky's father as a friend (no contact since the divorce eight years ago), I regret more deeply my own and Margaret's meddling in Dan's affairs, and the pain that caused him. How or why Becky changed I don't know, but I trusted implicitly Dan's confession as to their unhappiness. After that he was single for quite a while, so when he called from Honolulu to tell me that he'd married again and that he and his new wife, Vanessa, were coming for the weekend to visit me, I was happy but apprehensive. Vanessa's maiden name is Soriano, she's an island girl from the Philippines.

I was at my post, awaiting their arrival. My post is at my father's old desk, in my study, positioned so that I have a clear view through the window of our driveway and the front lawn, and across the street old Snoke's house (I haven't met the new owners). Dan and Vanessa flew in to Los Angeles and then on to Washington, where they rented a car, arriving here in the late afternoon. Dan is a big fellow and he climbed out of the car and opened the door for Vanessa. My first impression of her, there at my window, was—and Dan's a big fellow as I've said—well, I confess it looked like Dan had married a coffee-colored midget, and I was shocked. Thus commenced, for me at least, thirty-six hours of nonstop turbulence.

Margaret was of average size so I'm not used to tiny women. I opened the front door for them and Vanessa—she wore flat shoes, blue jeans, and a T-shirt—immediately stepped across the threshold, took my hand, said, "Happy to meet you, Dad," kissed my chin as I bent down to her, and gave me a hug. I don't think she weighs a hundred pounds and is no taller than a twelve-year-old American. She was also exquisitely beautiful, her thick shoulder-length hair parted down the middle, with high regal-looking cheekbones and slightly upslanted, exotic almond-shaped brown eyes. Was this a quality of tiny women, to make a whole room bristle so with energy? Dan looked fine, fit and trim and healthy, and clearly very proud. He put their suitcases down in the hall and took my hand.

I had put on a pair of gray flannel slacks with a blue blazer and a regimental tie, thinking perhaps that I might take them out to dinner, but fifteen minutes later I was sitting at the kitchen table where I always eat, with my tie loosened and my blazer on the back of my chair, chatting with Dan while Vanessa prepared soup and sandwiches. She had changed into a pair of baggy shorts and was barefoot now as she moved about the kitchen. I wasn't permitted to help, I was only glad I'd remembered to stock up on things that morning at the store. Vanessa's feet were flat and splay-toed; against her other skin their undersides were pale, as if she'd stepped into a thin pool of chalky liquid. Dan talked of Navy things: his next ship, or whether they might be moved from Honolulu to Norfolk or San Diego. Every now and then as Vanessa passed he grabbed at her and then as she laughed and slapped at him he nuzzled at her belly, this great crew-cut son of mine who was clearly happy, who in his leisure clothes looked somehow ill-composed, who looked so wonderful in his uniform. I wondered if Vanessa was pregnant but they hadn't said. She gave me glasses and ice and I went to the little bar in the living room and fixed Dan and me a drink, which I needed. Vanessa drank iced tea. She had small hands with long elegant fingers and sitting at the table her gestures were precise and neat.

We went to bed early, though whether this was for their benefit or mine I wasn't sure. Of course they were tired from their trip. Margaret and I built this house eight years ago, with the master bedroom on the first floor and double guest rooms upstairs. I didn't bother to put my clothes away. Under the covers, in my pajamas, I saw my white shirt and tie and blazer on a chair, dropped there as if by a man in a hurry to undress me. The phone woke me sometime after two o'clock.

Old men, even retired doctors, don't get phone calls after midnight unless something has gone wrong. I suppose this was in my mind as I groped for the light and the receiver, but by the time I got to it someone had already picked up the extension upstairs. Vanessa? The line was thick with static. Someone—a Martian?—giggled. "Hello?" Vanessa said. "Hello?" Her voice was heavy with sleep. Then someone spoke in a child-like singsong voice. A question, or supplication? Vanessa asked a question back, pop-bang-pop—she must have been awake now—in a language I'd never heard. Lilting, soft-voweled, if it hadn't been for Vanessa's haughty tone of rebuke, as if she was tolerating an unruly infant. Question, answer, question. Vanessa's response was like someone grinding out a cigarette. "Please," said a female voice, perhaps from another planet. I felt like I was intruding so I hung up the phone.

It was foolish, but I wanted to cry then or talk to Margaret. Where was Dan, and who was this woman he'd married? How had the calling party gotten my number, were these calls now going to be a regular part of my life? I looked at my rumpled blazer on the chair and turned off the light, then drew the covers up to my chin. Dan said Vanessa's father, Mr. Soriano, owned a steel mill; Dan had met Vanessa at a reception at the U.S. Embassy in Manila. So what? Foreign cities were part of his life and it was natural that he should meet people. Indeed she was a dark-faced beauty with flawless skin, but there were valuable things in my house, silver, clocks, and crystal, so why like some old fool did I feel these things slipping away from me?

A toilet flushed upstairs. Perhaps it was only that—and a dream—that had awakened me.

— ❋ —

Everything was fine the next morning. It was a beautiful day, I rose early and made the coffee, and Dan, already dressed and shaved, cooked bacon and eggs for me and Vanessa, her dark self thickly swaddled in one of the rich white terrycloth robes Margaret had put upstairs for guests. There was no mention of the phone call. Did I have plans? "No," I said, "only dinner this evening with my son and his wife at the Club downtown." This seemed to please Vanessa. Dan had an errand to do; afterward he'd return to get Vanessa and then show her around our county.

"You want to come, Dad?" said Dan.

"I've seen it."

"I know you've seen it," he said. "You live here, don't you? I thought you might like the company."

"You two go," I said. "I'll catch up with you later."

The truth was I didn't want to get downtown—or anywhere else, for that matter—where I might remember some trivial detail and commence to weep and embarrass everyone as I had at the library that afternoon with Margaret. That's my only gripe about my little stroke, or growing old: my unpredictable emotional incontinence, this sense of myself I have of someone not entirely to be trusted. Still, Dan was right: I should have spent the afternoon seeing the sights with them. What could I accomplish in wary solitude, at my post?

Of course I'd brought this on myself, this situation. Couldn't I have chosen just to take them to a restaurant, and not the Club? Like everyone else they'd been forced to integrate and take Jews, but neither Jews nor men of color had exactly flocked to the Hamilton Club downtown, our local haunt for businessmen and professionals. But Vanessa wasn't black. She was well-born, it seemed, and certainly exotic, not as dark nearly as the island women from Barbados that I've seen. Then I remembered that Margaret and I had given a party for Dan and Becky, his first wife, at the Club. Would Dan remember this and resent me?

"You'll wear your whites?" I said to Dan. Vanessa had gone upstairs and he was rinsing out the skillet at the sink.

"I do have a coat and tie," he said. He turned off the tap. "Why, you want me in my uniform?"

"Yes," I said. "I'd like it." When people saw us, wouldn't it be clear: here was the fast-track Navy man with his Oriental wife? "I'm proud of you," I added.

"Then whites it is," said Dan. That's another thing I like in him: so unthreatened by me he's amenable to my whims.

Dan left on his errand and I was in my bedroom straightening up, berating myself a little for this foolishness about the Club, when the telephone rang again. I waited, hoping Vanessa would answer it. But no one answered so after five or six rings I picked it up.

"Hello?"

"De-bas. Va-ness-a, ow?" Static, interplanetary sizzle.

"Hello?"

"Va-ness-a?" Plaintive now, and worried.

"Hold on, please. I'll get her."

I left the bedroom and walked through the living room to the front hall and called up the stairs. There was water running and I could hear a radio playing up there behind the closed door as well. The music surprised me because I didn't remember there being a radio in either guest room. I called again, twice, but there was no answer. I finally climbed the stairs and called to her through the door, which was open a few inches. I heard the shower running in the bathroom and the radio must have been in there too. I guessed it was an international call and they were waiting. I wondered, had my new daughter-in-law gone deaf? I pushed the door open a little and saw the familiar pink-striped wallpaper Margaret had selected, the open suitcases, the wide bed in disarray, the waiting telephone on the night table. Then—and here's the mistake—I took a step into the room and once more called her name.

At my age it sometimes takes a few moments to absorb things, but the sudden fact of Vanessa's nakedness before me was overwhelming. So much data! It didn't look like she'd been in the shower yet because her hair was dry and now that the door to the bath was open and the music was really loud, it didn't surprise me that she hadn't heard me. Was it customary in her country for in-laws to see each other naked? She gave a whoop, one thigh turned inward, her hands flashed as they tried to be everywhere at once, this small-breasted dark person who was so tiny that without clothes she seemed almost to disappear, my son's wife, who shrieked with embarrassment as I retreated from the room.

"The telephone," I said. "There's a call for you, I'm sorry."

I spent the rest of the morning and the afternoon at the desk in my study with the door closed.

At about five-thirty I commenced to dress for dinner. Dan and Vanessa had returned from their tour and I could hear them upstairs doing the same. Margaret would have laughed at me, at my excruciating embarrassment—to hear her chuckle would relieve me. In the afternoon I had paid some household bills and read again from the old herd book, strictly to distract myself. At some point, as I read about the famous colonel's frustrated retreat at the Battle of Long Island, I recalled an old expression of my father's: "If the bait is right, even an old fish will bite." Might I remarry? I wondered. The very notion was like trying to start a reluctant car on an icy day, but then again, why not? Too, there were the Chinese, who on the one hand worshipped the ancients, their forebears, and on the other—the emperors, at least, so I'm told—took younger and younger concubines to rejuvenate them. What, like Mr. and Mrs. Frankenstein, lying side by side and mute as the boiling blood is tubed between them? It would take a squalling infant to reinvigorate me, and with a crying child I could never sleep. Then I was at the hall closet to fetch my overcoat, and I wondered, where on earth had Margaret put my hat?

You are a lucky father to have a tall, good-looking son in the crisp white uniform of his country, accompanied by his tiny fierce-looking but utterly exquisite wife. Vanessa wore high heels and a snug-bodiced shoulderless white dress, a pearl necklace aglow above her clavicles. Nothing was said of my morning's misadventure; Vanessa claimed that seeing our old town had been fun. I sat in the back and let Dan do the driving.

The Club is housed in an old Victorian mansion downtown, across the street from the courthouse. Carl, who has been the barman there for thirty years, is my former patient. Gallstones, and when he was younger, treatment for burns when a deep fryer in the kitchen at the Club exploded. I remember removing his dressings and seeing his skin coming back quite nicely, though white—the pigmentation and his natural cast would come back soon enough. Observing this, Carl laughed.

"What?" I said. I touched the tissue lightly. "Does it hurt?"

"Not at all, Doctor. I was only thinking what life might have been like if my skin had looked like that."

"Different," I said.

So here was a man, my former patient, who had spent thirty years of his life in polite servitude to my kind and me, and myself, not yet infirm but clearly nervous, what with my handsome son and his pretty wife, her skin the even hue of milky chocolate. What did Carl do? Other club members beheld our entrance; I felt their eyes upon us as we ordered drinks and dinner. Did Vanessa notice too? How stupid of me, how inconsiderate to have brought them here to begin with! Still, the meal was fine. As we were waiting for our coffee Vanessa excused herself to go to the ladies' room. As she didn't know the Club I suggested that Dan accompany her, to show her the way.

"Doctor?"

It was Carl, standing at my elbow.

"Your meal, was everything all right?"

"Perfect, Carl. Thank you."

"Your son, he looks wonderful."

"Doesn't he? Marriage seems to suit him."

"If you don't mind my saying, Doctor. His wife, she's something special. He's a very lucky man."

I looked up into Carl's face, conscious of the compliment: not that Vanessa was beautiful, which she was, but that a dark-skinned woman was now part of my family, as if in bringing her to the Club in this narrow-minded town it endorsed the manner in which Margaret and I had tried to raise Dan and all our sons.

It had been a fine meal with excellent company, and the night was brisk. I felt that all was right with the world—Margaret would be proud of me. Vanessa and I waited on the steps of the Club for Dan to bring the car around.

"Those are beautiful pearls, dear," I said.

"Aren't they? Dan gave them to me at our wedding."

My heart sank. There was no tone of remonstrance in Vanessa's voice, but it was clear to me I'd failed. I had forgotten completely to get anything for them for their wedding.

— ❈ —

As a surgeon, I was always quick on my feet. That's a talent quite unnecessary to the tedium of a lung resection, say, but came in handy when things went wrong or when a life depended on the swift application of an alternate strategy. The ride home from the Club only took ten minutes, during which, I felt, I'd achieved a fine solution, something so appropriate that, thus conceived, it fit snugly into the preordained scheme of things, like the final piece in a puzzle.

There was also news, as Dan drove. His errand that morning had been to Western Union, to send money to Vanessa's sister, Anja. Was I right, that Dan had entered into some dangerous liaison with the tiny leader of some third-world family, whose financial needs would drain him dry? Hardly. While Dan and Vanessa were visiting me, Anja was staying in their apartment in Honolulu. What with the wedding, their honeymoon, and travel, Dan had forgotten to pay the rent (call #1), so Anja did and Dan promptly reimbursed her (call #2). I could begrudge Anja only her failure to speak English to me, plus her poor appreciation of the notion of international time.

"I have something for you," I said, as I unlocked the front door. "Just wait, please, and I'll be with you in a minute."

It was too big and too awkward to wrap, and anyway I couldn't recall where Margaret kept that kind of paper. In my study I took off my overcoat, my suit coat, then rolled up my sleeves. I carried the old field desk out into the living room.

"Vanessa," I said, "I want you and Dan to have this. It's a wedding gift from me."

"My God, Dad," said Dan. "That thing?"

Then I learned about tiny women. Vanessa gave Dan such a dark and venomous look it utterly froze him. As if that wasn't enough, out shot her elbow, nailing him neatly on the wrist. Tiny women have sharp elbows, and Dan winced.

Vanessa strode graciously to me. She put her hands over my hands as I

held the old lap desk, then craned upwards on her tiptoes and kissed me
on the lips.

"Thank you, Dad," she said. "It's beautiful. You'll have to show me how
it works."

"It's an old field chest, isn't it?" Dan said. "An Army thing. There used
to be letters . . . "

"Maybe we could just sit down," said Vanessa. "Here on the sofa. It's
heavy, isn't it? You'll have to tell me what's inside. Come on, Danny, please?
It's a lovely gift and I just want you to humor me for a moment."

We sat down then, the three of us, my family at the moment as it was. I
thought Margaret would be pleased. Whether my gesture was a sudden save
or the result of careful planning really didn't matter. I felt like I had launched
things in the proper manner and that I was ready for the next thing.

# True Believers

It was midnight when Maggie and Peter arrived at Indira Gandhi airport in Delhi. The terminal was almost empty, and after they'd cleared customs and retrieved their bags they took a taxi to the Maurya Sheraton.

The clerk at the front desk was nattily dressed and wore gold-rimmed glasses. "You will be checking out early?" he asked.

"A driver is meeting us here tomorrow to take us to Agra," Peter said.

Their room, it turned out, was enormous—with a brass chandelier and lime-green carpet. Maggie crawled onto the bed and with a dark look slipped under the covers. For her, it had not been a very good year: she had turned forty in October, and then her father had passed away in December. She had become so remote and gloomy, so withdrawn, that Peter had been distracted by a dalliance of his own. Well, all right, it was more than a dalliance—he'd had an affair with a young package designer in the office next door to his, but it had been a limited thing, like taking his tie off, clapping his hands, and putting the tie back on again. It was nothing, in fact, except it was sex with a woman who wasn't mired in gloom, and once in a while, for God's sake, he had needed that. It was over now, but Peter still felt rather tarnished.

Coming to see the Taj, he hoped, might help turn things around for him and Maggie. He had been there himself ten years before, when his business had brought him to India, and he'd realized at the time that it shouldn't be a solitary adventure—he'd vowed to return again someday with his wife.

— ✸ —

The driver was a skinny Sikh, who wore a yellow turban and a red-striped shirt and yellow driving gloves that matched his turban. Peter and Maggie sat together in the back of the old-fashioned sedan, too tired and jet-weary to talk.

Later the slowing of the car awoke them. They were entering the town of Agra. The driver put his electric window down, and presently the traffic edged forward and the rust-colored Yamuna River appeared outside the window.

"This is the great Taj Mahal," said the driver, though they were still stuck in traffic. Yet they were so close now Peter could feel his heart pounding with anticipation. For him, coming here with Maggie had been an inspiration, one of those romantic dreams that gives you no rest until it's fulfilled. Peter was in the mood now for some miraculous sign or confirmation of their undying love.

After several twists in the road the car turned again, pulling up behind a truck, and then the truck moved and they were suddenly confronted by that wondrous apparition in marble, arguably the most beautiful building in the world. In the early morning light its marble was pink and so delicate-appearing it looked like the inside of a seashell.

"Oh, my God!" Maggie gasped, grabbing Peter's hand.

The Sikh pulled into the parking lot and Peter and Maggie climbed out. They walked through the archway to the ticket windows, then entered, and looked past the reflecting pool at the Taj, which glowed golden now as the sun struck its dome.

Maggie grabbed Peter's hand and he saw that she was crying.

"It's so beautiful," she said.

She turned to him to say something more, but her face swelled and she began to sob in earnest. Peter hugged her and told her that he loved her.

"Oh, I love you too," she hiccuped, then laughed.

After a while she stopped crying and they walked on, spending an hour or more looking around inside the mausoleum. The Taj looked immaculate from a distance but up close it glittered with rough borders of inlay and carved leaves, and the shimmering marble had a smoky hue that was pearl-like.

When they returned to the car the driver was lying across the backseat fanning his face with a newspaper.

He sat up as they approached. "So, is it not exquisite?"

"Oh, it is!" Maggie exclaimed. "Thank you for showing us."

It was only a five-minute ride to the Taj-View Hotel on Fatehabad Road. From the outside, the Taj-View gave off gleaming seductive hints of more comfort within: its name engraved on a polished brass plaque, and beyond the glass a foyer like a moghul palace. Peter and Maggie squeezed into the same wedge of the revolving door, winding their arms around each other as they crossed the lobby. Peter wondered if the front desk clerk was accustomed to seeing similarly love-locked couples who, moved by the aphrodisiac of the Taj, couldn't wait to get into their rooms.

In fact, once they were inside, Peter had no more than tipped the bell-boy and locked the door before he and Maggie were glued together, stumbling toward the bed. On the wall above the headboard was a print of the Taj, and laughing, Maggie scooted across on her knees to get a closer look at it. As she did so, she pulled up the back of her skirt.

— ❀ —

When they awoke, it was wonderful to find the towels thickly stacked and a plentiful supply of hot water. Through the gauzy curtains, they could see the Taj beneath an overcast sky about a kilometer away. At dinner time they exploded from their room, because they were famished. Maggie hung onto Peter's arm as he steered them through the lobby. There were all kinds of couples staying at the hotel—French, Germans, Italians, plus wealthy Indians with their grandparents and kids.

They entered the hotel restaurant. Inside, tables of radiant people chatted and laughed under heavy clouds of cigarette smoke, wine, and the exotic curry-laced smells of Indian cooking. Everyone seemed to love it here. How delighted they were with their food, and to be eating it within a kilometer of one of the world's great wonders!

A hostess in an orange sari showed them to a table for two near the back of the restaurant. Glancing around, on every side Peter saw couples who seemed completely in love, staring into each other's eyes, letting go of each other's hands only long enough to dive into plates of tandoori chicken or rich curried lamb.

"Oh, Peter," Maggie said. "Isn't it wonderful?"

A waitress in a yellow sari brought them each a glass of chilled white wine and two menus. Both of them felt ravenously hungry, and it would be torture, they agreed, to pick only one dish for each course. Together they ran through a series of possibilities and decided just as the waitress reappeared. They ordered and then the two of them sat back and basked in the promise of an excellent dinner. Peter watched happily as the candle-light flickered over Maggie's face.

"I was thinking about making love to you all day," she said.

"You were?"

"I know I've been a bit of a bitch lately, and I wanted to make it up."

Moments after delivering their soup, the waitress began to crowd the table with savory dishes. It was unlike any food they had ever eaten.

"What beautiful chicken," Maggie said.

She was right. The tandoori chicken was ravishing: it looked like it had been marinated in henna, and small wedges of it were flecked with mites of parsley, onion, and garlic. Maggie sliced off a chunk and put it into her mouth and chewed. As Peter watched her she looked ecstatically happy.

Later Maggie scrubbed the last streaks of curry gravy off of her plate with a thick chunk of naan and then chewed it slowly. When the waitress reappeared, she ordered coffee for them both.

Maggie hung onto Peter's arm as they squeezed out of the restaurant. The entryway was crowded with people. Eager to get in, couples were pressing against the podium where the hostess in the orange sari stood. Farther on, four or five wheelchairs stood in a line outside the restaurant. Peter saw that these people were all Americans, gray-haired men and women. Some kind of retirees' group, he assumed, because the women all wore sweat pants and jogging shoes, and carried their purses on long straps around their necks.

Just as he and Maggie were passing through the group, Maggie slowed—a woman was staring at her. The woman had absolutely white hair cut in an attractive pageboy style and was staring at Maggie with her blue eyes.

"Excuse me!" the woman said. "I'm sorry, but aren't you Maggie Grant?"

The woman's use of Maggie's maiden name startled Peter and drew him up. He could feel his wife's hand tighten around his arm.

"I'm sorry?" Maggie said.

"I'm Elaine Chapman," the woman answered. "We're from Osterville, on Cape Cod. I could swear you were Maggie Grant."

"Oh, yes, it's me!" Maggie cried, and Peter could feel his shoulders sag. He suddenly felt like they were being dragged down from their carefree dinner and planted squarely where real things rest.

"My husband, Bill, and I are visiting here with our little troop," said Mrs. Chapman. "I used to know you when you were a girl growing up. Your parents used to rent the place next to ours."

Maggie leaned over and gave the woman a hug. "Is this your husband?" she said.

Hasty introductions were made among them all around.

Maggie laughed gently, her hand resting on the old woman's arm. "I can't believe you came here!"

"Oh, we're not alone, dear. Our group sticks together and takes whatever comes our way. Isn't Agra wonderful?" Mrs. Chapman was not looking at Maggie now, but over her shoulder toward the hostess by the entry. Just then there was a general commotion and several people filed past.

"We should be going too," Maggie said, suddenly distracted. Peter noticed that she wasn't looking at Mrs. Chapman, either; in fact, there was a faraway expression on her face. She seemed unsure of herself, and her eyes were shining.

"You'll have to come out to the Cape to see us," Mrs. Chapman called, as she began to push her husband's wheelchair through the crowd.

"Good-bye!" Maggie said over her shoulder.

Leaving the restaurant, Maggie leaned on Peter's arm. Peter felt relieved, happy now that they were alone again; he was proud that he and Maggie were a couple, proud of her easy charm, proud that the day had made her happy. As he pulled her to his side, the first touch of her body, redolent of their lovemaking that afternoon, sent through him a keen pang of lust.

Once they were inside their room Peter closed the door and locked it. He could hear the thumping of his heart against his ribs. He put the key on the bureau and when he turned he saw that Maggie had dropped her purse on the bed and was standing before the mirror.

"Well, what a coincidence," he said.

Maggie didn't answer. Instead, she turned away from the mirror and walked toward him. Her face suddenly looked so serious and weary that he wondered if she might be sick.

"You look tired," he said.

"I am. It must be jet lag."

Then she went to the window and stood there, looking out. Peter waited for her again and, fearing that their silence was about to divide them, said, "You know, those old Chapmans are something." But he stopped, feeling foolish.

What on earth was the matter with her? Peter was trembling now with annoyance. He was beginning to feel so exasperated that at first he didn't hear her turn away from the window and approach him. She stood before him, resting her hands on his shoulders.

"You're a good husband," she said. "This has been a wonderful trip."

Strange though her remark was, Peter was delighted, and he put his hands in her hair. She was right: hadn't it been a perfect day for them?

Peter slipped one arm around her and drew her against his chest. "What are you thinking?" he said.

Suddenly, in an outburst of tears, Maggie said, "I was thinking about the Chapmans."

Maggie pushed his hands away from her and ran to the bed and, throwing her arms across the pillow, hid her face. Peter stood for a moment in astonishment. He felt less like a man talking to his wife than like some bewildered physician with a case so confounding that it bordered on the metaphysical.

"Why are you crying?" he asked.

Maggie raised her face from the pillow and dried her eyes with the back of her hand. "I was thinking about someone I used to know."

"Who?"

"It was someone I used to know on the Cape when we went there in the summer."

"Someone you were in love with?" he asked.

"It was a boy," she answered. "He was the Chapman's neighbor, or his parents were. Daniel Keyes. He was a sophomore in college the summer I was nineteen."

"Were you in love with him?"

"Yes, we used to take long walks on the beach."

A thought flew across Peter's mind. "Was that why you were talking about going to the Cape to visit the Chapmans? Maybe he still lives there," he said.

"Don't be mean," said Maggie. "He died in a car accident."

Peter was stung. He felt humiliated by her evocation of this long-dead boyfriend. While he had been full of amorous intentions, she had been thinking of this dead man. How silly he was, and how stupid to bring Maggie here to try to rekindle their romance!

"Well, it must have been important," Peter said, trying to keep up his mild tone, because he wanted her to confess.

"Oh, he was," Maggie said. "And there's another thing I didn't say."

Maggie was not looking at him, and a vague terror seized Peter. "What was it?"

"It was over Thanksgiving," she said. "We had just gone out to the Cape for the holiday, to the summer house. Daniel was supposed to be driving out from Boston to be with us for the holiday. He and I were very stuck on each other and had been since that summer. Peter, I was only nineteen years old!" Maggie paused. "I'd just discovered two weeks before that I was pregnant."

"Oh, God!" Peter said.

She paused for a moment to get herself back under control. "The night before Thanksgiving," she said, "I was in the house alone. Someone came to the door and I thought it was Daniel, coming out from Boston. I'd already told him I was pregnant. Peter, he was the first boy I'd ever been in love with! I didn't know what we were going to do, though he'd told me he wanted to marry. But it wasn't Daniel who'd come to the door. It was a Barnstable policeman, come to the house to tell us that there'd been an accident. The weather was bad and a truck had crossed over the median."

"Oh, I'm sorry!" Peter said, reaching out to put his hand on Maggie's shoulder.

Numbly, Maggie said, "A couple of weeks later I went down to Albany with my mother and had an abortion. My father hated it, but it was a decision we made. They didn't want that kind of a life for me, they wanted the kind of life I have now."

Peter sat down beside her. "How come you never told me?"

"I was ashamed, I suppose. It's not the kind of thing I was very proud of. And after it was over, it was as if it had never happened."

Maggie stopped and flung herself down on the bed again. Peter felt so overwhelmed that he let her hand fall and walked over to the window.

— ☀ —

Peter went to the bed and stretched himself under the sheets. Leaning on his elbow, he looked for a moment at Maggie's matted hair and open mouth, listening to her as she slept. How could it be that she had never told him these things? She had been in love and lost her firstborn. Peter's eyes rested upon her, and as he thought of what Maggie had been, and of what she had lost—her father, Daniel, her first child—a tenderness for her filled his heart.

Damn those Chapmans, he thought. Why did they have to remind her? Disillusion stung Peter's eyes as he thought again of how Maggie had kept her secret, choosing, of all nights, tonight to dash his dreams. Well, he supposed it was true what people sometimes spoke of: how foreign travel could help crystallize your life. So what had he learned? Only how difficult it was to cross that unbridgeable distance between two people, for how could he assume anything when he knew so little about the woman with whom he had lived all these years!

A splatter of pellets against the glass made him turn. Peter could sense, rather than hear, the imminent downpour of rain. Sure enough, as he rose from the bed and went to the window, the sound of it was like the sky turning on. Across the plain he could see indistinctly the Taj, that he and Maggie had come so far to see.

Suddenly, Peter tried not to breathe. He did not want to move, or to disturb Maggie, out of respect for her and out of awe for what he beheld— for that grand impossible hope, living proof of a love that wouldn't die. After a moment he backed away quietly and stood looking down at his wife in the bed.

# Overture from a Faithful Booster

P oor VanDam: he hadn't, Warhol-like, been shot, or even threatened in the grand manner of a Rushdie. No, in his writing life VanDam had never been provocative. As one critic or two had observed, he ruled the supple image—another had even praised his dazzling lapidary style. Still, as an author, he was rather too often confused, he felt, with the other two more famous writing Johns—Updike and O'Hara—perhaps because they also had been born in Pennsylvania. Nonetheless, at fifty-two, VanDam was much awarded, prized, anthologized; his reputation, such as it was, had been made. All of which was fortunate, since he now wrote very little.

He also drove poorly, inattentively at best. Presently he was behind the wheel of his wife's new Taurus, speeding down I-76 through Lehigh County, on his way to Dr. Delaney's office in Paoli to have his sutures tweezed out. The trip was deeply private and thoroughly domestic, not unlike his fiction; his recent surgery had been a chancy attempt to reverse an eight-year-old vasectomy. During the procedure, Dr. Delaney had discovered a fatty lump in VanDam's groin, which he'd insisted on removing. "It's likely just a cyst," he'd said, though his frown belied a deeper concern. "We'll have a biopsy to be certain." Excised from his groin, the thing itself had looked no more threatening than the inside of a grape. Still, VanDam was worried; who wouldn't be? Was it cancer? Well, what if? God, the stitches in his groin had been burning for a week!

Reversing the vasectomy had been mostly Glenda's idea, not his. VanDam's wife (his third) was only thirty-nine, yet she was sweetly clamoring for another kid, though he had two boys already, she a girl, all of them in college. Of course, VanDam was deeply moved by Glenda's wish. He was very much in love with her, and excited by the prospect of another fatherhood, though he was also frankly scared. He wasn't sure he'd been a bad father, exactly, to his two boys, but he knew he could do better. And maybe that was it: with all her sweet insistence, Glenda was offering him another chance—tendering the lightness of their future together against the shortcomings of his past. And what an irony that would be—to have it all snatched away from him, if he was really sick.

The day as VanDam planned it had a twofold attack: first, to stop in at Dr. Delaney's office to get the ratty stitches out, and then to meet, in the parking lot of a MacDonald's, Mr. Michael Thomas Morandini, or more familiarly, Max, so that VanDam could autograph for him a copy of his most recent book—a collection of essays on writer's block that was already two years old. But what the hell, Max Morandini had been faithfully collecting VanDam's books for almost thirty years, and the plea to meet in person had moved VanDam a lot. What's more, arranging the meeting, through the mail, had allowed VanDam to plan as though he had a future. Well, didn't he?

Over the years, Max Morandini had been slavishly attentive to the ups and downs—mostly downs—of VanDam's career. More recently, he'd taken to writing not to VanDam's publisher, as he had before, but directly to VanDam's home, which was mildly disturbing. How had he gotten VanDam's address? Still, VanDam had a weak spot in his heart for the old man—and by now Max Morandini must be old, for over the years there'd been no more faithful collector of VanDam's work. Together, in fact, the two of them had grown old. Max Morandini's first letter had come after the publication of VanDam's first novel, in 1968. And all through the years, the invisible Morandini had kept up with VanDam's scanty yield, even acquiring such inessentials as VanDam's high school yearbook and old copies of the *Harvard Lampoon* on which he'd worked. Morandini tracked down these things, and they all came, in time, for VanDam to sign—more constant, really, than anything else in the author's chaotic life, his vagrant migrations from state to state, from one temporary college teaching post to yet another, the aftershocks of two failed marriages crashing about his head like shattered crockery.

In his letters, Max Morandini's voice had remained unchanged: respectful, scrupulous, and earnest. Until, that is, just recently, when the latest missive had arrived direct from Morandini to VanDam's home. It was as if the old man had violated the private terms of their agreement and somehow meant to up the ante. Also, there was the unusual request, in a typed post-script to the letter: "If you're ever in the Philadelphia area and can spare a few moments I'd really love to meet you. It would do me such an honor." Van Dam had found himself wondering about old Max more than he liked. For example, why was every letter typed, even down to the signa-ture? Was the old guy sick, perhaps? But the idea of stopping off to see such a faithful fan was heady stuff: in his mind's eye, VanDam appearing in the flesh seemed like a fine way to round out the old collector's life. His own, too, for that matter.

On the whole, VanDam preferred not to know his readers. Pressed as he was financially, he spent much of his time giving readings and workshops at colleges, although he vastly preferred the massed anonymity of a crowd-ed lecture hall to classroom visits or the disarmingly personal questions posed by increasingly young and ever more precocious students. Once on campus, he was inevitably hauled from the creative writing class to the alumni cocktail party to a dinner with trustees, then to a reading in a hall, more drinks afterward at a reception, and finally dumped, well liquored, back at the Holiday Inn. When he'd been between marriages, these trips had been made more bearable by the occasional graduate student with long hair and a batik skirt, but from these trysts VanDam had generally emerged, the next morning, headachy and gnawed by self-disgust.

Meeting Max Morandini, of course, would be a different tale. That is, so long as VanDam was healthy.

— ❊ —

Dr. Delaney was in his mid-seventies and pretty much retired, though he continued to see old patients like VanDam. He shared office space now with several much younger doctors, in a gray-walled office block behind the Paoli Hospital. He had been, back in Easton where VanDam grew up, a dispenser of tetanus shots, had sown up the occasional split knee when VanDam was a boy. Seeing old Delaney in his white coat and stethoscope always made VanDam feel a little younger, because to him Delaney always had been old. The waiting room with its straight-backed chairs, the harried nurses, the smell of antiseptic, all conspired to remind VanDam of his boyhood visits to the doctor's long-vanished office.

"I don't understand you, John," the doctor said. "Why, at your age, the two of you want to get pregnant, or think you do."

They were in one of the examining rooms and VanDam was unbuckling his pants. "We'd like to do it right this time," he said. "Or try."

"What are you talking about, raising kids? You have children of your own and so does she. Brenda, isn't it?"

"Glenda," VanDam said. "Yes, that's true, but we'd like to have our own. I'm excited about it, really."

"Ah," Delaney frowned. He grabbed a goose-necked lamp and pulled it over, then switched on the bulb. "Your undershorts too," he said. "Let me have a look."

VanDam scanned the ceiling as Dr. Delaney gingerly fingered his scrotum, then touched the tender spot upon his groin where the other, second incision had been made. "What about it?" VanDam asked. "I've been kind of worried."

"The cyst?" Delaney said. He had taken out a tweezers and was tugging gently at the stitches, prior to snipping them and sliding the stitches out. VanDam felt the doctor's hand slide up his thigh. "It was benign," the doctor said.

"You mean, I don't have to worry?" VanDam felt a tremendous rush of relief, then a vague tickling in his crotch as the doctor withdrew the final sutures.

Delaney dropped the tweezers back onto a metal tray. "Well, I wouldn't go that far," he said, as he snapped off his rubber gloves. "By the way, you'll have to have a sperm count. You want to leave a specimen for us now?"

"No thanks," VanDam said. "Anyway, I thought I was supposed to refrain from sex for another few weeks."

Delaney nodded vaguely. He was utterly bald but had copious hairs sprouting from both ears. "You can do it at home, then," he suggested.

"Pleasant thought," mused VanDam. "I miss Glenda a lot."

"How long have you been away?"

"Just three days. Last night I had a reading up in Kutztown."

"So what's she do?"

"Glenda's a social worker," VanDam said. "She's taking some time off this year, though. Her ex was an orthopedist so she did okay. I mean, she doesn't have to work. I'm driving her car, in fact. I didn't have to rent one."

Dr. Delaney clasped his hands behind his back. "So other than the improvement in your finances, how've you been?"

"Okay, I guess. Worried, though, about trying to get pregnant. And that cyst had me pretty damn distracted. Now that I'm finally happy, I think I'm scared that it's all going to be snatched away."

"That's only anxiety," Delaney said. "It's natural. Have you been doing any writing?"

"Not really," VanDam said. The funny thing was, he had often thought of using old Delaney as the model for some character; but like lots of things, nothing had come of it. Well, he was alive at least.

"Pull your pants up and you can go on home," Delaney said, as he opened the door into the hall and held out his hand. Evidently the interview was over.

— ✳ —

"Mr. VanDam?" a young man's voice said behind him.

VanDam turned and saw a longhaired man approaching him across the parking lot. The fellow was far too young to be Max Morandini. He wore a white shirt with blowzy sleeves and seemed to be favoring one leg. His black hair, ponytailed, hung nearly to his waist.

"You look younger than on your jacket shots," the young man said, smiling and offering a hand. "I'm Max Junior, sir. It's a pleasure to finally meet you."

Something, of course, was wrong. And what had confused VanDam was that little Max had offered up his left hand, not his right. Max's right arm appeared to be somewhat shorter than the other, and though it was difficult to see beneath the puffed sleeves of the Hamlet shirt, the hand looked crabbed and no larger than the forepaw of a dog. VanDam took Max's left hand and shook it gently.

"I hope you don't mind," Max said. "I left your books at home."
"Oh?"

"I thought maybe you could just follow me over to the house in your car. Since we last wrote, we've managed to get a hold of a bunch of your other titles. If it wouldn't be too much trouble, sir?"

"Oh, I don't know," VanDam said. He was feeling much relieved by Dr.

Delaney's report and was eager to get home.

"Gosh, I'm really sorry," said Max. "I guess I should have brought your books along." He shouldered out, slightly, his withered arm. "They were kind of tough for me to carry."

VanDam studied Max's face. "Is it far, the house?"

"Five minutes," smiled Max, turning toward his car. "And don't worry, sir. I'll drive slow so you can follow."

"Your father, is he at home?" VanDam called after him. But evidently little Max had failed to hear. After a moment VanDam climbed back into Glenda's Taurus. Well, the kid looked harmless enough. Max Junior was driving a brown Toyota, which VanDam followed into traffic.

The Morandinis lived in Frazer, a village southwest of Paoli, which wasn't far. Michael Thomas Morandini, 2811 Meadowbrook Lane. The address had been made familiar to VanDam by over thirty years of envelopes sending back his books. VanDam had even thought of it, of Frazer, as a vaguely bookish town, but as he followed little Max's brown Toyota, the stark reality of the place, the sad little close-built working-class homes, and the grimy sky began to sour him. Couldn't he just abandon his present route, hang a quick left or right in Glenda's car and speed away?

But already they were there. Max's Toyota pulled up against the curb on a haggard, leaf-strewn street. VanDam pulled in behind him and climbed out. Number 2811 was actually a half-house made of brick, with a flight of cement steps divided down the middle by an iron railing painted red.

"Come on in," Max Junior told him with a grin.

VanDam followed him up the sidewalk, past the railing, and was admitted into the little house. Immediately, the interior was a shock to him, as though he'd entered the command complex at some military installation. VanDam had imagined a dusty Victorian interior: shabby carpets and overstuffed chairs, a failing chandelier. But in an instant he saw that he had misimagined everything, because it was not, in fact, a proper living room at all. The room looked like a place of business, with a broad desk and shelves and a lot of computer gear on tables.

"It's nice you came around," said Max, too casually. It was obvious the kid was nervous. But still, what did the young man think, that VanDam came to visit Frazer every day and had the afternoon to burn? For VanDam, home and Glenda were still hours away.

"Where's your father?" VanDam blinked. There were high-intensity lamps hanging on wires from the ceiling, a large screen TV against one wall. What, was the old man sick? Or maybe Max Senior was simply shy, unable to believe that the object of such long devotion had at last appeared.

"That's something I guess I need to tell you," Max said. He pointed to a bulletin board over by a bank of phones. A black-and-white photo hung there, and VanDam crossed the grayish carpet to have a look. It was of a thin man with dark trousers, a white shirt and suspenders, who stood staring at the camera. His dark hair stood straight up, and his face was oblong, eggplant-shaped, the mouth deeply creased. Below it on a shelf were an old wedding photo and a crystal dish filled with decaying mints.

"He's dead?" VanDam asked, unable to hide his shock, his disappointment.

"He sure is. And I apologize for not saying so at first."

"How long ago?"

"Four years," said little Max.

"And you've been writing to me ever since?"

"Yep," admitted Max. "I didn't want to threaten the efficacy of the collection. I mean, I wanted to be able to finalize what my dad had started, maintain its currency."

"Where are they?" VanDam asked indignantly. "I mean, my books?"

Max led VanDam into another room beyond the former parlor, a windowless vault-like chamber with closed steel cabinets, which rose from floor to ceiling against the walls. Max opened up one door, hastily closed it, then opened up another and pointed to a shelf. Indeed, here was a treasure trove of the author's work—VanDam's old novels in dated jackets from the Sixties, plus paperbacks with loud typography that looked lurid today. As the author's eyes moved along the shelf—My God, now here's the rub!—similarly exhaustive and beautifully maintained collections of nearly every contemporary author he could think of appeared, rank after rank. Quickly Max closed the cabinet before VanDam could see all the other authors he had conned.

"Watcha think?"

"This isn't a collection," VanDam groused. "It's a cottage industry."

"Yep," said little Max, nodding in agreement. "It was pretty much all the old man had. Other than me, I mean. This room keeps out the light and protects the jackets, too. The air is purified and the temperature's kept constant."

"I see," VanDam said. But what he saw, really, was only his own hurt feelings, the crush of disillusionment after all these years. To think, how foolishly he'd allowed himself to envision the elder Max, earnestly maintaining this collection of his works! What's more, the further insult was to find his own stuff jammed onto shelves between authors he mostly didn't like—all in the name of commerce! What a mistake it had been, to intrude into these people's private lives! In the process, evidently, he'd also offended the young entrepreneur.

"You're really pissed," said little Max, bristling with affront. "Aren't you?"

"This collection's worth a fortune. You make me feel like I've been tricked."

Now little Max leaned in, so close to him that VanDam could see the pores in the young man's cheeks. "You begrudge me it, don't you? You begrudge us our hard work. What, you think these things grew in here, these books? You don't like it that I picked up where my old man left off? You think someone like me is going to get a job, like as an electrician or a plumber?" Max waggled his withered hand free of the Hamlet shirt, and VanDam saw in horror that the tiny fingers had cuticles no larger than those on an infant's hand.

There was a long silence while VanDam pondered Max's question and hung his head. "I'm sorry," he said, at last.

"Always the last word," said Max. "Mr. John VanBigshot."

Presently Max moved away from VanDam to a steel-legged table in the center of the room, on which a pile of newer volumes lay. "There are eight books here," he said. "It would really save me a lot of trouble if you agreed to sign them here. Then, once you're finished, maybe we'll have a cup of cocoa together before you split."

While Max busied himself in the kitchen, VanDam waited in his office. My God, such collections! Lines of reference books on antique coins, first editions, and 45 RPM recordings lined the shelves. Inside Max's command module, behind a richly padded swivel chair, on a wide counter were stacked small crimson boxes, all catalogued and labeled, which evidently held coins. Two telephones, two faxes, and a copier machine far outstripped the humble accouterments of VanDam's little study in his and Glenda's home.

VanDam stood restlessly, taking in the room. Behind him, he heard a spoon drop on the Formica counter in the kitchen. The door to the storage room, now, was closed. He had autographed, with some reluctance, the manipulative little Max's books for him. VanDam felt glum, picked clean, depressed by the dwindling commodity that had become his life; was this all that being an author brought him?

To his right, beside Morandini's computer, VanDam saw a small pile of correspondence. There was a screen saver on Max's monitor and across it floated small neon fish. The document on top of Max's neatly piled papers was a letter from a dealer in Toronto, acknowledging the receipt of a large shipment of coins. VanDam noticed that the envelope was stapled to the back of the letter, and that a date was written on it by hand. How neat he was, how thorough! Curious, VanDam reached down and with his finger deftly touched the space bar on the computer keyboard.

A document appeared, a letter. VanDam leaned down and surreptitiously began to read. He was shocked to see that it was a letter from Max to another author he vaguely knew, a woman who, he thought, now taught at Rutgers. She was ferociously productive, annually spewing out novels, short story collections, and reviews, all in all a bit too frantic and voracious for VanDam's more managed tastes. The woman herself was small-headed and puff-haired, with enormous glasses that dominated her bird-like face. "Dear Miss Barley," Van Dam read. "Thank you for your recent letter and the autographed copy of All I Want. I am writing to extend to you yet another invitation to visit us here at our home. There are a number of your fans here in town who would be most eager to meet you. Perhaps . . ."

"Sorry for the wait," said little Max, holding out to VanDam a saucer with a mug of cocoa. "It's hot," he said. "You better sip it first."

"Oh, I will," said VanDam. "I'm just in sort of a hurry to be on my way."

At that moment the front door opened and a very tall, good-looking young woman entered the front room. She was carrying a grocery bag under one arm, and from her hand hung the strap of a purse.

"This is Penny," said Max. He had taken a seat in the director's chair behind his desk and was observing VanDam coolly. "She's my sister," he explained.

"Beautiful," VanDam said, as much in recognition of her as of his own increasing exasperation. What was next, anyway? Couldn't he just leave? Indeed, Penny was attractive, yet once she'd deposited her sack on Max's desk her handshake was cold. On closer inspection the young woman looked ill at ease, unhappy. VanDam sensed, immediately, that things between Max and this woman were not good. Penny had a mountain of auburn hair and striking green eyes. Presently she removed a six–pack of bottled beer from her grocery sack and planted it on Max's desk.

"Want one?" she asked, as she uncapped a long neck with her fingers.

"No thanks," said VanDam.

"You know, I never met a really famous hack before," she said, then laughed nervously. "You surprise me, you know? You don't look at all like most of the other folks Max has come up here to visit."

"Penny," Max said.

"What other folks?" VanDam asked.

"Hey, where's the camera?" Penny said. "Isn't it about time you have me take his picture?"

VanDam had already placed his cocoa on the desk and was retreating toward the door. "No," he murmured. If there was one thing he didn't need, it was a snapshot to commemorate his disillusion.

Penny stared at the author amusedly, just long enough for VanDam to wonder if what she'd told him was the truth. Other authors, come to visit? Or was she just putting him on as a tease?

"I've got to go," VanDam said, his fingers fiddling with the door. "I have to say, you people disappoint me."

He stepped outside the house. It was raining now, and the narrow side-walk to the street was damp and slippery. Back inside the car, at last, VanDam realized he'd been weeping. To have once imagined and com-posed fiction, it seemed, laid him open to this curse: the people who admired him filled him with displeasure. Stymied in his craft, producing nothing, VanDam's life seemed to be turning into some dark joke—but wait—there was Glenda now to help him bar the way. Suddenly, VanDam was overcome by a need to be held, tightly, in her enfolding arms. Oh my God, how much he missed her! How lucky he was, how eager he was to be her husband and a father once again. Now VanDam eased himself back into the seat, her seat, and felt the Taurus all soft and cozy and soundproof all around him. He couldn't wait to get back home.

Glenn Burgoon

SAMUEL ATLEE attended Duke University and the University of Iowa Writers' Workshop, where he was a Teaching-Writing Fellow. He was a Peace Corps volunteer in Tunisia and worked in Hong Kong for *The Wall Street Journal*. His stories have been widely published in literary magazines, and he's received a grant from the National Endowment for the Arts. He is the father of three children and lives in Lancaster, Pennsylvania.